Queer Taiwanese Literature

QUEER TAIWANESE LITERATURE

A Reader

EDITED BY
Howard Chiang

Literature from Taiwan Series
in collaboration with
the National Museum of Taiwan Literature and
National Taiwan Normal University
General Editor: Nikky Lin

CAMBRIA PRESS

Amherst, New York

Copyright 2021 Cambria Press and
the National Museum of Taiwan Literature.

All rights reserved.

No part of this publication may be reproduced, stored in or introduced into a retrieval system, or transmitted, in any form, or by any means (electronic, mechanical, photocopying, recording, or otherwise), without the prior permission of the publisher.

Requests for permission should be directed to
permissions@cambriapress.com, or mailed to:
Cambria Press
100 Corporate Parkway, Suite 128
Amherst, New York 14226, USA

Library of Congress CIP data on file.

ISBN 9781621966982

Front cover image is *Self-portrait* (1963) by Shiy De-jinn, reproduced by permission of the Shyi Der-Jinn Foundation and the National Taiwan Museum of Fine Arts.

Table of Contents

Foreword vii

Note from Series Editor ix

Introduction: Representations of Queer Diversity in
    Contemporary Taiwanese Literature
    Howard Chiang 1

1: Late Spring
    Li Ang (translated by Yichun Liu) 17

2: On Her Gray Hair Etcetera
    Tsao Li-chuan (translated by Jamie Tse) 45

3: Howl
    Ta-wei Chi (translated by Yahia Zhengtang Ma) 109

4: Muakai
    Dadelavan Ibau (translated by Kyle Shernuk) 139

5: Violet
    Hsu Yu-chen (translated by Howard Chiang and Shengchi Hsu) 169

6: A Daughter
    Lin Yu-hsuan (translated by Shengchi Hsu) 199

7: A Nonexistent Thing
    Chen Xue (translated by Wen-chi Li and Colin Bramwell) 217

About the Editor 231

About the Translators 233

Cambria Literature in Taiwan Series 235

Foreword

Taiwanese literature, like its history, reflects the island's hybrid ethnic diversity and unique culture. Due to its geographical proximity to the Chinese Empire, Taiwanese literature has been greatly influenced by the ancient tradition of classical Chinese literature.

In 1895, Taiwan's fifty-one years of Japanese colonial rule began. During this period, the groundwork for the development of modern Taiwanese literature was laid. The end of World War II also meant the end of Japanese rule, but it was not a time of peace for Taiwan, which found itself caught in the escalation of the Cold War. The result of this was thirty-eight years of martial law. However, through political activism and the persistent efforts of the Taiwanese people who sought to revolutionize and refine the island's political system, martial law ended in 1987 and the island was transformed into Asia's most liberal country, and one with a strong, democratic political system. The struggle for democracy also set the tone for increased responsiveness and acceptance in the literary sphere.

As such, it is important that the world learns about the distinctive brand into which Taiwan literature has evolved. This book is part of the Literature from Taiwan Series, which comprises a varied selection of literary works showcasing exemplary Taiwan literature. It is part of a systematic and measured attempt to introduce Taiwan's distinctiveness to the rest of the world.

All the literary creations featured in the series have been composed by writers who were afflicted or confined by the societal pressures of their time. If one reads a single work of Taiwanese literature, one can easily sense the exuberance of Taiwan's literary masters. However, when one reads a collection, one can experience the force that is driving Taiwan forward.

Since the Taiwan Ministry of Culture's launch of its promotional project, "Books From Taiwan (BFT)" in 2016, the Taiwanese Ministry of Culture has taken on a proactive role in establishing an international copyright information platform and has been an active presence at international book fairs. The Ministry of Culture, furthermore, has been inviting international translators to Taiwan and assisting in the facilitation of translations of Taiwanese books into various languages, measures which have proven fruitful thus far. The National Museum of Taiwan Literature (NMTL) is affiliated with the Ministry of Culture and its structural organization/structural mechanism aligns with that of the BFT, with both parties focusing on the promotion of important Taiwan literary creations.

In addition to this book series, the NMTL has been working on creating a long-term database of translators of Taiwanese literature. It has also conducted a Taiwanese literary survey in various countries with the aim of promoting Taiwanese literature internationally as well as raising awareness for Taiwan's literary excellence, thus giving it a well-deserved voice on the international stage of world literature.

—Su Shuo-Bin,
Director,
National Museum of Taiwan Literature

Note from Series Editor

The painting on this book's front cover is *Self-portrait* (1963) by artist Shiy De-jinn. Born in 1923 in Sichuan Province and settled in Taiwan in 1948, Shiy De-jinn is considered one of the first and most well-known Taiwanese queer artists. His self-portrait is an attempt to explore his sexuality within the constraints of a sexually conservative society. Reproduced by permission of Shyi Der-Jinn Foundation and National Taiwan Museum of Fine Arts; copyright restrictions apply.

I would like to thank Greta Hagedorn for her editorial assistance on the translations, as well as Yi-Chia Lee, Kirsten Klitsch, and Chein-Sen Peng for their assistance on this project.

—Nikky Lin,
General Editor,
Literature from Taiwan Series

Queer Taiwanese Literature

Introduction

Representations of Queer Diversity in Contemporary Taiwanese Literature

Howard Chiang

Taiwan is one of the few Asian states known for actively promoting the rights of its lesbian, gay, bisexual, transgender, and queer (LGBTQ) citizens. In 2003, it became the first country in the Sinophone world to hold an official annual gay pride parade, and, sixteen years later, it became the first in the world's largest and most populated continent to legalize same-sex marriage. The roots of these twenty-first century breakthroughs, however, can be traced to the changing sexual configurations of the post-WWII era and the militancy and vibrancy of *tongzhi* 同志 activism in the 1990s.[1] The word *tongzhi* literally means comrade or common will in socialist China, but gay and lesbian activists in Sinophone regions such as Hong Kong and Taiwan began to use it to refer to queer subjects in the 1990s.[2] Much of the political energies behind this social movement was agitated by a crucial turning point in Taiwan's recent history: the lifting of martial law in 1987, which ended the hegemony of the Nationalist Party on the island.

The political liberalization that followed enabled the development of oppositional political movements. Different strands of social activism emerged to provide a space for imagining radical sexual politics and the principles of gender inclusion and egalitarianism. Sometimes under the aegis of feminism and sometimes not, an increasingly vocal cohort of *tongzhi* activists began to organize more systematically to challenge the homophobia and heterosexism propagated by the ancillary apparatuses of the state. One of the most famous episodes of this struggle occurred in 1995. Lesbian and gay groups lobbied against the Taipei city government's plan to subject New Park, a historic cruising site for gay men, to urban replanning. From December 1995 to June 1996, the Tongzhi Spatial Action Front coordinated a series of demonstrations and cultural events, rendering Taipei New Park as both a rallying cry and an urgent site for *tongzhi* memorialization. Even though the government ultimately redesignated the park as the 228 Peace Memorial Park in 1998, the Front made clear the significance of a new form of cultural citizenship grounded in queer sexual desire.

In the years leading up to 2000, Taiwan's *tongzhi* movement blossomed with an extraordinary momentum. The first lesbian and gay religious groups, the Tong-Kwang Light House Presbyterian Church and the Buddhist Youth Abode, were established in 1996. Founded in December of the same year, the Tongzhi Citizen Action Front, or the "Second Front," was a reincarnation of the earlier Spatial Action Front. The police raid of a house party on Changde Street in Taipei in July 1997, also known as the Changde Street Incident, prompted the Tongzhi Citizen Action Front to document and disseminate the unjust treatment of gay men arrested by police. The Front unleashed a resistance force to interrogate the legitimacy of such discriminatory practice in social governance. This in turn set the stage for the formation of the first *tongzhi* consultation group, the Tongzhi Assistance Association in November 1997. Another organization, Queer'n Class, which later changed its name to Gender/Sexuality Rights Association for Taiwan, soon followed in 1998. By the time that various lesbian and gay groups came together to cofound the landmark Tongzhi Hotline Association, the first *tongzhi* corporation officially registered with the Ministry of the Interior in June 2008, many activists fostered a growing alertness to the way subcultural communities—including the transgender, bisexual, and BDSM communities—had been marginally positioned in relation to the mainstream gay and lesbian movement.

In addition to social activism, the 1990s also witnessed the flowering of queer cultural production. In 1994, students at National Taiwan University formed Taiwan's first-ever lesbian society—the Lambda society. Academic queer theory suddenly became a hot topic of study across university campuses. The first edition of the earliest queer magazines, *G&L* and *Together*, were released in 1996 and 1998 respectively. A thriving queer-themed academic and publishing culture came to characterize much of the decade. The surfacing of a series of queer-focused special issues of scholarly journals, including *Chung-wai Literary Monthly*, *Unitas*, *Eslite Book Review*, and *Isle Margin*, shaped a self-conscious *tongzhi* reading public. Increasingly, a generation of *tongzhi* authors—Qiu Miaojin, Tsao Li-chuan, Chu T'ien-hsin, Chu T'ien-wen, Wu Jiwen, Lin Yuyi, Lin Chung Ying, Hong Ling, Chi Ta-wei, Hsu Yoshen, Chen Xue, Dong Qizhang, Ping Lu, Lai Hsiang-yin, Li Ang, among others—wrote popular novels and short fictions, which consolidated a subgenre of Taiwanese literature that came to be known as *tongzhi wenxue* 同志文學 ("tongzhi literature").

Not only did this growing interest in *tongzhi* texts lead to the opening of Taiwan's first dedicated gay and lesbian bookstore, Gin Gin's, in 1999, notable *tongzhi* fiction began to acquire prestige in the literary establishment by claiming almost every single literary prize available.

As cultural studies scholar Fran Martin has noted, "In fact it seemed at times that not a literary competition went by without at least one prize being awarded to a tongzhi themed short story, novella, or novel."[3] Most notably, Chu T'ien-wen's *Notes of a Desolate Man* won the 1994 *China Times* Novel Prize, Qiu Miaojin's *The Crocodile's Journal* was awarded the 1995 *China Times* Honorary Novel Prize, and Chi Ta-wei's *The Membranes* received the 1995 *United Daily News* Novella Prize. In addition, Tsao Li-chuan's "The Maidens' Dance" won the first prize in the 1991 United Daily News short-story competition and "On Her Gray Hair Etcetera" (included in this volume) received the 1996 *Unitas* Honorary Novella Prize; Ling Yan's *The Silent Thrush* was awarded the 1991 *Independence Daily* Novel Prize; Dong Qizhang's *Androgyny* won the 1994 *Unitas* Award for New Fiction Writers and *The Double Body* received the 1995 United Daily News Special Novel Prize; and Du Xiulan's *Rebel Woman* was awarded the 1996 Crown Popular Fiction Prize.

Against this backdrop, this book is best understood as an extension of the legacies of queer activism and cultural enterprises in Taiwan. In fact, readers can easily treat this volume as a companion to the collection *Angelwings: Contemporary Queer Fiction from Taiwan*, edited and translated by Fran Martin. That landmark collection included ten stories written in the 1990s by those whom we may consider as "trailblazers" of queer fictional writing. In selecting the stories included in this book, I aim to showcase the exciting diversity that has come to characterize queer Taiwan itself. This can be considered through the prisms of generational and topical depth. Not only do the seven stories featured in this book span five decades from 1975 to 2020, but they also deal with various dimensions of sexual experience whose relation to the category of "lesbian and gay" is neither protean nor exclusive. In this sense, the diversity of themes represented in the book highlight the way erotic inclinations and identities intersect with other forms of social and cultural transgression: bisexuality, asexuality, aging, HIV/AIDS, indigeneity, recreational drug use, transgenderism, and assisted reproductive technology.

Introduction

The first story in this collection, "Late Spring" (1975), is written by one of Taiwan's foremost feminist writers, Li Ang. Born in 1952 in Lukang, Changhua County, Li Ang's real name is Shih Shu-tuan. After studying philosophy at Chinese Culture University, she received a master's degree in drama from the University of Oregon. Li is perhaps best known for her novella *The Butcher's Wife* (1983), which brought forth a critique of Chinese patriarchy, aroused controversy, and established her as an eminent critic of gender politics in contemporary Taiwanese society. Among Taiwan's third-generation writers, Li's work often displays a bold depiction of female sexuality.

This candid engagement with sexual representation can be seen in "Late Spring," which is a rare early fiction, written in the 1970s, that enfolds female same-sex sexuality into its plot development. The protagonist Tang Keyan is more accurately understood as bisexual, as her self-understanding traffics with complexity between two contrasting systems of "sexual knowledge": her past relationship with an old girlfriend, Anan, and her more current relationship with the first man she has ever slept with, Li Ji. Other writers, including Chu T'ien-wen, Ouyang Tzu, and Pai Hsien-yung, had also experimented with the theme of female homoeroticism in their stories around this time, but Li's blatant portrayal of bisexuality, especially in the various moments of "competition" and "tension" between Tang's heterosexual and homosexual intimacy, stand out among this group of writers. Springtime is typically considered the season of flowering, but it is also the time of rebirth, renewal, and rejuvenation. Although both *tongzhi* and straight critics have raised issue with Tang's "genuine" sexuality, the description of her most climatic orgasm in the story as the moment of "late spring" implies that neither hetero nor homo is fully adequate to capture Tang's sense of self. This important story goes a long way to spotlight sexual fluidity precisely in a historical era when the space for women's movement—both private and public—had been deeply restrained.

Most queer stories tend to feature a coming-of-age narrative. In contrast, the second story, "On Her Gray Hair Etcetera" (1996) by Tsao Li-chuan, offers a refreshing perspective on a middle-aged butch lesbian. Born in 1960 in Changhua, Tsao graduated from Tamkang University in New Taipei City with a degree in Chinese literature. When her "The Maiden's Dance" claimed the first prize in the 1991 *United Daily News* short-story competition, Tsao emerged as one of the most noted authors of lesbian literature in Taiwan. Five years later, "On Her Gray Hair Etcetera" won another major literary prize, and, in her personal life, Tsao both entered and left a heterosexual marriage in between.

Adding to the richly layered plot, the protagonist Fei-wen embodies a certain degree of sexual ambiguity and potential asexuality, a phenomenon that has been underacknowledged in queer literature. Tsao explores queer sexuality and sex in a very explicit and introspective manner, not a common feature of the queer fictions produced in the 1990s. It is particularly intriguing that the plot unfolds around a lesbian's distress toward aging and her sexual epiphany, instead of tragic or bittersweet stories of star-crossed queer lovers. Though fictional, "On Her Gray Etcetera" paints a lively picture of a lesbian's life in Taipei.

While queer teenagers struggle to find their voices and establish their identity in the heteronormative society, Fei-wen, who is already in her 30s and has been in a platonic relationship with several women, is somehow still confused about her sexuality. Though she has been exposed to nudity and sex from a young age, Fei-wen barely even knows her own body and cannot picture herself having sex or, as the case may be, forming genuine connections with anyone. The story begins with Fei-wen having her period, and she is in great pain. This anguish is also symbolic and foreshadows her inability to come to terms with her sexuality within a woman's body. In contrast to her self-perception, both Jessi, the woman to whom she is attached, and Fei-wen's own mother have bisexual orientations, as they were both once married to a man and had kids. As a butch lesbian with zero interest in men, Fei-wen cannot orient herself toward nor against anyone around her. And despite the fact that one of Fei-wen's brothers is gay and that she has her own "lesbian clique," she always appears detached and her emotions displaced. When Fei-wen becomes fed up with her repression, she opts for the most extreme catharsis and drowns herself in pornography. The bodily sensations on the screen give her comfort even though, again, she gradually becomes sick. It is somewhat ironic that she has not any ordinary sickness but an ovarian cyst. Ovaries are an integral part of the female reproductive system, and Fei-wen's reluctance to part with them, despite the cyst, symbolizes her troubled reconciliation with her female body. Tsao's style, as evident throughout the story, adds color to Fei-wen's story—sometimes with despair, at times with humor, and still at other times with fear and resignation.

The author of the next story, "Howl" (1998), is Chi Ta-wei, a preeminent scholar of *tongzhi* literary history in Taiwan. Educated in the Department of Foreign Languages and Literature at National Taiwan University, Chi received his Ph.D. in Comparative Literature from UCLA in 2006. In fact, before doing doctoral work in the United States, he had already built a name for himself in the Taiwanese literary scene. In the 1990s, he published seminal queer science fiction works, such as the prize-winning *The Membranes* (1995) and devoted time and energy to raising awareness of queer theory and discourses in Taiwanese academia. In 2017, he published the most authoritative treatment of queer literary history in Taiwan to date: *A Queer Invention in Taiwan: A History of Tongzhi Literature.*[4]

In his writings, both fictional and scholarly, Chi places an emphasis on the playfulness of language, especially with respect to the representation of non-normative sexualities, identities, and bodies. The last decade of the twentieth century, during which time the "Howl" was first published in Taiwan, saw the groundbreaking encounters between Western terms such as "queer" and "AIDS" and the use of *tongzhi* in the Chinese language. From the story title and the peace sign to the direct quotes of Allen

Ginsberg's poem with the same title "Howl" and the allusion to San Francisco, Chi uses "Howl" to denote not only approaches critiquing the minoritizing model of homosexuality and subjectivity but also possible ways of having translingual, inter-semiotic, and transnational encounters between Taiwan and the United States.

The language is further complicated when it comes to the translation of the story, the difficulties in linguistically and culturally translating the peace sign, the name of the pub San Francisco, the (unspecified) man's name "□ □ □," the body, and the re-translation of Ginsberg' poems—all of these transcultural and translingual practices exemplify a series of queer translation: itself both a critique and execution of representation, transformation, and sexualization. Even though the "sexualization" of translation may not be immediately obvious, "translating" the body (e.g., "*Without putting on the hand-dyed T-shirt he had been wearing, he had my bath towel wrapped around his body after the shower*") reminds us of another reading of the concept of a "hidden" body, a redressing of the body with another language. In the end, the depiction of the "borrowing" of the poems (both of the author's quote of Ginsberg's poems and the characters' "borrowing" and "returning" of the collection of Ginsberg's poems) alongside the handover of Hong Kong to the PRC and the parody of the "Blue Sky, White Sun, and a Wholly Red Earth" are symptomatic of more fundamental issues in relation to the imaginings of queerness as mediated between identity politics and the politics of language.

Most of what we call queer Taiwanese literature today features a sustained attention on Han-Taiwanese writings. In contrast, the next story, "Muakai" (2001), provides a rare perspective from the indigenous experience. The author Dadelavan Ibau, an ethnically Paiwan woman of Taiwanese nationality, was born in 1967 to the Tuvasavasai tribe located in Pingtung county. She graduated from Hualien's Yu-shan Theological College and Seminary in 1991. A prominent focus of her career has been the promotion and education of Paiwan culture and tradition, and, to that end, she has worked as a scholar at Academia Sinica and affiliated with a performance art group called U-Theatre. "Muakai" narrates a female college student's perception of a Paiwan lesbian, Muakai, who adopts Hsiu-hsiu as her Han Chinese name when living in Taipei. The story explores the tropes of gender transgression and homoeroticism through distinct nodes of cultural differentiations between Han cosmopolitanism and Paiwan indigeneity.

Three elements of the story distinguish itself in the way queerness emerges from its translation: narratology, language, and Paiwaneseness. Regarding the problem of narrativity, how does one tell a story in general, and how does one tell a story of queer subject formation in particular? These are important questions to which "Muakai" offers interesting answers. Elements of mythical time and the Paiwan storytelling tradition are built into the narrative that complicate the otherwise linear trajectory of the standard work of short fiction. These are not unrelated temporalities, though, and might be described as palimpsestual—the "modern" reality seems built on top of the mythical one that informs Ibau's broader worldview. From a queer perspective, it is also this mythical level that makes it align with other queer building narratives. Although it is presented in a broken and piecemeal fashion, it nevertheless challenges those models by identifying the source of this composite identity not as a fractured, single, modern identity but as multiple, competing epistemologies that are fused into one.

With respect to language, Ibau's narratology is reinforced through several moments of linguistic confusion in the story. When Muakai explains the nature of the relationship between a same-sex female couple to the protagonist who is also from her tribe, she refers to them as "girl-girl friends," which is how it might be expressed in Paiwanese. There is a moment of confusion, but they work through the linguistic awkwardness. There is a different moment that highlights the layered (settler) colonial nature of life in Taiwan as well, when the protagonist tells two older Paiwan women that most people call her "College Student" (*daxuesheng* 大學生), but they can't produce the strange sounds of the "Beijing-ese."

Consequently, the multiple linguistic registers also gesture toward the various social and value systems queer and aboriginal subjects must navigate.

A related theme concerns Paiwaneseness. However porous and diffused this term may be, Ibau's story unambiguously explores "what it means to be Paiwanese" in both literal and transformative forms. A large portion of the queer trauma of the story (separate from an unsuccessful and slightly emotionally abusive relationship) is that Muakai is forced to marry a man from another tribe due to tribal cultural expectations. She eventually runs away from this marriage to reunite with her female lover, who it seems has also abandoned her. The conclusion of the story has Muakai telling the protagonist that she thinks that the mythical Muakai, after whom she is named, has always loved women, which subverts contemporary Paiwan social expectations in a way that aligns in an unlikely way with contemporary queer values. Muakai is both a modern Taiwan and Paiwan woman, for whom those traditions' dual legacies shape her final outlook. Queerness is represented in the story through the work of narratology, language, and Paiwaneseness.

The next pair of stories feature the work of two young, talented, and up-and-coming authors: "Violet" (2008) by Hsu Yu-chen and "A Daughter" (2014) by Lin Yu-hsuan. Born in 1977, Hsu graduated from the Department of Motion Picture at National Taiwan University of Arts and received numerous recognitions, including the 2006 *Unitas* short story competition honorable mention. A graduate of National Taiwan University, Lin originally majored in finance until chancing upon an introductory course on literature. Then, after visiting a gay bar with friends and joining a queer studies society, he developed interest in *tongzhi* literature. Lin began his journey of creative writing in the second year of college. "A Daughter" won the 2010 *United Daily News* Short Story Prize.

By diversifying the meaning of *tongzhi*, the work of Hsu and Lin can be viewed as a response to both the golden decade of queer literary production at the close of the twentieth century and what was then considered as the most representative themes and tenets of *tongzhi* experience. Both authors seek to address the subjectivities of individuals who have been "hidden" from the mainstream queer representations in the post-Martial Law era: recreational drug users and transgender people. Although this may at first seem like a nominal gesture of inclusion, the bringing out of these figurations from the shadow of the *tongzhi* movement suggests in fact a more fundamental politics of redistribution. Not only does it denote new kinds of legible desire interlacing with *tongzhi* subjecthood, but the attention on drugs and trans also continues to pose challenging questions about the forms and legitimacy that a fictional depiction ought to take, especially in light of ongoing struggles in the social sphere such as the legal battle for rights and equality. In this sense, both stories imagine a universe, even a utopian one, in which alternative modes of belonging are not stigmatized but respected.

In "A Daughter," the narrator's in-your-face and somewhat unapologetic tone is a huge step away from the commonly known bleak and sorrowful tone in Taiwan's LGBTQ literature. This is representative (and reflective) of all the advances made on the fronts of gender and queer movements in contemporary Taiwan. However, this sense of pride is not necessarily felt or enjoyed by people of all ages. Through the lens of the narrator, we see the gradual transformation—or "coming out" if you will—of the mo-father (in the story, the narrator discovers that like herself, her father is also interested in cross-dressing), whose process of becoming suggests that despite all the advances, there are still people who "dare not to speak their love" for reasons such as family bonds and social moral values. While it is important to celebrate all the achievements Taiwan has made, "A Daughter" reminds readers of the continuing fear and suffering experienced in the queer communities. As the narrator states at the end of the story, "There is still a lot to learn." There indeed is still a long way to go to achieve recognition, acceptance, and ultimately that ideal sense of equality.

Hsu's "Violet," on the other hand, approaches Taiwan's contemporary queer life with a much more downbeat and somewhat pessimistic tone. In contrast to the upbeat and in-your-face (somehow confrontational) voice in "A Daughter," the voice in "Violet" is reserved, quietly meditative, and philosophical. The narrator's solitary existence appears to reflect the sentiment of many Taiwanese people, queer or not: mundane, non-changing, and stagnant. "Journeys," physical or fantastical, seem to be the only way out of these traps and constraints of life. The narrator's philosophical investigation of his fantastical experiences—under the influence of substance—brings about realizations that everything in spatial and temporal distances is after all connected, and history repeats itself, déjà vu. Above all, this story raises universal humanistic concerns that go beyond gender and queer issues. It is in this way that the story underscores the issue of the changing (or changed) dynamics of contemporary Taiwanese society (and this is why the invocation of the "entrance" in the story is so crucial): searching through and coming out of darkness, queer movements have gained prominence and achieved milestones in Taiwan, but it is important not to become complacent and rest upon these achievements. There are still blank corners in the mural —that impressionistic rendering that both introduces and concludes the story—waiting to be filled.

Chen Xue, the author of the last story in this book, is one of Taiwan's most prolific writers of lesbian literature. Born in 1970 in Taichung, Chen graduated from the Department of Chinese Literature at National Central University in 1993. As mentioned previously, her work has won numerous literary awards in Taiwan, and she was one of the foremost architects of *tongzhi* literature in the 1990s, although most of her novels appeared in the twenty-first century. Her short story collection, *Book of Evil Women* (1995), is often considered a classic in the field and includes a well-known story "Searching for the Lost Wings of the Angels" that inspired the title of Fran Martin's translated anthology *Angelwings*. In 2011, Chen served as the ambassador for the first annual LGBT prize in Taichung City.

Introduction   13

Chen's "A Non-Existent Thing" (2020) is included in this book to showcase her ongoing engagement with the changing landscape of queer life in Taiwan. In particular, the story addresses the issue of surrogacy, assisted reproductive technology, and, by extension, new meanings of family and kinship that are taking shape in contemporary society. The milestone event to which "A Non-Existent Thing" responds is the legalization of same-sex marriage in 2019. Readers may find three striking features of the story of particular interest. Firstly, there is something very direct and practical about its content. The story speaks to some of the legislative loopholes regarding conception in Taiwan that gay marriage legislation, as welcome as it is, does not yet solve. There is an argument in the story for reform that would be relevant to the Taiwanese judiciary (in the case of the woman who conceives a child with her embryo and then has no rights to see the child after the breakup). Not foreign to the genealogy of *tongzhi* literature, "A Non-Existent Thing," in this sense, embodies the historical linkages between queer writing and civic duty (in particular arguments in favor of pro-queer legislation and reform) in Taiwanese literature. This has been a distinctive facet of Taiwan's queer cultural production.

Moreover, the story also paints a credible representation of queer women and queer friendships. All of the characters claim varying perspectives of their own sexuality, but their differences do not disrupt their closeness; there is a comfort in this, and a sense that these women are looking out for each other and care deeply about each other. At the same time, there are discussions of domestic abuse within the queer community too, which shows that the community is not reducible to some kind of cuddly homogeneity. These are real people, and, although the route they take to conception is quite different from that of straight women, they do face the same issues. Notably, the women in the story are all from fairly bourgeoise backgrounds (e.g., Chen constantly quotes specific amounts of money, ranging from a half million to one million TWD). So, the story implicitly acknowledges that queer women of more limited means will not be able to afford to reproduce. This returns us to the social context in which the fabric of queer life is imbricated with economic conditions—a longstanding theme in queer women's literature.

Finally, Chen Xue also, as any exceptional writer does, puts a human face on deeply politicized issues. "A Non-Existent Thing" delivers a strong sense of the individual stories that lie behind certain decisions. This is especially the case on the topic of abortion. While everyone has their own opinion on the subject, the story portrays a sense of the real-life consequences of terminating a child, how difficult this decision can be to make, the lasting consequences of abortion on a woman's mental health, and how the non-existent life can be grieved for too. Moreover, the story clearly outlines the journey to the discovery of one's sexuality for each character: all of them feel differently about conception, and all their opinions are valid, which heightens what we know about them as characters. The subject of conception will always remain controversial, but "A Non-Existent Thing" demonstrates the urgency of having stories like this, which humanize the subjects, thereby showing them as real people with hopes and regrets.

Chen's short story serves as a good outro for this book because it both extends and challenges the genealogy of queer Taiwanese fiction that we have been exploring. It embodies forms of naturalism predominating this history, in particular the crossover between fiction and forms of life-writing. Qiu Miaojin's novels come to mind immediately; readers of Qiu's work are often left with the impression of a kind of biography that steps closer to reality than it does to fiction.[5] Chen's story gives this longstanding leitmotif a present permanence by speaking to the current situation of Taiwanese queer politics, and it does so in a more global sense: the notion that real stories are important and worth telling without too much embellishment. Perhaps this could be identified with certain literary currents in the West, a kind of warts-and-all approach to biography that is only semi-fictionalized (consider Karl Ove Knausgaard's work, for instance.) Taiwan is of course its own place, and its literature does not need to reference Western contexts to be valid, but the relationship that Taiwanese literature has to that of the West continues to fascinate literary producers and consumers. In the context of criticism on queer writing, we see this surfacing once again in the writings of Ta-wei Chi and others. Taken together, the stories collected in this reader show that gender and sexual diversity is not incidental to a vibrant branch of contemporary Taiwanese literature but sits at its very center.

Notes

1. Howard Chiang and Yin Wang, eds., *Perverse Taiwan* (New York: Routledge, 2017).
2. Howard Chiang, *Transtopia in the Sinophone Pacific* (New York: Columbia University Press, 2021).
3. Fran Martin, ed., *Angelwings: Contemporary Queer Fiction from Taiwan* (Honolulu: University of Hawai'i Press, 2003), 5.
4. Chi Ta-wei, *A Queer Invention in Taiwan: A History of Tongzhi Literature* (Taipei: Linking Publishing, 2017).
5. Ari Larissa Heinrich and Eloise Dowd, "In Memoriam to Identity: Transgender as Strategy in Qiu Miaojin's *Last Words from Montmartre*," *TSQ: Transgender Studies Quarterly* 3, nos. 3–4 (2016): 569–577.

1

Late Spring

Li Ang
(translated by Yichun Liu)

1

Tang Keyan had not visited the memorial since its opening. Occasionally, she passed the place, gazed through the luxuriant foliage enshrouding a neoclassical Chinese shrine. It was different from the flamboyant brick and tilework of a typical Taiwanese temple. She found it lacking something.

It was an internationally renowned symphony that first brought her to the memorial. But it wasn't simply to hear a concert that she set foot in the park. She was sure that Li Ji, music lover that he was, would be sure to attend. Perhaps they'd even cross paths.

Indeed, the first night, Tang Keyan caught a fleeting glimpse of him through the crowd. He passed by without seeing her, nor did she acknowledge his presence. The papers had advertised concerts on two consecutive nights each presenting different masterpieces. As such, the next night when she returned to the symphony, of course it was to hear more of that deeply bewitching modern music. Thus, she was all the more unprepared, when she saw him in front of the fountain, with another woman in his arms!

The fountain with its tirelessly changing flow patterns was illuminated by multicolored lights under the water. Enormous colorful water drops falling from the fountain merged with the twisting streams, turning into various shapes and images that were almost recognizable. Suddenly, in the middle of the fountain, a stream shot up high into the sky—immediately scattering in the gentle breeze. Across the fountain, she saw him. The rainbow droplets reflected on his slightly raised head, casting deep shadows like a river of tears. She kept standing there. She didn't enter the hall until the whole fountain shot up again, filling the air with a curtain of mist.

Unexpectedly, the program was the same as the previous night. She felt deceived and snuck out hurriedly after the first piece. When she looked up and saw the fountain again, facing the empty square without the music to distract her, she couldn't help but pause for a moment as a wave of bitterness flooded her heart. Yet, almost immediately, her lips broke into a bemused grin.

She couldn't quite believe that she still had such feelings.

2

Tang Keyan knew that undoubtedly she had demeaned herself a bit that night. Her impression of Li Ji at first was mostly based on a few casual encounters and her brother's comments on his intelligence, his unfortunate preoccupation with work, and his insouciance. Apart from that, she knew nothing about him. Yet, she gave her consent, on that night, far from home.

Perhaps, not being familiar with each other had made things a lot easier. She was on a business trip to a reformatory school in a remote, southern town. Li Ji was heading to the same town for work, and Tang Keyan's brother asked Li to look after her. She followed him into the hotel room and let him have his way.

In that small town, the only place they could find was a comparatively clean hotel room with an old, sagging box spring. Tang Keyan kept her eyes closed the whole time, even through the pain as Li Ji thrust into her. She remained silent, sinking into the darkness, bearing every motion of the male body writhing on top of her. All those years of chastity, up in smoke.

So this is lovemaking.

She tried to ignore the man on top of her, telling herself that the whole thing was not as unbearable as she'd imagined it. Yet the physical pain still gradually tore her apart. His movements followed a steady rhythm. The pain *down there* spread wave after wave. Just when it felt like it would engulf her whole body, she raised her voice softly to stop him.

"Please..."

To her surprise, he actually stopped thrusting and pulled out. She lay still in the silent night with its gentle breeze. As the suffocating pain gradually receded, she felt as if her whole body was unfolding like a cavern. A breeze crept through the window and entered her body gently. She shivered and a spasm coursed between her legs.

"Ann..." she said to herself.

Once, she'd wanted to try one of those new-fangled sanitary products, but couldn't figure out the instructions or where it would go in her body. She thought of Ann, who had returned home from abroad and would know better about these kinds of imported products. She sought Ann's advice, and when Ann taught her how to use the tampon, she finally realized that she and Ann shared the same anatomy.

Although she knew there were two orifices theoretically, she wasn't sure where they were exactly, and whether she had the same body structure. Besides, she had read a medical study indicating that in some cases the two orifices could be merged. Even though the odds were one in ten thousand, she was still worried about it. After she met Ann, in spite of all her hopes, she reluctantly accepted that Ann couldn't help her clarify the matter directly.

Earlier, when Li Ji entered her with a few quick thrusts, she knew she was a complete woman after all. Yet, Tang Keyan did not feel like a weight had been lifted off her shoulders. Instead she sensed that she lost something she had kept for many years. It wasn't something she'd wanted to keep per se, nor did she particularly want to value it. She simply thought that her chastity, precarious as it was, might be something worth treasuring.

Still, Tang Keyan did not regret it. Li Ji, lying next to her, with his lanky frame stretching up toward the headboard, was silent. She lay beside him, her head reaching just up to his chest, and felt nothing but the special shame of being taken lightly.

Still lying on her back, she slid up the bed, closer to Li Ji and whispered as softly as possible,

"That is my first time, do you believe it?"

Li Ji lay on his side in the darkness. Tang Keyan didn't see an ounce of surprise in his expression. *He would never believe such a thing,* Tang Keyan thought to herself,

What kind of first time is this?

Indeed, she had never pictured it being in a room full of flowers, but she still hoped that there would be a wide and comfortable bed and a man who made the first night a kind of devotion. Only when she experienced it herself, did she realize that it would be in such a shabby hotel in a remote town with a man whom she neither hated nor loved.

Tang Keyan knew clearly that the reason she consented to it was simply because they couldn't make it home that night, and the timing was just right. Of course, considering her brother's close friendship with Li Ji, she knew things would be kept quiet. She was willing to give herself to Li Ji, and trusted that as a sexually experienced man, he wouldn't cause her excessive harm, pain, or embarrassment. Besides, she knew she was safe during those days. There was no chance of getting pregnant.

It was Li Ji who took the initiative and Tang Keyan accepted his advances without protest. Although she had no intention of holding Li Ji responsible, she just couldn't help but tell him that it was her first time. As his silence stretched on, Tang Keyan immediately regretted she'd said anything at all. She could have held her tongue. Her first time had nothing to do with letting the other party know, especially a first time like this one. The last thing she wanted was to let Li Ji believe that she had any designs on him.

After the two remained silent for a moment, Tang Keyan whispered again.

"I've heard that a man can tell if it's a girl's first time."

Li Ji, aroused by her words, replied with a hint of bravado,

"Oh yeah, it felt a bit different."

Tang Keyan couldn't help feeling amused with herself. She'd never imagined she'd seek proof of her chastity on a night like this. She smiled ironically and said no more.

Tan Keyan sensed that Li Ji seemed particularly agitated, but she didn't quite understand his arousal. When Li Ji asked her to make love with him for the second time, Tang Keyan knew that for her, this so-called "lovemaking" entailed nothing except pain and maybe a bit of numbness. She did not acede to his request.

Li Ji fell asleep shortly afterwards. Tang Keyan tossed and turned for a while before she too dozed off.

She found herself in a room with familiar furniture and decorations from her childhood. Her mother's dragon and phoenix washstand stood to one side of the big carved mahogany bed. There was a woman lying on the bed. It seemed that she was naked, but her body was partially blurred. The only thing that drew Keyan's attention was the woman's long protruding genitals, below which there also seemed to be an indistinct split orifice, seemingly neither male nor female. There was a man; a hired hand, or so Keyan inferred, for she had seen her brother bargaining with him. He stood beside the woman and prepared to treat her with his member. She couldn't understand what had happened, and why it was happening. The only thing she knew was that the woman was sick, and they wanted to treat her but she had no idea what they were going to do to the woman. She was sick. She was just sick.

Then, the man turned around, it was Li Ji. She felt no loathing or revulsion, but just a sense of defilement in knowing he had touched such a woman.

She couldn't forget the man's calm expression as he sat there peacefully, nor the woman splayed on the bed and her nether region. She couldn't fathom how he would "treat" the woman, either. He just sat there, apathetically, with his hand on the woman's thigh.

After what seemed like an eternity, the room gradually became illuminated, and a beam of light flitted across the woman's face; it was Ann. The light receded, and in a fleeting glimpse of something elusive and blurry, it was not Ann's face, but her own.

Tang Keyan opened her eyes to the dazzling sunlight, the memories of the dream, remained before her like an afterimage. A woman with long hair on thin shoulders.

It was Ann.

She slightly shifted her posture, and immediately felt a fullness between her legs, which reminded her of the events of last night. She promptly sat up, still preoccupied with Li Ji's expression as he sat beside Ann in her dream. At that moment, Tang Keyan didn't even dare to glance at the man next to her. She scrambled out of bed, only to find that she was completely naked. She didn't bother to sort through the tangle of clothes strewn across the floor; she stooped slightly, and dashed into the bathroom.

The bathroom was separated from the bedroom by only a drab floral curtain. Unfamiliar surroundings had always made her unsettled. Just the thought that Li Ji could burst in at any moment, and catch her off guard, was enough to give her pause. Tang Keyan hesitated briefly, then reached to turn on the shower.

In the dim light filtering in from the bedroom, Tang Keyan clearly made out two dark red blood stains on the floor. A pair of round, thin red moons, they stood out against the grimy white tile, strangely and ambiguously erotic.

The blood was still red, so the stains were obviously fresh. There was no chance that they came from a previous guest. Tang Keyan tried to recall what happened last night. They'd probably dripped out when she went to wash up after sex. Looking at those droplets that had fallen from her own body, Keyan was overcome by indescribable fondness for them, and withdrew her hand from the faucet.

When she went back to get dressed, Li Ji had woken up. He reached out toward Keyan, grabbing her from behind, gently caressing her.

"Who would want to do such a thing so early in the morning?" Tang Keyan retorted.

Even while she was trying to resist, she was nevertheless aroused by those blood stains—weirdly erotic in such dilapidated surroundings. She let him have his way.

Li Ji couldn't stimulate her and still failed to satisfy her. To her, that happiness somewhat needed to be learned. At first, she was willing to cooperate, so that he could call forth the hidden desire from the depths of her body. No matter how much the pain between her legs had diminished, she still felt uncomfortable, and it made her want to give up on cooperating. But Keyan didn't stop Li Ji this time. In his heavy breathing and rough thrusting, she cherished those pathetic overnight blood stains. Suddenly, a long-gone memory flashed through her mind.

She'd gone over to Ann's, but Ann was out. She took out the key and opened the door. The room was messy. She sat down beside the bed and gazed about absentmindedly. The brocade quilt with its dragon and phoenix pattern was twisted up in a white sheet, which was dotted with bloodstains. Ann was always careless and never folded the quilt. Keyan sighed, and began to fold it for her. When she flipped it over, she was startled to find the white bedsheet was streaked with waves of blood, like a crimson tide soiling a white beach. The blood had already soaked into the cotton fibers, forming stains with a serrated edge. Because they had been tangled up in the quilt, it seemed the stains had not completely dried.

She knew Ann was on her period, but how could she be so careless? A wave of disgust overcame her. Staring at the blood stains on the white sheet, she suddenly recognized a similarity between Ann and herself. At this point, what was there left to cling to? Like a spell that had been broken, the knot in her heart unwound; her passions faded into the distant corners of her mind. Keyan shuddered at a feeling of desolation churning in the pit of her stomach, she felt like vomiting. That was the last time she visited Ann.

Sprawling on the bed, Keyan let Li Ji ride her to his heart's content. Gradually, she felt more and more weary. Perhaps, this whole business with Li Ji was all because of Ann. After her passion faded, she was left in bewilderment, as if the whole world had turned to dust and any affection would only exhaust her further. The only thing that could validate her existence was a male body and all it implied.

Still, Li Ji's male form that distinguished him from Ann and also herself, disgusted her, especially under the light. When it was all over, Li Ji got up to dress himself. Tang Keyan lay there with her eyes squeezed shut.

Eventually, she had to get up. Even though she didn't really care about the act itself, she couldn't bear the thought of Li Ji watching her dress. She asked him to turn around, but he didn't take her seriously—looking back over his shoulder to ogle her. She had never felt so humiliated.

Throughout the journey home, Keyan was deeply preoccupied by a sense of depression, and she gazed blankly out of the window over the gently sloping plains of south-central Taiwan. She was unwilling and unable to look at Li Ji. Completely unaware of her feelings, he put his arm around her shoulder and whispered,

"I saw the blood stains on the sheet this morning! I really should have been gentler last night."

Li Ji's tone of voice suggested that if it weren't for the stains, he wouldn't believe that it was her first time. The thought of it all made Keyan miserable, but when she glanced at her reflection in the car window, she found she was smiling faintly.

In the following weeks, Keyan kept turning him down, except that they talked on the phone. She spent her days quietly drafting the plans for the reformatory, doing her best to apply what she'd learned. Occasionally, she sensed a huge change in her body, and was quite surprised that her family, especially her mother, didn't notice anything different.

In a strange turn of events, she bumped into Ann at an art exhibition tea party. When Keyan arrived at the venue, she immediately sensed Ann's presence in the crowd. Ann always exuded an aura of unique charm—an exotic appeal of sorts. For a moment, Keyan's chest tightened with surprise, the next, she felt crushed by utter desolation. Ann was still very thin, and her hair hung loose over her shoulders. She could not help but draw closer to Ann. Looking at Ann's porcelain face, and her languid but comforting smile, Keyan suddenly recalled that night with Li Ji. Abruptly, a series of vague impressions and fragmentary memories strung themselves together.

In her memory, her mother had that same porcelain complexion. As a child, Tang Keyan had lived in a mountain retreat with her mother. She was roughly six years old but had yet to attend school. She remembered her mother lying in bed for a long time. A mahogany bed, decorated with seasonal flowers, dragons and phoenixes. That bed; deep red, and so tall that even when she stood on tiptoe, she could only see a small part of the porcelain face—framed by disheveled hair in the gloom. She was both frightened and curious for no reason at all. She didn't know why her mother had to lie in bed like that.

A few days later, a serving woman, hoisted little Keyan up to the mahogany bed. Under the heavy quilt, looking out at her, were her mother's porcelain face and endless tears.

The servant's name must have been Cai, because Keyan was told to call her Cai-Guan out of courtesy. She vaguely remembered Cai-Guan as a very stout middle-aged woman with a fat waist and pigeon toes. Her arms were strong, and her palms were as rough as sandpaper. So rough they often hurt her, especially when Cai-guan dragged her to get her hair washed.

Every time she saw Cai-Guan put a wooden bucket under the running tap, she'd try to hide. Even if she hid behind her mother's bed, it was so tall that, she would never be able to see her mother. Eventually she would be caught, laid across Cai-guan's lap, her head locked firmly under a plump armpit, then forced into the water.

The water was often too hot and splashed into her ears and eyes. Cai-Guan's hands were wet and heavy. If she struggled to escape, Cai-Guan would hug her more tightly to her chest, and her whole face would be smashed into Cai-Guan's saggy breasts. She thought she just might suffocate.

Finally, she was taken back to the city by her father, to attend school. Immersed in the novelty of everything at school and the storybooks, the memory of her mother's narrow porcelain face faded. Her father never took it upon himself to fill the gap.

She had the impression that it was dusk; she was playing house with her friends. It was the first time she had taken out the precious plastic playset sent by her mother. The miniature stove, kettle, dishes, and cutlery were strewn across the floor. All of a sudden, a foot in Japanese-style clogs came crunching down on a spoon, smashing it to pieces. In that moment, the foot seem extremely huge, like a giant's. She lifted her head in tears and realized it belonged to her father. He hastily passed her without looking back.

But there was no shortage of new distractions, especially when there was no fear of being grabbed by Cai-Guan and suffocated by those breasts. The young stylists at the beauty salon had soft and gentle hands. When she lay on the chair getting her hair rinsed, their breasts exuded a faint fragrance as they drew near. Like the aroma of an unknown flower on the spring breeze—its source a mystery.

As she grew older and taller, the breasts of the beauty salon ladies got closer to her face. Hard at work, they inadvertently leaned over her; sometimes brushing against her, tender and warm.

Then, she kept searching for it eternally—while she was persistently escaping from Ann and other names, except that she hadn't fallen deeply like this time before. Even when she understood that she might only be the continuation of Ann's "lifestyle abroad," she was unable to eradicate her emotional attachment to Ann's completely feminine tenderness.

That night, Tang Keyan promised to go out with Li Ji for the first time since their return. They went to see "Cabaret" even though they already knew most of the plot.

Probably due to the gratuitous censorship, Li Ji did not even pick up on the subtext of the final scene. When Tang Keyan alluded to it, and Li Ji responded nonchalantly,

"Is there anything good about two men being together? I was just surprised. I mean I have all of the same junk. It's nothing new to me."

"What about for fun?" Tang Keyan said with a smile.

After a pause, it seemed that Li Ji hadn't finished what he wanted to say,

"Now, if two *women* got together…."

Tang Keyan made no reply.

They had made a reservation for a late dinner. Tang Keyan chose the twelfth floor lounge of a nearby hotel, not for its glamour or ambiance but only hoping that in the dim light, she might be able to tolerate sitting across from him. She still couldn't look at him directly, but it was not just Li Ji. In the past, any time any man, wanted to flirted with her, she always got annoyed and inexplicably overcome by the desire to escape.

It was only the two of them in the elevator. Li Ji pressed himself tightly against Keyan to let her know his sexual urges. As soon as they sat down, he awkwardly confessed his feelings for her.

"Just so you know, I don't do this with every girl."

Li Ji finally said with more than a hint of annoyance in his tone.

Initially, Tang Keyan was unmoved and found the whole thing rather ridiculous. It was hard to believe that the tall, muscular man sitting across from her could act like such a petulant child over something like this. The more she thought about it, the more she began to pity him a bit.

She let him to take her back to his studio. As soon as they entered the room, Li Ji started to kiss and caress her while he took off her clothes. He wanted her. However, the tiny lamp's dull light was enough to set Keyan on edge. She asked for total darkness, but Li Ji only adjusted the lamp's position to make things "more romantic." Keyan felt stung by his inconsiderateness, which brought back the memories of that night in the remote town and how the next morning, unexpectedly, he'd wanted her again.

Li Ji's techniques on her already healed body led her to surrender this time. Little by little, Tang Keyan became fully aware of a brand-new joy in Li Ji's movements. She vigorously entwined herself with him, aroused into satisfying the thriving lust he seemed to derive from her, its force strengthening with each thrust. In the end, she knew he would leave her.

After Li Ji pulled out, Tang Keyan collapsed and lay flat without shedding a tear. Like a streambed after the water dries up in autumn. A jumble of pebbles, and boundless sands, traversed by a crisp wind that moved slowly, silently, straight through without twists or turns. She was flat plain, parched by drought.

It wasn't until she got up to go home and dressed with her back facing him that she could spit the question out,

"How many women have you slept with before me?"

There was no answer. Tang Keyan turned around and raised her voice, "Well?"

"Is it really that important?"

The cigarette held in the corner of his mouth flashed scarlet. He inhaled heavily, and the tip bloomed briefly like a crimson flower in spring, only to be impatiently plucked up and crushed. Tang Keyan looked at Li Ji through the gloom, realizing that all the fire in his young body was naught but an afterglow. Tang Keyan pursed her lips and chuckled softly.

Although abusing oneself was a pleasure, it was not entirely enough. With the last remnant of her smile, Tang Keyan deliberately asked again,

"How come you had the courage to do it that night. Weren't you afraid that my brother would ask you to take responsibility?"

"Then I would just take responsibility." Li Ji lit another cigarette, "I'd just marry you."

Tang Keyan froze; then retorted incredulously, "You'd marry me?"

Li Ji nodded.

His sudden commitment made Keyan feel that he was being flippant, as if there wasn't a thing in this world he'd bother taking seriously.

Time after time, they were always in bed talking about the same kind of questions. Over and over, in different locations.

She often met him in his studio where he'd wait for her. They had a mutual understanding. As soon as she arrived, he started to undress her. Only now, Keyan would lend him a hand. Especially garments with buttons, or clasps which were comparatively tricky, and thus always provoked an eager desperation. She savored this sensation coursing between them. In fact, she had learned from experience how to lose herself in the heat of the moment. She'd focus all her energy on the space between her legs, waiting to be aroused. She hardly thought about it and hardly cared, nothing could inhibit her passion. Li Ji often complimented her on her unbridled lust in bed. They were a good team and their extasy seemed boundless.

She also got used to enduring the aftermath. She always wanted him to fully satisfy her, even though her lower body ached when it was over. By virtue of the pain, she had proof of those moments, during which something *real* had occurred. With Li Ji's youth and superior technique, achieving it always seemed effortless.

Every time after sex, they'd lie in bed and she refused to let him fall asleep first. She was afraid of lying there awake and alone; but not because she was worried about thinking of Ann. She hadn't thought of Ann and other things for a long time. Especially, since she got to know this kind of ecstasy, it was even more difficult for her to give up. Thus, more than ever before, she believed in her own conviction—that faith she embraced in the most hopeless moments—that only sex between a man and a woman could bring true fulfillment; maybe even a kind of redemption.

She was afraid that as soon as he fell asleep, none of this would exist. The moment's glory would vanish in a puff of smoke. That was why she nagged him with questions, even provoked him on purpose.

Each time they saw each other, Tang Keyan always asked,

"Did it ever occur to you that it could be my first time that night? How could you be so bold?"

Initially, Li Ji wanted to dodge the question, but he was no match for Keyan's needling, and eventually responded,

"I didn't expect it to be your first time."

"Why not?"

"How can you ask such a question?"

Keyan started to giggle.

"So, you thought I'd slept with all kinds of men?"

"Not really, but I supposed that I wasn't the first."

"Do you regret it?"

Li Ji shook his head.

Keyan often encouraged Li Ji to talk about the other women he'd slept with. She would ask him about all the explicit details and then repeat them back to him.

"It's not fair. You've slept with so many women and had all kinds of sexual experiences. But that was my first time, and I was basically in the dark."

Though her voice seemed cutting; deep down, Keyan was actually completely indifferent. All she felt was distant solitude and a hint of wry amusement.

To her surprise, this provoked Li Ji's sympathy and sense of responsibility.

In fact, Tang Keyan was not a high-maintenance woman. She basically followed Li Ji's every order and instruction in bed. All of this was like a game. The rules were obvious and simple. Yet, Keyan had to admit that this kind of happiness dwindled bit by bit as she became accustomed to it. Often, she came to Li Ji hoping that her needs could be satisfied, but ended up feeling nothing in particular; and sometimes she didn't even feel anything at all.

It occurred to her that she would leave him one day.

She was unwilling to consider how their first night might affect everything afterwards. Especially since each time they met, they hardly left the bed, which suggested that Li Ji wanted nothing more than to sleep with her. Meanwhile, her self-preservation instincts made her resolutely believe that she was staying with him for the same reasons. She felt it increasingly difficult to hope that the sex in that remote town hotel had established an emotional bond between them. Especially in light of Li Ji's persistent lack of concern for her feelings.

By now, Keyan already had enough experience with Li Ji that when she thought back on it, she could roughly understand why he was so callous the first night. Perhaps, it was his frustration at being interrupted at the peak of arousal. Afterwards, sometimes she was not able to embrace him sexually. Li Ji's restlessness and insecurity in those moments, deepened her belief that he wanted nothing more than sex. What she really couldn't understand was why Li Ji always wanted to take her to hotels.

Keyan didn't need to make up any excuses for herself to explain her own behavior that night in the remote town. She didn't even have to use Ann as an excuse to redeem herself. She was a good girl after all. She did it for vanity after she'd became so helpless and hopeless. She accepted her fate; her new identity, and she couldn't care less about how Li Ji occasionally disrespected her. However, the fact that their trysts all occured in comparatively discreet places, gave the whole thing the tinge of an illicit affair. At least, there was some room for entertaining possibilities. But staying in those purely commercial hotels brought Keyan to her senses—Theirs was an utterly vulgar relationship, purely about carnal pleasure.

She could surmise why Li Ji wanted it this way. It was probably because he got bored easily when it came to sex. Out of pure curiosity, she pressed him about the actual reason, but he only retorted skeptically,

"Don't you think having sex at the same place is rather boring?"

After the two had been together for quite a while, Keyan was keenly aware that Li Ji was, in many respects, still like a boy. He was fairly uninterested in everything, except for *that*. Which explained why he was always changing places and focusing on cheap tricks.

The thing Tang Keyan found most insufferable was how Li Ji broached the topic; he never addressed it explicitly.

"Can I take you somewhere?" Li Ji asked, smiling mysteriously.

"Where?" Keyan inquired, although she already understood what he was implying.

"Somewhere nice."

"As long as it doesn't embarrass me too much." Was her only reply.

A few hours later, Li Ji would lead her down some narrow side street, since he hadn't the courage to book one of the fashionable tourist hotels downtown. The places he chose were invariably cramped, secluded hotels whose business obviously survived on guests who came for "a rest." Indeed, some of them were tasteful, but this merely made Tang Keyan feel filthier than ever. She couldn't help but think that if Li Ji was more transparent, it might be easier for her to accept.

One time, after Keyan had repeatedly refused, Li Ji simply started up the stairs of a hotel and then glared back over his shoulder, expecting her to follow him. Keyan immediately turned around and rushed away. In the past, she'd deemed this kind of behavior dirty and inferior. But this was the first time those feelings came back to her since she'd acknowledged their relationship. In that moment, Tang Keyan not only felt insulted, but also experienced a profound aversion to the whole thing.

As Keyan hurried away with her head down, a group of young men sitting on motorcycles in front of the hotel followed her with their eyes. It seemed that they habitually followed girls with eyes only, as they didn't so much as jeer.

Tang Keyan was beginning to feel rather bored.

After that night, she didn't meet Li Ji for a long period of time. To be honest, as her lust subsided, separation was not completely unbearable. Only on certain days did she feel an urgent need, especially now that she knew what she was missing. At the same time, she felt she'd already experienced all that sex had to offer. Caught between memory and amnesia, she became increasingly jaded. Sometimes when she looked back on it, it seemed there were no memories worth clinging to.

Although she could banish her lust, there were many things she had yet to work through. Keyan waited in a daze. She knew that other men like Li Ji would enter her life. Every one of them would be a traveler, who might leave his mark on her body. When it was all over, maybe she would have discovered another part of herself; or maybe she would be right back where she started.

In a daze, she was waiting for herself to be clarified. Precisely, she was waiting for another man, who would use another method to awaken the femininity that had lain dormant in the depths of her soul. When that moment came, she'd be truly *completed*.

Soon after, another man came into her life. By now, Tang Keyan found the romantic relations she thought unbearable in the past were actually not so arduous as long as she didn't seek to escape. He was a meek and slightly gloomy boy, a friend of a friend. She had seen him several times, but only had a vague impression of him. In fact, she often failed to recall his name. He was younger than Li Ji and obviously a virgin.

Friends talked about how he had a rather ambiguous relationship with another boy, but he wasn't brave enough to pursue it.

"People like them are all entangled with each other in a confusing mess," said a friend. "Truly, it's masochism."

She was overcome by a déjà, then a distant memory appeared before her, like the vision of a past life. Ann had a habit of teasing her just like that,

"You're really such a masochist."

Looking back on it later, Keyan realized that was the moment she decided she wanted him.

She met up with a few acquaintances, which of course meant drinks and plenty of sexual gossip. After a few rounds of toasting, everyone was tipsy. Keyan was a little under the weather, so she stayed off the hard stuff. In fact, ever since she lost touch with Ann, her passionate mood swings had all been subdued. In the midst of all this raucous debauchery, she was but a sober onlooker, gazing at an empty horizon.

Keyan immediately observed his unease, and she knew only too well how those emotions could torment one's sanity. Watching such a delicate boy, silently drinking along with everyone else, she felt a mix of pity and compassion. Beginning with the typical erotic topics, Keyan obliquely alluded to the possibility of same-sex attraction. She glanced up to see his response, and caught a glimmer of light in his eyes. Alas, it was only ephemeral.

Tang Keyan asserted that unless two people actually had sex, most of these affections might just be a kind of confusion or conjecture. Especially among intellectuals, who were constantly exaggerating and scrutinizing their personal attachments. It's like they've caused an epidemic of 'questioning'.

"Of course, some people say it's a lifestyle, and there is absolutely nothing wrong with it," Keyan continued. "If you don't accept your fate, or try to struggle against it, you'll just end up suffering more. It would be better to clarify things from the start. You are who you are. You can't become who you are not."

Keyan went on to argue that she firmly believed that for people who only had homosexual tendencies, heterosexual intercourse could be a means of 'adjustment'. Through sexual contact, one could gradually eliminate one's doubts and aversion to the opposite sex and eventually achieve a state of clarity.

"The most important thing is to try it out. You'd realize it's no big deal."

Keyan continued her series of eloquent arguments, but noticed that he hadn't said a word in response. He just sat curled up, arms fold across his chest, smiling faintly.

At that moment, Keyan felt quite jealous of him. She begrudged him the solemnity with which he guarded his misfortune. This "misfortune" if looked at another way, was rather a kind of blessing for Keyan. After breaking off her entanglement with Ann, and through sex with Li Ji, she discovered that she had nothing to show for it but an apathy born of emotional desiccation. After a brief respite at the oasis, she would have no choice but to confront the fearsome dunes.

She envied the boy's misfortune and pitied his unhappiness. She hoped in her own way to remove some of the confusion from his heart. Subconsciously, she began to seduce him.

Given her complete disregard for her own mind and body, she effortlessly gave him an opportunity. After blowing out the candles, everyone lay around on the floor. Tipsy as he was, he finally leaned over and kissed her.

She immediately realized he was not good at kissing. A delicate, young man like this probably had never kissed a woman before. She gently guided him, leaning into the kiss. The boy felt encouraged; one of his hands hugged her tightly and the other slipped under her thin clothes. At first, he clumsily hesitated but soon started stroking her breasts.

Keyan kept her eyes closed. His touch did not arouse her at all. She felt flattened and her body seemed to stretch on endlessly like a prairie caressed by a gentle wind. Every pore in her body was brimming with an unspeakable comfort. She sensed that she was waiting for something. Not waiting to be fulfilled; just to let him lay upon her—to embrace and absorb him wholeheartedly.

Perhaps because she put up no resistance, his caresses gradually grew more passionate. He continued to lick and suck her nipples, but his clumsiness made his kisses seem rough to her. The pain brought it all flooding back to her: the memory of her first night, the grief for her lost virginity. Keyan desired him intensely, but the pain had also triggered a sadistic desire for revenge. She wanted to plunder his unexplored completeness. She'd exploit him—both to compensate for her loss and to seek redemption. She was sure it was his first time, so when he slid his hand down her panties, she frantically and desperately loosened his trousers and fondled him back.

But he was unable to do it. At that moment, Keyan had no time to consider the underlying reasons; she just kept trying anyway, but it was no use. He could do nothing but stubbornly suck at her nipples.

Then they were interrupted. One of the others had thought up a new drinking game, and got up to relight the candles. They disentangled themselves. He straightened his clothes and walked out unsteadily.

The next day Keyan heard that he'd vomited all night, and even a few times more in the morning. He evaded her questioning eyes and never spoke to her again. When recalling that night, she sensed an odd connection between his sucking her breasts and his vomiting afterwards.

The events of that night gently brushed past her and faded away. Besides they had never had a *real* relationship, so she didn't feel the need to delve into his reasons for vomiting so violently, or to consider whether such an unpleasant experience, for such a melancholy boy might have lingering effects. She could not care about any of this because she just kept hurrying forward, inexplicably propelled by a turbulent and restless lust, not knowing to what ends it might lead her. In the back of her mind, she knew that raging libido had changed her. She had become selfish and could think of nothing but her own satisfaction.

Even so, her actions that night disturbed her, it was as if in that moment, she became a woman desperate enough to do almost anything. Keyan's faith in her self-discipline was completely eradicated. She felt that she had fallen apart but was still waiting in a purposeless trance. Alone in the fog, she couldn't fathom what else she could possibly wait for.

Then it came, out of blue, and shocked her to the core. She heard about it through the grapevine. Some friend inadvertently mentioned that Ann had been getting very close to another girl recently. No one knew what kind of relationship Ann and the girl really had, and no one dared dig into the details. Maybe it was nothing serious. Nevertheless, for days afterward, Keyan felt gripped by an unbearable anguish.

A year had passed since their separation. And yet, just the thought of Ann could still profoundly incapacitate her. Tang Keyan shook her head in disbelief. She desperately needed consoling, so she called up Li Ji.

The two got back together and began frequenting hotels. You could say they were inseparable—at least from the bed—though Keyan felt completely unmoved. Trailing Li Ji, she walked into lobby after lobby and without even glancing around to check if anyone might recognize her. They stood in front of the counter and waited for the keys. At first, she felt a perverse pleasure in degrading herself, but once she grew accustomed to the blank indifference of the staff, she found it no fun at all.

The hotels of this metropolis, large and small, all had their own tricks. Sometimes, they'd be led by the staff through a side door labeled "Employees Only." Then, onward down a shabby corridor, to another counter and a much more racy atmosphere. In Keyan's opinion, the illicitness of this adventure and the thrill of being chased out by a hotel hostess if they failed to check out in time were at least as exciting as the sex itself.

Of course, there were some poignant moments. One night, when Li Ji was rocking on top of her, she suddenly felt attached to him more than ever before.

"You know, I do love you....I do love you."

Stubbornly, she repeated it over and over.

After she said that a few times, her heart was flooded with sadness, and tears gushed from her eyes. At that moment, she hoped that he would stop and comfort her. She was willing to believe that he was sincere and to some degree would like to cherish her after all. Though he leaned in to kiss her, he kept thrusting away, without missing a beat. She choked with sobs for a moment; then, feeling that weeping during sex was rather ridiculous, Keyan dried her tears. *After all it was nothing worth crying over.*

She still sensed that she was waiting for something. It became progressively clearer to her that she just wanted to use Li Ji as a sort of vacation. As soon as she got back on her feet, and felt ready to face the setbacks like before, she knew that she would leave him.

Around that time, Keyan received an offer to fill a vacancy at the reform school. She'd depart for the south in a few weeks. Her days with Li Ji were numbered.

After playing the hotel circuit for a while, Li Ji finally asked her to over to his parent's house. It was an afternoon, and Li Ji's family was out of town. He gave her a casual tour, and then brought her to his room. He wanted her, and he was ready.

The new surroundings weren't exciting for Tang Keyan at all. She knew that no matter how well-decorated the room was, in the end, everything was about the bed. She went through the motions as always, all of their usual routine. Yet, this time she was surprised to find some new sexual delight.

As soon as they walked in the room, Li Ji immediately put on a record. At first, they merely moved along to the rhythm; then just when she was getting there, the record finished playing. The needle stayed on the turntable, scratching incessantly in the grooves. That staticky crackling, circled around the room like an age-old blues.

Li Ji noticed it, of course, but he kept pumping away, unwilling to get up from the bed. After a while though, his motions slowed a bit. Apparently, the sound disturbed him. Tang Keyan listened quietly:

K'cha K'cha K'cha
K'cha K'cha K'cha
K'cha K'cha K'cha

That same sound, repeating itself in those equal intervals. Gradually, the sound synced up with Li Ji's movements, like the clicking of an abacus.

K'cha K'cha K'cha

Tang Keyan felt that motion itself had never been so real before. In a trance, Li Ji was still inside her, digging deeper and deeper, inch by inch along with this sound. Suddenly, she realized that he truly penetrated her deepest possibility. An unknown, hidden part in her body had been awakened and explored.

It wasn't like before—that searing pleasure she'd had to accept with clenched teeth. No, this was a gentle and tender suction. It was as if she was being slowly submerged into the river of life. Encased in this comforting warmth, a profound sense of relief washed over her and her cheeks flushed.

"So, this is it" she sighed softly to herself.

When Li Ji pulled out of her, Tang Keyan closed her eyes and lay quietly—feeling a sweet black wave flood over her and swirl thickly around her. Her body was full of fatigue—rippling, like water that turned into hundreds of millions of particles and slipped from her grasp. Soon after, she sunk into a deep sleep.

She woke up to the sound of the rain. She had no idea when it began. Li Ji was out cold next to her. She looked out the window from her place on the bed. The little yard, shrouded in the late spring shower. Her gaze drifted over to walls of the neighboring properties. An idea came to her, like a waking dream. She got out of bed gently and tiptoed to the backdoor. As soon as she opened it, the cool wind threw a curtain of rain over her naked body.

Trembling because of the piercing chill, she instinctively folded her arms across her chest and recoiled slightly, but the rain kept tempting her. The memory of twisting on the faucet to bathe in the remote hotel, flashed before her. Keyan shivered and strode into the rain.

It was not a torrential rain, more like a gentle drizzle. The rain splashed in tiny beads over her hair and across her naked body; then, like a light puff of smoke, it seemed to diffuse. At first her whole body was shuddering uncontrollably. Suddenly, she felt the rain getting warmer, and she slowly uncrossed her arms. The bone-chilling droplets permeated her core, gradually distilling into a soothing clarity.

Finally, she stood upright in the rain and let the droplets converge on her body to form small streams of water, flowing down her breasts, lower abdomen, and down between her thighs. She stood there, occasionally opening her arms, or raising her face to the rain. After a while, she felt the rain was getting heavier. She had no idea how long she'd been standing there. Somehow, she remained still, standing in that late spring rain. If she had thought to look down, she might have noticed that she stood in a sea of clovers, their purple blossoms bobbing beneath her feet.

3

Tang Keyan sat there in front of the fountain for a long time, watching the streams twisting and twirling from one formation to the next. When the concert was about to end, she stood up and headed home. She walked more slowly than usual, so it was already past midnight by the time arrived at her apartment. She hesitated slightly, then picked up the phone.

After a few rings, someone answered. Li Ji's familiar voice filled her ears.

"Did I wake you?" Tang Keyan asked.

He hesitated for a moment, and then exclaimed with surprise: "Tang Keyan!"

She was startled to hear her full name.

"Were you asleep?"

"No, no," he hurriedly replied, "When did you come back?"

"A couple of days ago."

"Is everything okay?"

"Busy, as usual. How about you?"

"Same. Real busy. Can't catch a break."

She didn't know how to bring it up. It seemed like the first time she'd wanted to discuss something with Li Ji deliberately. Keyan fell silent. Li Ji was surprisingly curious about how she'd been doing. She answered his questions one by one, and after the two of them finished exchanging platitudes, it seemed they had nothing to say.

After a short pause, Tang Keyan asked, "Are you still painting?

"No, I'm too busy with work. I gave it up a while ago."

"Oh, that's a shame."

"It's hard to say." Li Ji replied as if he didn't want to talk about it anymore.

He hurriedly changed the subject, "That day, you came to my house. When did you leave? I was fast asleep, and didn't even realize you'd gone. I called you the next day, but your folks said you'd left for the south."

"I want to get a feel for the place."

The way he talked about those days made her feel close to him. She wanted to ask him something, but she couldn't help hesitating.

"Li Ji—"

Eventually, she went for it,

"I went to the symphony tonight. By the fountain. I saw…"

"Tang Keyan" Li Ji interrupted her, calling her full name again.

Then he paused for a moment and said slowly, decisively, "In the past few months, after you left for the south, I did some thinking. I'm telling you something that you may not believe. But I do love you, in my own way. Not because I was your first time, that's not important. It's just that…" Li Ji trailed off, unsure how to proceed. "It's because I learned something new about you, especially when we got back together the second time around. It made me realize that I could start to get to know a person in a different way."

Then, the words came out in a rush, "Tang Keyan, let's get married."

In the still of the night, the voice on the phone struck her word by word. Keyan raised her head in horror. The scenes from that evening flashed through her mind. Li Ji by the fountain; his head slightly raised to catch the spray. The sparkling mist settled onto his face…tiny droplets with shadows like tears.

2

ON HER GRAY HAIR ETCETERA

Tsao Li-chuan
(translated by Jamie Tse)

"With one foot in the abyss, there is no returning, no stopping, only gravity and the speed of the fall. Unless someone throws her a rope. Alas, she doesn't even have time to pray for a rope—or learn how to make one—so she is unlikely to ever get up. Her body is burning up, and she lets out a last gasp. As Fei Li-wen tosses and turns in bed, her once-black locks finally turn all gray."

1

The Devil.

The Devil is a whip, a chain, the tangled skeins twist around her like the shuttle of a loom. One loop, then another......wrapping around and around her until all that is left is her head—only her head—Ah, help!....... It's as if she has traveled back across eons to save her splintering frame.

Teeth chattering, the veins at her temples are bursting as she closes eyes tight. In broad daylight, she lies on the white bed. She doesn't appear to be having a nightmare, however. It's more like her soul has detached from her body and entered an ecstatic trance.

She sweats and moans. She trembles and, after what seems like an eternity, her dry eyelids finally crack open—*Damn, where am I?*

Drifting in zero gravity. *Come on, come back.* Reaching for the fragments of her consciousness—spiraling and stopping—she tumbles down. Falling all the way, through layers on layers of purple light, white light, blue light, into an endless abyss. Suddenly, a flood of golden light floods over her. An endless void of glimmering light.

Emerging from the trance, she makes out her alarm clock. Rays of sunlight reflect off its brass frame, dancing around her small room like glistening knives and flashing swords. Out of the blue, the smell of gun smoke assails her senses.

Outside her window, a strangely hued mushroom cloud hangs in the corner of the sky. Remaining still, she stands upright, not budging an inch, coming to a deadlock with the cloud. Checkmate. Sunrays permeate the room like the dust from a nuclear fallout. Her left eyelid twitches three times.

"Shit, that's apocalyptic......" Her right eyelid twitches too. A sunbeam takes aim at the spot where her eyebrows meet, striking like a cleaver, "Fuck!" She suddenly sits up.

The mushroom cloud is nowhere to be seen.

She feels something is off, looks down at her crotch and realizes her period has arrived, like a ruptured aneurysm, staining the bedsheets red. Great! Really. Fucking. Great! Some luck. It's like losing a bet without even placing one in the first place. Her periods were never on time like this! She gets out of bed, shuts the window, grabs any scrap of fabric or piece of cardboard she can lay her hands on, and seals off every light source. Her tiny room, now a cave—her personal lair. She bows her head and starts pacing—back and forth, back and forth—letting the blood trickle down her legs, dripping onto the floor—one step, one stain, one step, one stain—speckling the floor like tears.

The room is spinning. Her lips are parched like cracked earth after a long drought. She can't help but wonder if perhaps her blood has already run dry, her body already mummified—bone dry. There is a stinging pain in her throat—when she swallows, it's like a piece of silk getting torn. Her whole body is so dry that a doctor probably couldn't extract even 0.1 milliliters of fluid from her lymph nodes.

Opening the fridge to look for water, all she finds is a couple cans of beer. Well then. She cracks open a can and chugs it—then, immediately staggers to the sink and throws up.

"Yeah, go ahead! Puke yourself to death!" She curses herself. If only she could puke her guts out; puke her brains out; hell, just puke her whole body inside out—purge all the crap cluttering her up inside, until her body becomes an empty vessel, that she could fill with a little something else......She straightens up, turns on the tap to flush away the filth, and grabs a few Antacids, and some painkillers; swallowing them down with tap water.

Pain is the One. Pain is the Overlord. Headache. Backache. Sideache. Stomachache. Cramps. *Damn, it fucking hurts. What a useless wimp—can't even take a little pain.* She laughs dryly. Tracing her way back along the trail of blood, she staggers back to her bedside and picks up the phone.

2

Fei-wen is photophilic and has nyctophobia. Everyone knows. On a cloudy day, she wilts. On a rainy day, she withers. Sunlight is her elixir of life. Just to sleep at night, she needs to light her seven-square-meter flat with a dozen 100-watt bulbs. Her clothes come in two colors—yellow or white. She only uses porcelain or metallic dishware. Her flat? White walls, white floors, white bathtub, white toilet, and white vanity. Half of her furniture is painted chrome yellow. Her friends joke that she'd be better off just building herself a greenhouse and planting herself inside so that she can soak in enough solar energy.

"I'm not a plant!" Fei-wen retorted, "Besides, people need to practice moderation."

Obviously, no one protested—everything in moderation. How is a person supposed to live a long life without moderation? They had promised each other that when they all got old and had no appetite for food or sex—almost like plants—they would build a mansion and live in it together, worshipping a naked goddess. When the time came, they would vote on which goddess this would be—they might as well make it their late comrade, Gai Shu-ting tongzhi. They would keep a bunch of wild sows, hens, bitches, and female cats. Most importantly, they'd keep each other company, enjoying their old age together and would live it up until they're really old—old, old—old enough to be like the legend that goes, "Once upon a time, there was a coven of hundred-year-old witches and female demons......" For this alone, they had to practice moderation. Those who did not practice moderation do not live long. If it weren't for self-control and moderation, Fei-wen would not have ended things with Jiao-jiao last night.

"Let's break up, Jiao-jiao." Last night Fei-wen made up her mind to spit it out.

Last night....... The countless same-old last nights. Memories forged through collective desire are much more vivid than those made masturbating. She remembers. She remembers too. They all remember. One Saturday night years ago, they took to the streets, barefoot and scantily clad. Emma ended her "solo era" with a black lace petticoat. Jesse went grannie-style with her sleeveless cotton nightdress. She was like someone selling vinegar in wine bottles. Good girl! Good girls! The good girls softly smiled like balloon flowers blooming—hazy and clustering, in a translucent kind of blue...... Blue is distant, sorrowful; so damn clean—

like a wet dream with no excretions. Then, the female beasts went into battle, strewing casualties across the wastelands of memory, like manure.

Spare no one. Winds, blossoms, frost, moonlight. They had the roaring thunder as their battle drums; their hunting songs sliced through the night like raging sand.

The sisters took off their bras and draped themselves in thin lingerie. Swinging their breasts, big and small, they went in formation to patrol Keelung Miaokou. Like queens, they slayed with every step, turning trees to charcoal stumps with one searing glance. The two cosmic demons Emma and Jesse led the way—one yin to the other's yang. Big and small breasts stood at attention, they strode down the street, catching the eyes of those hunters and hustlers, and dragging them along like fish on a string. *Left, right, left, right, left,* marching in step. They were valiant, fierce, feisty. The onlookers' eyes crunched under their feet like pebbles —ke-cha, ke-cha, ke-cha—like a string of firecrackers.

It is said that even the pilgrims at the Shibawang Shrine lit a thousand and one incense sticks of incense for them. Arriving at the gates of the temple, they were dead wasted. A gale was blowing over the bay. As the winds picked up, Fei-wen flipped her skirt up over her head and squatted to light a cigarette. She could taste the salty moisture of the tides, its aroma mixing with the scent between her legs like a fine wine. She was mesmerized by the fragrance, cast out of time, enchanted......Suddenly, someone pulled her skirt off from her head. She looked up in a daze, it was Jiao-jiao. Jiao-jiao's eyes were bleary from the wine; she began to dance, wiggling her waist to summon the tides. Seductively caressing herself, twisting her limbs and curving her fingertips, shaking her hips like they could flow with the tides. Jiao-jiao's long hair met the wind like an inky water snake swimming into the heavens. Her red robe billowed up in the winds like a war banner, slicing through the sky. Unfurling, sinking its fangs and claws into the racing winds—riding their currents along the coast into the distance. Jia-xian cried urgently, "Jiao— Jiao—" She grabbed the wine bottle, threw her head back and drained it. Then she rushed and held Jiao-jiao by the waist. Their lips met, wine flowing between them. Boy, what a kiss that was...... Gai-zi said......

The founding members were Gai-zi, Jiao-jiao, Yong-lin, and Man-qing. At the time Gai-zi was with Zhang Ming-zhen, Jiao-jiao was with Jia-xian, Yong-lin was with Jesse, and Emma was with A-bao. Fei-wen was with no one—she used to be with Man-qing but then one day Man-qing finally packed her bags and left. It was enough to ruin the appetite of even the most adventurous eater. Fei-wen is a pro at that, the others said.

Eventually, there came Miss Jesse, Queen of luxury. Yong-lin was the one who brought her into the fold. No one had a good first impression. Emma stared at Jesse with raised eyebrows for two good minutes before finally catching sight of her ears, "Argentina amethyst. Hand-made. Nana at Long-men, is selling them for five hundred and fifty." She was referring to her gigantic pagoda-like earrings.

"You bought them for five hundred and fifty?" Jesse replied, scooting closer, her eyes searing. She seemed oblivious to the icy stares from the room, "How dare they sell them to me for eight hundred dollars!"

"You didn't bargain?" Emma was getting into it, "She first made an offer of eight hundred, right? Let me tell you, you have to bargain whenever you shop there......" That was it, they hit it off right away. Three minutes and they were thick as theives.

A-bao whispered to Yong-lin, "The way I see it, this woman is just as decadent as Emma, maybe even worse."

"She's spending her own money, so it's none of my business!" Yong-lin replied.

At the time Yong-lin had just started working in a publishing house. Her starting salary couldn't have been more than nine thousand. If she went without food or drink, and bargained the price down, she could buy sixteen pairs of pagoda earrings and still have twenty dollars left to spare.

Fei-wen sized up that enchantress from a distance. She had a different color of nail polish on every finger and toe. Black. White. Yellow. Blue. Pearl. Moss. Snake bladder green, and pig's blood red. Standing out against her face—pale, like a porcelain doll—that bloodstain at the corner of her mouth was actually—Guai-guai betel nut juice! Her hair, straw-blonde and hip-length. Her body was draped in hundreds of strings of beads, rings, bangles, earrings, which all rattled so loudly that they shook the heavens even when she was just breathing. This woman also carried a massive, yellowed cloth sack around with her. So full and bulging, one couldn't help but speculate about what strange things it might contain. Fei-wen frowned, took two steps back, frowning, something was off……

This woman set up camp at Yong-lin's place the very same day. And the mystery of the cloth sack was revealed, in it were all of Jesse's belongings—a sleeping bag, a steel cup, and some clothes. She didn't even have a toothbrush or a towel. The sack was soon emptied. She picked it up and shook it, out fell a few bundles of dry herbs, a ball of copper wire, some stones, a pair of pliers, a pocketknife, and some super glue…… The creepiest thing was a small gourd-shaped canister—jet-black and shiny—no one could tell what it was.

"Where did you pick up this woman?" Gai-zi finally broke the silence, "Wanhua railway station?"

"Ran away from home." Yong-lin answered.

"What does she do?"

"Just dropped out. Was in her fifth year in college. Couldn't graduate."

"So, will you be feeding her then?"

"Ha! It should be her feeding me!"

"You watch out!"

"We'll see."

Back then, Fei-wen had to report to her mahjong masters Yong-lin, Gai-zi, and Jiao-jiao every weekend. Ever since Man-qing went back to Japan, they were short a player, and since Fei-wan was the culprit, everyone had agreed that she should be the one to sit in. Fei-wen originally was counting on A-bao—who would return from the newspaper office at midnight—to bail her out, but A-bao was only a casual gambler. She'd eat and shower and have a few drinks; maybe even take a quick nap before she'd sit down to play. What's more, "napping" for A-bao usually meant sleeping until sunrise. For Fei-wen, it was like sitting on a pin cushion, and she'd beg Emma to save her, over and over, to no avail. Fei-wen's "masters" quipped that when it came to mahjong, Emma was like a rotten beam that can't be carved. So Fei-wen should just focus on mastering the art of the game, and they would never let Emma sit in. After Jesse came on the scene, Emma did not so much as spare them a parting glance before heading out with her partner in crime for an unforgettable night on the town. As the weeks stretched on, Fei-wen forked over enough "tuition fees" to buy few grade-A suckling pigs, but her mahjong skills didn't seem to be improving.

The mahjong party went on like an endless loop. Meanwhile Fei-wen got addicted to something else.

Her ears were getting sharper. She sensed a frequency and craved it more each day. There was something in her body that was eager for action, and she was getting familiar with this feeling—too familiar. Like a well-trained hound, aroused at the scent of blood, she was on her mission: pursuing the prey. Diligent dogs get the most bones. In those years, only she could hold a candle to A-bao. The number of lovers she'd had was more than Gai-zi and Yonglin combined. How does A-bao's poem go again? ...... Like the currents in the earth's core, streams bubble up from glacial pools in spring...... No, deeper than the earth's core and more springlike than snowmelt. No depth. No temperature. Undetectable. She heard it, that's all, she just heard it.

Heart racing, hands icy, ears burning. The sound carried from five floors below and one hundred meters away. At the mouth of the alleyway, *her* footsteps and the rustling of her clothes, even her breathing. As the frequency increased, Fei-wen became more and more agitated—the Dots, the Characters, the Bamboos, the Dragons, the Winds—the castle built by tiles crumbled in front of her eyes. Brick by brick, tile by tile, flushed away in the rapids, swallowed by the whirlpool. She was helpless. Her ears are her body, her heart, her universe. Ah, so strong was her impulse to howl and rush to the door wagging her tail. Just holding it back left her drenched in sweat.

Next to escalate was her sense of smell. She'd developed a canine's nose, and she began to sniff the scent of her master, the scent of her prey, the scent of the gods—but at the same time she also heard the gods say, no, no, child, you are just inviting a ghost to possess you.

"...... *Now it's been said, I have to forget. Old love's a lingerin' day and night, night and day, can't get you out of my head......*" On that night of the monsoon, Jesse's singing struck her ears like thunder, "*I know you're a player, heart like petals in the wind. Why oh why'd I fall for you again ......*" Fall for you...... In the midst of her reverie, Fei-wen fell for a three of bamboos; hesitating, she just couldn't bring herself to discard it. "Asleep at the wheel? Go ahead and play already!" Yong-lin tried to snap her out of it. Ah...... Not thinking of you, not thinking of you, not thinking......you......

An bomb exploded in Fei-wen's ears, shattering her.

The dreams of youth are broken. There's no hope for you and me...... Yes, no hope at all with this lousy hand....... *I know you are a wildflower with thorns, because I won't regret, no way, no how.......* "Hula! I won!" Gai-zi turned over her hand, Yong-lin was the last to discard, and thus the loser. Fei-wen got off scot-free, but it's hard to change the habits of an old dog, she raised her head and sniffed the air.

"What perfume do you have on today?" Yong-lin took the chance to nuzzle Jesse's chest while taking a whiff as they were shuffling mahjong tiles.

"*Poison.*" Jesse replied.

Fei-wen kept her head down and focused on stacking the mahjong tiles. Suddenly she felt woozy because of the overwhelming poison. That poison's the real deal! It turned out that when Jesse bent over while facing Yong-lin, she covertly stretched her left leg under the table so that its tip gently brushed against Fei-wen's calf, again and again and again ......Millions of tiny vipers nibbling on her, with miniature fangs that tickled as they sunk into her skin. The venom rapidly coursed through her blood vessels, reaching her heart. It got to the point that Fei-wen suspected everyone in the room could hear her heart pounding, putong putong, like the staccato of battle drums when two armies clash on a theater stage. Millions of troops charging forward, shouting war cries that would fright both humans and gods, "Kill!......"

Fei-wen came out of her stupor like a corpse awakening. Her ears could not hear, her eyes could not see, her mouth could not speak. Poison! Damn, it was poison! At any rate, Fei-wen was not cut out to be a thief. When she saw that Yong-lin didn't have a clue, she became more and more restless. Eventually, she finally realized she'd drawn an extra tile, playing right into her opponent's hands. It was too late to stop the damage, which proved to be so catastrophic that she was still in the hole eight rounds later.

Poison soon perfumed the streets of Taipei. Jesse still had more than half a bottle left, but she just poured it all down the drain. As for that little purple glass bottle once filled with Poison perfume, years later Fei-wen noticed it at Yong-lin's place. *Yong-lin and Jesse had been broken up for ages.* A few more years later, Man-qing married an American Jew in Japan whose Japanese was ten times better than hers, and everyone laughed at the news. Man-qing wrote in a letter that her old husband was nineteen years her senior. His ex-wife was Japanese, and his ex-

ex-wife was Korean—in a nutshell, he worshipped "Eastern Goddesses," and worshipped Chinese cuisine even more. She served him meat every day. His favorites were pork, chicken, beef, lamb, and human—especially the fat ones. Man-qing, plump, pale, and delicate, never missed any opportunity to shag the old man—day or night—shagging him until his legs gave out, which just made him crave her more. This woman was so callous; her heart was already set on the inheritance.

Man-qing kicked off a "wedding fever" in the group, from A-bao and her childhood sweetheart, Gai-zi's ex and her ex-ex, to Yong-lin's older classmate, who always said their connection was "spiritual not sexual." The most bizarre was Emma's latest lover Hong Mei-hua, the manliest-looking tomboy in Taiwan who would most unexpectedly wear a white wedding gown and don a bridal veil. A-bao couldn't believe her ears, so she attended the wedding banquet to see for herself. Afterwards, all she could do was sigh, "Got played by the amateurs!" As it turned out, Hong Mei-hua had gotten engaged two years ago. The others asked A-bao if she'd given them a wedding gift. She said she did, just like Emma instructed. Everyone turned to scold Emma, who coldly replied, "A stack of spirit money, the perfect gift. No?" Emma wished for Hong Mei-hua's death, out of spite. In the six months they'd been seeing each other, who knows how much gold and silver jewelry—not to mention cash—Emma had showered on this woman?

Hong Mei-hua didn't die, but someone else did. Slit their wrists but survived. Tried overdosing on pills and rushed to the E.R. to have their stomach pumped. Saved their life. So, what did they do? Snuck up to the hospital roof, jumped off, and ended up like a smashed plate of eggs and tomatoes—no way to put that back together again. Yong-lin went to identify the body—it was her sworn brother, Gai-zi.

Yong-lin didn't cry; she just drank, drank like the alcohol was water. She didn't eat, sleep, or speak—she just drank herself blind, to being on the brink of death. Yong-lin and Gai-zi had both studied philosophy. In university, they were like two outlaws against the world. They shared everything, their spoils and losses, glory and shame. They'd have been willing to kill for each other or burn the whole place down......that was the kind of love they had. A couple days later, Yong-lin managed to pull herself together sufficiently to help Gai-zi's parents with the funeral arrangements. The day of the wake, she finally fell apart, Yong-lin cried even more hysterically than Gai-zi's parents—her heart broke when she saw Gai-zi's peerless face stitched back together like a broken net. She had a fit when she saw the burial clothes. She was furious to the point that she nearly dragged Gai-zi from the coffin to change her back in men's clothes. Nobody could contain her, so they had to carry her out of the mourning hall. "Didn't even bother to tell me shit when she was planning to die. Now I don't fucking know who to kill if I have to kill somebody!" She said at the end of the day.

"The T University Suicide Incident: Graduate student Gai Shu-ting jumps to her death," marked the end of an era. The living had to go on living. If we can't learn from history, then we may as well forget it. No one knew what Gai-zi was thinking before she died. She didn't leave a suicide note. No last words, not even a diary. Not the faintest trace. The only lead was her lover Zhang Ming-zhen who had not showed up at all, and they reached out to her eventually. "I wouldn't know more than you guys do." Zhang said, "We hadn't fought, there wasn't somebody else, nothing was weird between us. She even told me that we could find a house and live together as soon as she got out of the hospital, and that once she passed the oral examination, we could save up and go abroad......" Zhang Ming-zhen, always the gentle and patient type, actually broke into a sneer, "Wanna know what I was doing when she jumped? Buying her some sneakers! She said she wanted a half size bigger; comfortable, best if they were jogging shoes. Ha! Can you believe it?" Laughing, she swiftly wiped away her tears.

Dead or alive, they all need a place to go. In or out, old or new, the cards keep getting shuffled. At this point it's Jia-xian and Xiao-qing, Emma and Yong-lin, Fei-wen and Jiao-jiao. A-bao is the most perverted;

she likes 'em young and cute. Since Hong Mei-hua got divorced, A-bao has bumped into her a few times at the T bars. Apparently, she was with a different girl every time, were all the spitting image of Emma—dark complexion, big tits and lips. Hong Mei-hua kept asking A-bao for Emma's number. Emma told A-bao, "You just tell her to go to hell."

That's it, go to hell. Jesse had said the same thing to Fei-wen. It's seared in her mind. What does it take to move a mountain? Wrong! It's not perseverance, but time. It's Jesse's motto as well, another line Fei-wen would never forget. The power of time is boundless. The first two years after Gai-zi died, they'd all get together and visit her grave on her birthday to offer flowers and burn incense. After a while, they all got busy and forgot. Last year when Zhang Ming-zhen got married and they all went to the wedding banquet, no one, especially Yong-lin, brought up Gai Shu-ting. Everything changes as time goes by, like mists over fields or fog on the sea. No more cutting it up in front of Shibawang Temple, Jiao-jiao no longer dances to summon the tides. In fact, she hasn't danced at all in a while now. Their nights have grown shorter. Sleep is important to people over thirty.

From time to time, someone new would come around, and everyone would rally a little, but it wouldn't last. Some things take time to materialize, it doesn't happen overnight. Besides, it would be too long of a story to tell, how they'd slashed through forests together, wallowed in each other's sorrows......and sometimes tore each other apart. Newcomers would always be outsiders.

Like the brat A-bao dragged in last night. Outsider doesn't begin to cover it, more like a total alien. "Pretty damn terrifying!" Jia-xian sighed once the kid had left. The kid spoke "Alien" all night; nobody understood what she was on about—Crayon Shin-chan, Saint Seiya, Kanji and Rika, The Cranberries, Tori Amos......it was like she was chanting a spell. A-bao reluctantly played along by bringing up the Grammy Award-winning singer K. D. Lang, "What about her? You know, the one who was in

Salmonberries?" The kid just curled her lip, "Her? Ha! Too old!" As if she couldn't see they were almost as old as K. D. Lang.

The kid then gave them a brief introduction to all the T bars, like she was pointing out constellations in the night sky. East Side, West Side, South Side, North Side. Polaris serves great cocktails but it's pricey. Spring Fever has a dance floor and karaoke. Orion is full of "old uncles." Sensory Zone is the most boring. All they do is hold talks day and night...... The kid has short shaved hair, and a few strands of her bangs are highlighted, dazzlingly white. Dangling from her left ear is a little double-headed axe. The kid said the double-headed axe is a symbol of lesbianism, in Greek mythology, but the story was boring, so she doesn't remember how it goes—Anyways, it was about a bunch of girls fighting people with this type of double-headed axe and they'd just fight 'til they're *hai*— Fei-wen thought for a second until she realized she meant "high" not *hai*.

"A-ma-zon......" A-bao did her best to enunciate clearly and help the kid finish her story, "A horde of women, so valiant and fierce, that they once conquered Athens. Had to have been about three thousand years ago......."

"Isn't it tight?" The kid was too busy playing with her earring, totally ignoring A-bao's words like they were nothing but air. The double-headed axe hacked at her neck again and again, "My friend got this for me in San Francisco, on Castro Street."

Listening to her speak Alien made everyone sleepy, but the brat's next sentence startled them awake, "I am vers!" From her tone, it seemed like bragging. Nobody knew what she was talking about. A-bao jumped in to explain to the group that being "versatile" means she can be with both butch and femme. Jia-xian still didn't get it, so A-bao said, "She can be with you and she can be with Xiao-qing, got it? 'Vers'—completely breaking through the dominant hetero stereotypes—just two female bodies facing each other. Returning to their truest most original selves......" A-bao was entranced by the sound of her own words; her tone sharp, and trembling like one of the crazies at the Chiang Kai-shek Memorial Hall, who hold up *Quotations from Chairman Mao Ze-dong* and yell "Destroy the Four

Olds." Yong-lin narrowed her eyes, as if she was questioning if A-bao was on the kid's side or theirs. Eyes wide, Jia-xian made no comment. She just grabbed the lime wedge from the rim of her Corona and went to town on it. Fei-wen shivered just looking at her.

The kid drank Vodka with Rum, with salt around the rim of her glass. Yong-lin said we don't serve that, so the brat slid herself back behind the bar and made one herself. She and Yong-lin were not exactly the petite type. Brushing shoulders and bumping elbows, the two squeezed behind the counter. Yong-lin tried her best to act the mature adult, keeping a straight face as she made space for the kid, but whad'ya know, the kid spun around abruptly, almost knocking over the Long Island Iced Tea in Yong-in's hand. The glass teetered, ice cubes clinking about dizzily. Yong-lin responded with withering side-eye.

"Do you know there's a drink called Rainbow?" When the kid made it back to her seat, A-bao had to play her favorite trump card, "Rainbow. Popular in the 1960s. Made with seven types of spirits, all of different densities, so each layer floats above another without mixing. One color for each layer—red, yellow, green—just like the rainbow. You have to set it on fire when you drink it......"

"Old uncle" A-bao's outlandish story finally got the kid to shut up and listen, but even so, she couldn't help but cut in, "Where do they sell it? Do you know how to make one?"

"Hong Kong." A-bao replied, the wind gone from her sails, "Word is, they got someone at the Shangri-La who knows the recipe."

"What about Taipei? Anybody know?"

A-bao shook her head.

"No worries." The kid reassured her, "I'll look around, when I find one, I'll let ya know."

Seizing the moment when the kid went to take a leak, Yong-lin warned A-bao she'd better tell that little twerp to scram. Besides, Yong-lin said, no one was interested in playing nice in front of this 1970s baby. Even when Navratilova retires, she'll always be "Bionic Woman." It's like casting Ken Takakura and Miyuki Nakajima for "17 Sai -at Seventeen-."

"Like oil and water!" Jia-xian said to A-bao.

Fei-wen chuckled, not at A-bao but Jia-xian's words. Well said, like oil and water.

"Let's break up, Jiao-jiao." Fei-wen finally made up her mind to say it. She made up her mind just as she cracked her fourth Corona. It was an inebriated epiphany—a drunk person getting her head on straight —and she wasn't even drunk yet. In fact, she's never had the guts to get drunk. "Let's break up, xx......" It's not the first time she's said this to a woman. Ten years. For ten years, the lot of them have been like fish stranded in a dry stream, spitting on each other just to stay moist and breathing. Like fish, scooped up and twitching in a net, tangled up into an absurd, spectacular food chain—A preys on B. B mooches off C. C provides for A...... Fei-wen is the only "vegetarian" among them. A Kelpfish, a White Whisker.

"Let's break up, Jiao-jiao." Fei-wen said it with her eyes. She surveyed the room. Yong-lin's hand was around Emma's waist, massaging the small of her back. Emma was already nine months pregnant. In the past year, she and Yong-lin agreed to look for a suitable sperm donor. Emma, the eternal perfectionist, just happened to find a man with the same blood type and horoscope as Yong-lin; the guy even has monolids and a philosophy degree to boot. The I.V.F. worked; Emma got pregnant. Apparently, the sperm donor doesn't even know that he has been treated like a disposable coke can, use and discard. Not to mention that there is another human inheriting his DNA and growing up in this world. Emma and Yong-lin are probably going to settle down since they've got it all— money, a car, a house, and now a baby. Fei-wen is a bit mystified by the whole thing; this is not the Emma and Yong-lin she knows.

Ah, they have yet to grow old together—so struggle on, comrades, for it doesn't count until all our hair turns gray! Fei-wen sighed. She looked at Jia-Xian's face and was shocked to see two deep wrinkles traversing her brow.

With an air of unusual solemnity, she raised her Corona and drank a toast to Jia-xian, "To longevity!" Poor Jia-xian had been transferred to Dongguan, on the Mainland, for three months and lost a whole 4kg. "I'm not going there ever again! Not even if they double my salary." Jia-xian said, "Talk about flyover country. If I were a bird, I wouldn't so much as shit there!"

No one knew when Yong-lin had gone to the kitchen, but she suddenly appeared with a steaming plate of fried tripe. She set it in front of Jia-xian. Yong-lin's joint never sells any stir-fry dishes. If lamb tripe isn't exactly easy to buy, it's even harder to prepare. Fei-wen did a double take. It was like seeing a whole new Yong-lin. Jia-xian didn't even offer a word of thanks; she just grabbed her chopsticks and dug into the fried tripe, one of her favorite dishes.

The kid finally left after Yong-lin closed up for the night. Jiao-jiao suggested that they all head over to the underground pub near her record company and keep drinking. She said……What did she say?

Decadence……. Right, that seems like the right word, decadence. She said she "really dug" the decadent vibe there. Fei-wen shook her head. Ah—decadence! Ah—Jiao-jiao……

Following in the footsteps of Decadence, they crossed over the post-modern threshold. The ornamentation, the irony, the frivolity, the hedonism, the senses…… The currents of decadence have long been part of the global trend cycle, roaming on the border of two centuries. Roaming, yes, roaming. Fei-wen was struggling along on the borders of her conversation with Jiao-jiao, straining to receive the endless string of codes she sent out; painstakingly converting them back into plain speech. Fei-wen sized up the room. The place was filled with geometric pastel-toned tables and chairs, the crisscrossing ventilation ducts on the ceiling looked like a giant circuit board. The photographs hung here and there along the walls were all close-ups of lips—wide, narrow, thin, plump; open, closed, teeth, no teeth; men, women, young, and old; all sorts of races—actually, it was repulsive to have so many lips. Lips and only lips. Lips like the piles of fish on ice at the supermarket. At least you knew for sure the fish there was food, but a bunch of lips? Talk about a buzzkill.

Fei-wen felt her breathing tighten. The lighting there was so dim. Sun-crazed Fei-wen could feel herself wilting. The group of statues standing in a corner were so poorly made that they looked like chimimoryo, and an entire wall at the back of the bar was taken up by a mosaic mural of naked men and women getting it on: *Portrait of a Hetero Orgy*. She didn't have a clue what constituted "decadence." Even if she did, it wouldn't mean anything. All she knew was she had to call it quits with Jiao-jiao. No question.

Jiao-jiao ordered five mugs of millet wine, one for each of them except Emma. The owner, Arian, had the hots for Jiao-jiao for a long time, so he always gave her special treatment. Jiao-jiao told them Arian was half Ami and a first-rate saxophone player and guitarist. Not only that, Arian could sing better than any of the male popstars in Hong Kong or Taiwan. "And look at his complexion—Hiroshi Abe's eyes, Hugh Grant's chin, Keanu Reeves' kind of 'cold on the outside and warm on the inside' vibe—he definitely will make it to the big time!" According to Jiao-jiao, a whole mess of producers have been trying to sign Arian, but, alas, to no avail. He's way more passionate about brewing and bartending than trying to be some kind of star. "His millet wine is first-class, artisanal stuff. He's super meticulous about it—even grows his own grain." Jiao-jiao said.

"Really?" Jia-xian glanced at Jiao-jiao mischievously, "Isn't mixing rice wine with Mr. Brown Coffee the trend these days?"

"I'm afraid you're behind the times." Jiao-jiao smiled angelically, "The trend now is Dao-xiang with Gu-Dao Green Tea, or beer with tomato juice."

On Her Gray Hair Etcetera 63

"How much does a person make selling wine? He'd sell out for sure if he could sign you as a wife!"

Jiao-jiao paid her no attention and got up to look for Arian.

"Back so soon? Is it a done deal?" Jia-xian said when Jiao-jiao returned.

Jiao-jiao turned to light up a cigarette, not sparing her even a glance.

From across the room, Fei-wen saw Arian switching CDs and suddenly Fei-wen's stomach turned. Here we go again! This woman! Even if she'd been struck blind and deaf on the spot, she'd still have been able to guess what CD it was. Jiao-jiao had been playing it nonstop for her for the past six months, and she had even taped the music video for her to watch. She had listened to it so many times that she just wanted to puke just hearing the first notes. How was Jiao-jiao not sick of this yet?

"Return to Innocence," oh yes, how delightful, returning to innocence. The problem is, what the hell is innocence other than a noun? "What ever happened to moderation, Jiao-jiao......" Fei-wen thought to herself.

Heh—Ee—Yah—Hi—Ya—Hi—Hi—Ye....... Listen. Listen to them calling, what an innocent call. Come my child, hold hands, and form a circle. Now I'm passing on to you the wisdom of our ancestors, you have to remember with your heart, never forget.......

What Fei-wen couldn't forget was the look on Jiao-jiao's face when she first introduced her to this song, "Return to Innocence," by Enigma. "Listen!" She was so pious and solemn, as if this was the damn Sistine Chapel and she was pointing out the beauty of a real Michelangelo, "Heh—Ee—Yah—Hi—Ya—Hi—Hi—Ye—" Jiao-jiao was belting it out along with the CD. As a matter of decency, Fei-wen put on her best show of "piety" and endured the rest of the song. "How come they can pull this off and we can't?" Jiao-jiao sighed. From Fei-wen's fogged out expression, Jiao-jiao could tell she was completely at a loss, so she quickly explained, "Enigma is this German band. They sampled this Ami melody and worked it into their own song, listen—" She played the CD again, "This is what the elders sing during the ilisin, which is pretty much the same as the harvest festival for us Han. All Ami young men have to participate in ilisin, which is kind of like a coming-of-age ceremony. All the men in the tribe form concentric circles; the elders in the innermost circle, and the youth in the outermost—layer on layer, just like…just like…The layers of an onion!" Needless to say, there was a limit to Jiao-jiao's imagination—that's probably what made her such a masterful secretary. Jiao-jiao couldn't help but laugh at her clumsy analogy. "Oh, who cares!" Swaying her head side to side, she started talking to herself, "Heh—Ee—Yah—Hi—Ya—Hi—Hi—Ye……. The innermost elders will start to sing like this, then they pass the melody from layer to layer, just like a choral ensemble, from the oldest to the youngest……" There were tears glimmering in Jiao-jiao's eyes.

"What does this 'oh—ay—yan' mean?" Fei-wen asked her.

"Hm…… Arian didn't say. Probably some sort of prayer to bring happiness and ward off evil spirits."

"We better learn it, so we can use it next time we have to perform an exorcism. Oh—Ay—Yan……" Fei-wen teased.

"Oh god, don't tell me you didn't feel a thing?" Jiao-jiao was horrified, "Innocence! The fountain of life! If we keep going on like this, we'e all going to stiffen up and die. Aren't you afraid?"

"How? Afraid of what?" Fei-wen giggled—innocently.

"You're hopeless, Fei Li-wen!"

Fei-wen looked at her but could not read a single thing from her face.

"Forget it! You got me this time." Jiao-jiao turned and left. Abandoning the faithful little machine which kept playing the tenor on a loop, again and again. Echoing and expansive, like the winds in a canyon.

Heh—Ee—Yah—Hi—Ya—Hi—Hi—Ye…….

Don't be afraid to be weak

Don't be too proud to be strong

Just look into your heart my friend

That will be the return to yourself

The return to innocence...

Jiao-jiao is the type who never tires of enlightening others, and so she did not give up on Fei-wen the delinquent. No, No. Jiao-jiao resorted to playing her videos. "I forgot that you aren't very musical," Jiao-jiao was all smiles, "Let's watch MTV, shall we? The images may touch you, and you'll see the light."

Fei-wen watched it, not just once. She did learn something—but she didn't really experience a return to innocence. It was more like a realization of what fucking terror is.

Return, return...... Fruits returning to the flowers, to the stems, to the soil; let tides return to the other side of the oceans; let the hooves of a horse return and backtrack so it would forever walk in place; let tears return to the eyes, to the tear glands, to non-existence; wrinkles returning to babyface; the inked returning to a blank sheet of paper; return...... Fei-wen could not help but question if the end point of return is shit returning to the mouth, humans retuning to zygotes, then back to Africa to Olduvai Gorge three millions years ago? Without self-discipline and moderation, then wouldn't all living creatures all just return to unicellular innocence and the world would just melt back into a pile of goo? "Chaos" to put it prettily......If it came to that, there'd be nothing. Nothing. The end of innocence is nothing.

And if you want, then start to laugh. If you must, then start to cry.

Be yourself don't hide. Just believe in destiny...

How horrifying! Fuck innocence! Fuck destiny! Fei-wen tilted her glass to the ceiling, desperately downing the last few drops of alcohol to expel all the horrible memories the music video brought up. Setting down her glass, she waved at Arian, he came over to the table and announced they had already cleaned him out of millet wine. So instead he handed Fei-wen half a bottle of Old Parr leftover from the last time when Jiao-jiao came around. Jia-xian ordered Taiwan Beer, while Xiao-qing made herself a Gin with lemon and Yakult (it was her secret recipe). Emma had a huge appetite. She'd already eaten half a loaf of multigrain walnut cake and two whole packs of beef jerky.

Jiao-jiao refilled Fei-wen's glass. Her miserable expression suggested that she knew what was coming.

Fei-wen could not bring herself to turn and look at her. A-bao's voice carried over from beside them, "...... Wanna know the scary thing? It was just a whole crowd of 1970s babies! Shit, are all the dykes over thirty dead?" Among them, only A-bao frequents the T and G bars, mostly for networking purposes—she's a reporter on the 'arts and culture' beat. A-bao says there are tons of 'comrades' in the culture industry. (That's odd. Fei-wen's field, broadly speaking, is the arts, but she has never met any 'comrades' at work). According to A-bao, Taiwan's tongzhi culture has been flourishing recently, all kinds of related organizations and publications were taking up arms—and among them, lesbians had greater voice than the gays, probably because they can ride in the wake of feminism. "Sooner or later, we will have to chart our own course," A-bao concluded, "The lesbian project cannot be achieved within feminism. It's incompatible."

A-bao finished her speech, the audience was nonplussed. Nobody even bothered to respond, not even Jiao-jiao. Jiao-jiao actually doesn't get along with A-bao. What's more, A-bao has told them the exact same thing countless times. What the hell does homosexual culture have to do with them? How is 'feminism' relevant to them? Haven't they managed to live to this point without all of that? It would be better to just get some sleep than having a talk like this at 2 a.m..

"Let's just go to bed." Yong-lin said. Fei-wen followed her gaze and saw Emma already fast asleep on a sofa in the corner.

The words "go to bed" immediately aroused Jia-xian, "How about it, Fei-wen? Shall—we—go—to—bed?" She was staring straight at Jiao-jiao.

"What a tart!" Jiao-jiao retorted.

Fei-wen hasn't slept with Jiao-jiao yet, and not just Jiao-jiao—she has never slept with any woman. In A-bao's words, she's "just fooling around." According to A-bao's system of classification, she, Yong-lin, Jia-xian, and Fei-wen are the "T" in lesbians—the tomboys, or the butches. In fact, these terms don't really mean anything to them, but they just make things a little easier to understand for the outsiders. It wouldn't faze them if you changed "tomboys" into "tomgirls"—it might fit them even better. Fei-wen has never been interested in labels. In her first decade as a "tomboy," she hadn't even heard the word before.

It is not about the labels, but the content.

"You are just fooling around! What are you doing if you aren't fucking?" A-bao was fed up with her.

"Hah! Fucking 'nothing' that's what she's doing." Jia-xian jumped in.

"Useless. What an ostrich. What a fence-sitter." Yong-lin concluded. She always said Fei-wen was useless, sexually useless to be more accurate, like an ostrich that kept its head in the sand to avoid dealing with sex —who knows, maybe if push came to shove, she'd even use this fact to "prove" she wasn't gay—too bad Yong-lin's reverse psychology never worked. Miss Fei Li-wen did not come over to the dark side.

Emma said she was "sick." Xiao-qing and Jia-xian had even given her a "tuition-free" demonstration. In an attempt to "awaken her." Someone else once told her, "Alas—woe to the great, mighty city of Babylon! The fruits you craved have left you. One day you shall fall, dear Fei-wen. Your Babylon will crumble into ruins. If you are unwilling to live among devils, you might as well off yourself now......" Just like Jesse said in her letter, "Dear Miss Fei Li-wen, if you can't figure things out yourself, then come, come to Jesse. Poison is the medicine you need."

Poi—son—you......

"Let's break up, Jiao-jiao." Fei-wen finally spat it out. She crouched on the sidewalk and dry heaved, and Jiao-jiao stood beside her gently patting her back. Fei-wen kept retching, but nothing came up. Holding her stomach, she turned and saw Jiao-jiao's long legs under her miniskirt.

"Actually, you can just go and be with Arian......" She said to Jiao-jiao's ankles.

"Fuck you, Fei Li-wen!" Jiao-jiao yanked her up, "Say it again! If you've got the balls!"

"Sorry, that's the thing, I got no 'balls'" Fei-wen was on the verge of collapse.

Jiao-jiao wouldn't let her drive, so she dragged her to a 7-Eleven to grab something to eat. Fei-wen filled her basket with beer, and Jiao-jiao sighed but paid anyway. Holding their purchases in one hand, Jiao-jiao ushered Fei-wen into a taxi.

"You two just can't break it off, can you?" Jiao-jiao broke the silence.

Fei-wen shook her head.

"So, you—" Fei-wen shook her head again before she could finish her sentence.

Jiao-jiao is a smart one, so she can understand, right? Fei-wen collapsed on Jiao-jiao's shoulder, fighting back the urge to vomit with all her might. She felt like she was riding a roller coaster, going through loop de loops. Reverse! Oil and water. Return to Innocence. The end of innocence is nothing. Go to hell, dear Fei Li-wen...... *Return to yourself, don't hide, the return to innocence......* All that could no longer be returned...... too late! Fei-wen finally threw up.

3

A-bao said that Fei-wen has the best features—broad shoulders, flat chest, narrow hips, long legs with high cheekbones, pretty cheeks, and a defined neckline—but most importantly, that fucking Fei-wen is heartless and completely oblivious to the consequences of a breakup. So, Fei-wen definitely has what it takes to wear pants, have short hair, and be a femme tomboy. What's more, until she turns thirty-five, she definitely has the best odds among them all to seduce those underaged girls.

"Better yet, she can promise them they'd still be virgins when it was all over. No need to worry about damaging their marriage prospects." A-bao had all the zingers.

Fei-wen wasn't sure if A-bao meant to praise or degrade her. It's true that she's not the type to promise to spend the rest of her life with someone; it's also true that she has never been one to bawl her eyes out, or attempt suicide over something as trivial as a breakup. Long before she met Jesse, Fei-wen realized that the more she acts like this, the more people would try to "awaken'" her, to mold her, to test her boundaries. She knows that they like her for her bluntness and stoicism; the blunter, the better. It's as if she is helping them test where they should draw the line.

She is the blessed one. How could she give Miss Fei Li-wen a second thought? Other than her teen years and learning to be heartless, for Fei-wen becoming a tomboy totally depended on being at the right place at the right time with the right people. She did not even have to make much of an effort. The winter when she was almost six, she lost her mother. Fei Li-wen was brought up by her father and her three older brothers. Ever since she was small, she wore her brothers' old clothes and went to the same barber shop as they did. Even whenever they had a fight with others, they never forgot to bring her along to learn a thing or two. What more could she ask for? Without lifting a finger, she inherited all of the tricks of the trade—starting from Year 3 of primary school, she'd follow her brothers around and learned how they would pick up girls. In Year 4, she began to running errands for them and buying them cigarettes. The corner stores were selling loose New Paradise—unfiltered. Sometimes they would even slip her one. The first time she smoked a cigarette, she almost choked to death. Her face became flushed and her eyes turned red. Her eldest brother punched her right in the chest, "How old are you? And you don't even know how to smoke!"

In Year 5, she had her first kiss with her eldest brother's busty girlfriend "Boba Boobs" A-Xia. In Year 6, her eldest brother brought home a soiled copy of *Playboy* for the brothers to share. Maybe it was because they were so nervous and excited…At any rate, they forgot to kick her out of the room. Later on, she accidentally came upon A-Xia and her eldest brother "fighting" between the sheets…… How's that for an awakening? Then, there was that one time when Xiao-qing and Jia-xian had downed two bottles of red wine, undressed, and spared no effort to "demonstrate" for her. They used their fingers, lips, tongues, and even several sex toys they had rustled up especially for the occasion. Secretly, Fei-wen wanted to laugh—her "enlightenment" had come way earlier and was way more detailed than what they imagined. She had learned everything too early, and also too late. During her final years in middle school, heaven knows, there were a couple times where she had thought of taking her third brother's scout rope to hang herself.

She had always been "enlightened" about the fact that she didn't have a penis or balls. Her breasts were small; they grew in late but still filled out their form. As for menstruation, the explanations in the health education textbooks had made her break into a cold sweat. When her best friends began secretly exchanging information about their "friend," Fei-wen was almost filled with grief and anger thinking her best friends had already formed another clique excluding her—for themselves, her best friends, Fei-wen would even pray for her period to come sooner; she wanted this so badly that she'd be willing to take a punch to the jaw and, without flinching, swallow the blood, spit, broken teeth in one gulp—anything to have her wish granted. Until she reached Year 3 at middle school, she had no one to turn to except for A-Xia, who offered her a "lesson."

Without saying another word, A-Xia took off all her clothes, guiding Fei-wen's hand across her body. Come on, let me show you. Here are the breasts, here, inside the tummy are the uterus and ovaries, and this is called the "vagina." If a boy inserts his cock here, you'll get pregnant, and the baby will come out like this...... Fei-wen snatched her shivering hand back. She understood. A-Xia, smiling, kindly handed her a pack of sanitary napkins and sent her home. A few days before the second semester of Middle School, Year 3, her first period finally came. What is meant to happen will happen; she was like a martyr ready to meet her maker as she calmly and solemnly stepped into the washroom to take care of the matter. When she was washing her underwear, she thought of her mother for the first time. From then on, until she left home for university, Fei-wen always doubly wrapped up her used sanitary napkins and disposed of them outside the house.

Other than menstruation and peeing, Fei-wen learned everything from her father and brothers. Although there were moments every month she felt all alone, it was not unbearable—before she turned thirty, she never experienced menstrual cramps, her bleeding was never heavy, and her period lasted for at most two to three days. She sometimes wondered if her father and brothers had forgotten that she is female. Perhaps even she herself had forgotten.

It is hard for her to relate to how A-bao and others have been "making an effort" and "training themselves" all these years. They always remember to have their shirts buttoned from the right—treating it as a matter of honor, like medieval knights abiding by their commandments. Fei-wen takes it even further—she wears an undershirt and, thanks to her small breasts, has never worn a bra, not even once. A-bao smokes Marlboro, Jia-xian is a loyal fan of Long Life (hardpack), but Fei-wen's preference, New Paradise? Sorry, they have never smoked it.

A-bao hits the gym twice a week for two hours every time—more frequently than Xiao-qing gets her facial treatments. Yong-lin jogs, Emma swims, Jia-xian plays tennis, Jiao-jiao does yoga, and only Fei-wen "the slacker" doesn't exercise. "The 1970s' babies are everywhere now, haven't you noticed?" A-bao warned her, "Don't be so arrogant, you are one of the elders!"

It was not arrogance but despair. Someone who has never worked hard to keep the things she has would not know where to start even if she wanted to.

She can only sketch a self-portrait in her mind—it all started when she discovered her first gray hair. She began having a recurring dream of her gray hair growing and flowing like a stream stretching on for miles, twining around her, and turning her into a mummy—hair silvery, eyes blurry, hunched with stooped shoulders. Tottering, (maybe she is thirty-nine, maybe forty-nine, she cannot imagine a number higher than this), she gets on her rusty motorcycle. The unrelenting, blinding sandstorm is like thousands of double-headed axes careening toward her, and her feeble flesh can no longer hold them off. Her forehead, the corners of her eyes, her cheeks, neck, and limbs, are marked with age spots and wrinkles. It isn't just her—all of them suffer the same fate.

...... At least, before turning thirty-five, she "has what it takes" to attract underaged girls...... But thirty-five is just around the corner, and the power of time is unstoppable. Fei-wen is not so naive to think that she can miraculously elude time's massacre. She already has gray hair, remember? Even if it's only a few strands, it would not take long for them to spread like wildfire or overflow like a bursting dam—all that talk about return to innocence is just bullshit! Isn't she innocent enough? All this time she has basically been stuck in the age of innocence, unwilling to move forward. Self-assured, she has been playing it safe with the same preteen game of handholding and kissing with her girlfriends, with no sex involved. Playing the role of a tomboy as if she is just playing pretend. But how the hell can she keep acting innocent after turning thirty-five?

She has been wasting her energy. From adolescence to her early middle-age years, she has been daydreaming and wasting her energy, about to age and wither away before growing up.

On Her Gray Hair Etcetera

The vermillion stream flows from her body. It's as if all the flow of periods that are yet to come have merged into one torrential current. Within half an hour, her overnight pad is completely soaked. Fei-wen remember the big chunky maternity pads that she bought for Jesse and realized that she has no choice but to head downstairs to the supermarket to buy some. As she makes her way there, her legs wobble like she is walking on water. After climbing the stairs and changing into the extra-large pad, she cleans up the blood-stained bedding, mattress, and bedsheets and collapses into her bed like a dead fish. Her lower abdomen continues to cramp up and throb with pain. She is covered in sweat, from head to toe, on a cool December day.

She has to call in sick to work, Fei-wen thinks to herself. She still has several layouts that can't be postponed. She'll just have to ask her colleagues to help finish them. She still has two jackets at the laundry. Isn't the due date of her credit card payment today? Her phone bill is already overdue; the service will be cut off if she doesn't make the payment. Her toilet has been leaking forever, and she's yet to get it fixed. The bulb in her table lamp needs to be replaced. She's almost out of spray glue. The bread in the fridge has gone moldy and needs to be tossed. On top of it all, her motorcycle is still at Yong-lin's....... Fatigued, Fei-wen crumples to the bed, thinking about this list of tasks. She begins drifting into a daze when she has an epiphany—this is it isn't it? This is all there is to her life. No, this sucks. She has a bad feeling about this. She picks up the phone and calls Jiao-jiao.

"Actually, why don't you just go marry someone—" She wants to say this to Jiao-jiao but hangs up after the first ring. This is not about Jiao-jiao, and Fei-wen knows it. Jiao-jiao has her own philosophy of romance — "absorbent and breathable, no leakage, no wetness"—the only one with anything to be ashamed about is Fei-wen.

"Go marry someone, Jiao-jiao......" Fei-wen is still thinking to herself, "Don't waste your youth on me......" Wow, damn, is she starting to sound like a mantra-chanting monk? Can't she say something new for a change?

Man-qing got married, Duan-ru got married, and so did A-bao's two exes Bei-bei and Lin Zi-qi, and so did Jia-xin's ex Hui-xin, and Yong-lin's A-ji—they all got married, thanks to Fei-wen. "Despicable and ignorant," that's what Jesse called her. If she's incapable, then why doesn't she just get lost? *You advise them one by one to get married and turn over a new leaf. Who do you think you are?* Guanyin offering salvation to all? Heaven knows who is the one who really needs salvation!

"You're sick you know!" Jesse fumed.

And Fei-wen knows she is sick because, for example, she used to wet the bed. She's an old pro when it comes to dealing with bedwetting. Since she was five, she would get up and get changed by herself, washing her pants clean and putting them out to dry on the bamboo rack, tiptoeing so as not to wake anyone. She wet the bed the night before her mother ran off. That winter when she was five, almost six, on that dark and stormy night she got up to clean and change her pants quietly, but this time even her mattress and blanket were wet, she was left with no choice but to go to her parents' room to sleep with them for the night. She stood at their door, and the first thing she saw was four feet, her father and mother's, then she recognized their naked legs above their feet. However, when her eyes moved further up, it was a clump of dark-yellowish flesh, which she didn't recognize at all. The clump of flesh quaked and undulated, sometimes slow and sometimes fast, as if something frightening was about to happen, but nothing happened. Once her eyes had adjusted to the darkness, she finally managed to tell that the familiar-looking round shape on top of the clump was the back of her father's head. She hesitated, not knowing if she should call for her father, and at that exact moment, her father suddenly buried his head underneath like he had gone mad, and a face emerged from under his underarm—it was her mother.

Her mother glanced at her for a brief moment but didn't say a word. Trembling, Fei-wen immediately turned and fled back to her room. The next day her mother disappeared. Fei-wen had a high fever for three days and three nights. She kept dreaming of her mother, who was dragging her by the hand. They were running, and her mother was leading her through a dark, shadow-filled maze. They took many turns and sprinted quickly as if there was some heinous monster chasing them. The sounds of their ragged breathing and hurried footsteps, along with a cacophony of noises, echoed loudly. Her mother kept dragging her forward, but they could never find an exit. Eventually, her mother let go of her hand and said, "Let's just fend for ourselves......." Then Fei-wen woke up and both the dream and her fever went away. Fei-wen returned to the real world and grew up, but she continued to wet the bed.

The last time she wet the bed was November 12, 1986, Sun Yat-sen's birthday. Fei-wen would never forget. It was 5:30 a.m. in the morning, and she was at Yong-lin's place. Waking up startled, she saw the carpet wasn't wet, but her underwear and jeans were done for. Arching her back in a catlike manner, she got up, trying not to make a sound, like a professional spy. She stepped over, one by one, Jia-xian, Jiao-jiao, A-bao, and Emma who were splayed out on the floor, and then she stepped on something hard and cold, the missing mahjong tile no one could find the night before. Feeling her way through the dark, she headed to the toilet to pee, but she was at a loss about what to do next. Damn. No spare underwear. Fei-wen used toilet paper to pat her underwear as dry as possible and then went out to the balcony for a smoke. It was quite cold for November. She fidgeted. *Standing still? No, doesn't feel right. Pacing? That's not it either.* In wet briefs, freezing her ass off. She shivered so much that she started choking on the smoke. *Fuck it.* She stubbed out the cigarette. *Might as well get going.* She fished around in her pockets for her motorcycle key. *Where was it?* Even her wallet was nowhere to be seen. *Great*, she muttered to herself, *just great*. She didn't even have cab fare!

In her vexed state, Fei-wen caught sight of a glint of light in the corner of the room. When she took a closer look, she realized that the light was bouncing off the rim of a glass. Someone was crouching on the floor in the corner, drinking a glass of water. Who could it be but Jesse? In the dark, her shadowy figure and her disheveled hair made her look like a ghost from a Japanese horror film.

"What do you think you're doing? Sneaking about in silence!" Fei-wen wasn't in the mood to humor her.

"You're the one sneaking about here! What are you doing up at this hour?"

"Piss. Did you smell it?" Who knows what had gotten into Fei-wen's head when she blurted that out, "I wet the bed."

"Oh—" Jesse didn't even flinch, "And—?"

"And I don't have another pair of underwear to change into, Lady!"

"Why didn't you just say so in the first place?" Jesse stood up and handed her the cup, before heading in and grabbing her a pair of underwear. In the restroom, Fei-wen examined the pair of tiny grayish-blue laced panties with little stars all over. The underwear was so tiny, and she doubted they would cover half her bottom. She put them on carefully, not wanting to rip them by accident. Once she had them on, however, she realized she had underestimated these panties. "So, Jesse wears this type of panties......" She started to imagine......but then she didn't know where exactly to begin—at that time, nothing had happened between them.

When Fei-wen came out of the restroom, Jesse looked her from head to toe and burst out laughing, "Why so short?" She pointed at her orange athletic pants. Fei-wen looked down, she had to admit, Jesse had a point! They barely reached mid-calf.

"Hey," Jesse scooted closer and poked Fei-wen in the butt, "Are they too tight?" She moved to tug her waistband.

"What are you doing?" Fei-wen recoiled. She already found it hard to get used to these low-rise panties and the way they left most of her belly exposed. The last thing she needed was something else to worry about. She pulled her pants back up, keeping a good distance from Jesse.

Jesse asked her to walk out with her and grab breakfast together. On their way there, Fei-wen, on a whim, decided to tell this woman every single detail of her bedwetting saga including what she'd seen the night before her mother disappeared. The whole time, Jesse seemed distracted. Fei-wen couldn't help stuttering; she'd never told anyone about this before. Both women looked straight ahead, avoiding the other's gaze. Suddenly, a motorcycle came flying by; Fei-wen heard it and instinctively reached out to pull Jesse toward her, but she was too slow. Jesse was hit by the bike's windshield and thrown to the ground.

"Fuck your mother!" In a heartbeat, Jesse leapt up and cursed the driver out. The way her voice projected her words made every passerby within a hundred-meter radius turn and give her a look of approval. "Where the hell are you going, driving so fast? And don't you dare pull that 'my mother's funeral' bullshit!" Jesse's rage was unabated. Grabbing some pebbles, she threw them at the motorcycle even though it was by now probably a kilometer away. Fei-wen wanted Jesse to head back and tend to her injuries, partly because her abrasions looked pretty bad, encrusted with gravel and blood, but she could also already tell that this woman was quite the piece of work. Jesse refused outright, "Come on—we're *almost there—!*" Damn. This woman could flirt.

They reached the crosswalk just in time for a yellow light. Jesse went for it anyway, "Come on, Fei-wen—let's go for it!" While Fei-wen was still hesitating, the light turned red. She stood there, watching Jesse dodging through the traffic like a cat with nine lives and fearlessly reaching the other side. For the next thirty seconds or so, there was a four-lane road between them, and they looked like a couple who got separated in a crowd. Fei-wen gazed through the traffic at the petite girl with two pigtails and red slippers on the other side. Submerged in morning sunlight, a faint shadow appeared at her feet. She smiled innocently at Fei-wen—Jesse wasn't wearing her glasses so she couldn't even see clearly. Her innocent smile was perhaps directed at nothing in particular . Even so, Fei-wen couldn't help but smile along with her,

"Atta girl, Jesse……," She called out to Jessie from her side, but she knew that it was completely impossible for Jesse to hear her.

Atta girl, Jesse……

"The Sun sets now to rise again tomorrow, my youth has flown by like a bird that won't return……" Jesse loves singing this song. *"The sun is setting, so let's make love"* is what Jesse likes to say. Fei-wen would never forget those shimmering eyes, red lips, white teeth, like a porcelain doll —innocent, without an evil thought in her mind. The toxic ones always look the most delicious…… Fei-wen hates herself for being so blinded and obsessed, for overreaching.

The purpose of youth is making love, Jesse said. The more, the better—for both your body and soul. Lovemaking is the ultimate act of vulnerability and generosity. Orgasm is the perfection of beauty—see, all those years ago Jesse had already been using her body to experiment with a "return to innocence" of sorts—she never hid her sexual desires.

Meanwhile, Fei-wen's love-making record is zero; her lust has never been ignited, so maybe she really is sick. If so, it is quite a serious condition indeed.

"Oh, poor Fei-wen……" Jesse once said with so much concern, like she wanted to save her. The problem isn't damnation though; it's their "invisibility." It is fine not being able to kiss in broad daylight, but even in front of their "comrades" they still have to keep a low profile and maintain the ruse. Fei-wen's way of putting friends before girls stemmed from her unwillingness to butt heads with Yong-lin, but she never knew it would lead her to this dead end. Jesse could never let go of this. Although it has been years since she broke up with Yong-lin, because of Fei-wen, to this day she still has not returned to the social circle they once shared.

"Have you heard how loudly cats call when they are in heat?" Fei-wen would never forget when Jesse said, "Saint Fei Li-wen, I'll sing your praises!"

"But Yong-lin really loves you……" Fei-wen's response sounded like she was reciting from the Four Anchors and Eight Virtues morality primer.

Jesse heaved a long sigh, "Ah! Miss Morality. You know what? Go —to—hell—!"

Dying……do you think it's that easy? Jesse's asked on the phone last night.

"I think I'm about to die, Jesse." Fei-wen had just sent Jiao-jiao away. Jesse was the only person she could confide in.

"For real?" Jesse was laughing, "Is it cancer or what?" She kept laughing, "Did you get in a car accident? You're more likely to be the one who kills someone in the car accident though……" And then she paused for a second when she was done laughing, "What? Is Jiao-jiao planning to kill you?"

"No, Jesse! I—have—gray—hair!" It sounded like a cry for help.

"Gray hair?" Jesse laughed even louder, "No big deal. Don't make a fuss about it! Don't you know how to pluck them? You know, you can always just dye it, or shave your head and go bald. Hell, some of my pubes have even gone gray, can you believe it? If dying is that easy, I'll go jump off a building with you tomorrow……"

Are we still talking about jumping off a building? Fei-wen is completely worn out, hanging on by a thread—where would she find the strength to jump off a building?

4

No one knows when the sneaky sunlight started seeping in. Fei-wen's cave is soon to be no more. She rummages through her house and grabs a thick blanket and covers up her window. The blanket then becomes half a wall of flowers. Things in the past start coming back to her.

Coarse weave fabric feels lumpy like it is mixed with cottonseeds, rough enough to exfoliate your skin, according to Jessie. Its texture is similar to that of soil. Rose mallows, the size of soup bowls, sprouting from the red earth; their cores and the edge of the petals are tinged indigo and laced with golden threads. Beneath the blossoms are stems and leaves, robust and luxuriant—clustering, entangling—emerald fades to inky black. Jesse dances among the flowers, smiling and waving at her, those sparkling eyes, red lips, white teeth, and porcelain skin. Come! Fei-wen, come to Jesse—bewitched, she marches toward her……

Jesse's blanket. Fei-wen once crawled on this blanket and kissed her for the first time. There was a sea of flowers in Jesse's hair, her clothes—all around her, inside and out. Fei-wen felt lost in the the sea of flowers, unable to stay the course. The sweetness was nectar—an elixir—which Fei-wen knelt and worshipped. She was possessed by an uncontrollable desire. Only when she snapped out of it, did she realize she was done for. Jesse's lips were already firmly pressed to hers. Nectar and Elixir—Poison's disguises. The sweeter it is, the more toxic. Blindly, she feasted on them and followed the road to her downfall—even though she didn't die, she became forever incomplete. This thing called "hate" had rendered her defenseless.

Hate. Yes, the type of hate she hoped never would stain her life. She runs from it as it were the plague. She can't hate, shouldn't hate, mustn't hate. Yet she has nowhere to retreat. Even love has abandoned her. There is no hate without love, according to Jesse's logic. Without desire, there is no soul—no light without darkness; no joy without sorrow. How could a soulless person hope to love with a soul? Such logic, so circuitous and indirect, almost drove her crazy. Jiao-jiao's words still ring in her ears, "Do you really not know or are you just playing dumb? She has slept with every single one of them, every—single—one—of—them!"

Really? She's slept with every single one of them? Fei-wen doesn't believe it.

However, Jiao-jiao is a woman of integrity and Fei-wen believes her to be trustworthy. She has helped Fei-wen to keep everything that happened between her and Jesse a secret for so many years. The first time they played footsie under the mahjong table, Jiao-jiao witnessed their adultery firsthand but promised Fei-wen that she would keep her mouth shut. She never pried for details or told anyone.

Then one day, Jiao-jiao became her lover and was no longer just a friend who kept her secret.

Never had Fei-wen imagined herself succumbing to someone like this—Jiao-jiao, Queen of the Fierce and Spicy, started serving up plate after plate of strawberry shortcake day after day, and Fei-wen, prone to indigestion, started to develop a fear of sweets. Overactive stomach acid wasn't what caused Fei-wen's pain. What really hurt was the resurfacing of the deep-rooted resentment she thought she had buried for good—about how she had slept with every single one of them, every single one of them—the flames of hatred flicker red in her eyes.

Jiao-jiao is at the end of her rope, and Fei-wen knows it.

Left with no choice. No choice. Yet, oh how bloody is the blade. No choice. Fei-wen cross-legged, on the floor, both hands fiddling with her toes, eyes blank. There is something in her body rapidly expanding. A voice in her head tells her, "Quick! Quick! Or else you won't make it......" *So what if she does not make it?* Fei-wen asks herself. Whether or not she sticks her neck out, the blade will catch her in the end. She knows better than anyone how fast hate can take over a life. Back when she was still inside the womb, still just an embryo, fate decided that she was to be infected by this hatred. That she has lived to be this age is truly remarkable.

Moving her numb legs, she stands up slowly and walks to the bathroom where she fills up the bathtub and gets in for a soak. Gradually, the hot water turns warm and then becomes cold. Fei-wen gets up, drains the cold water, and fills the tub up again. She repeating this cycle again and again. Clouds of steam flit about the room, guiding Fei-wen into a hazy dreamland—she is standing in a dank and gloomy cave in which the humid air is laced with the acrid smell of medicinal herbs. Lining the walls of the cave is a circle of glass tanks that surround her completely.

Inside the tanks, suspended in fluorescent yellow fluid are specimens—body after body, all in the fetal position, their skins wrinkled and tinged sickly shades of white, blue, or purple. These are human specimens. People with their eyes closed. Dead people. Tiny people. So very tiny that they look both human and like the young of an unidentifiable animal all at the same time.

These specimens are the bodies of stillborn babies. Some of these infant corpses have deformed faces while other have deformed limbs. For every one of them, the umbilical cord is wound tightly around the neck, limbs, and chest. A few of them are perfectly flawless, with fully formed faces and limbs. Fei-wen pauses, bewildered. Blink—a fluorescent yellow world—only now she is one of the tiny people in the tanks. The person on the outside looking is both her adult self and her mother. She floats in the bone-chilling fluorescent liquid. Her mother stares silently at the tiny Fei-wen for a while, then turns away and walks toward the mouth of the cave. Tiny Fei-wen calls after her, "Mom, I am not stillborn yet......" but her mother has disappeared without a trace, leaving adult Fei-wen's shadow shivering on the cave wall.

5

Cold! So fucking cold! This pair of psychos, she and her third brother, went all the way to visit their mother at the end of November just when a cold spell descended.

...... A-gui, your kids have come to see you...... The person their mother ran off with introduced them to the tombstone that read "Here lies Xu-gui of the Fei family." Fei-wen squinted to make out the characters engraved on the bottom left corner: "In tearful mourning, sons: Zheng-wen, Ming-wen, Hong-wen." *Come on, give me a break.* Who among them has ever come and wept? If they had to fabricate stories, they might as well just go all the way and put Li-wen down as a son. Truth is, she'd rather it read, "Erected by her beloved, xxx"—only if this Little Chen had the balls. Perhaps her mother and Little Chen were both afraid that they would be denied a place in the underworld. Fei-wen pursed her lips; before her icy sneer could form, it was blown away by an icier wind.

Her mother had been with Little Chen all along. They had roamed east to west and lived all over Taiwan. She died two years before Fei-wen's father; by then, she'd been on dialysis for years. On the way there, her third brother filled her in briefly, "There's a place called Xinshe in Taichung, you've heard of it, right? Little Chen has a corner store there, which doubles as a betel-nut stand, Mom is buried somewhere near the seedling farm......" Fei-wen didn't know when her third brother started searching for their mother, just like she didn't know when he became her comrade, a fellow tongzhi—that's right, two in the same family. Her third brother is gay—the scruffy kind who has a crewcut and stubble—a comrade who can walk down the street, undetectable to outsiders. All she knows is that he and his lover Xiao-long have been steady for five years now. They are both "versatile," though her third brother is usually a bottom. They have a tacit understanding that both would sometimes sleep around, but because of AIDS they have been fairly monogamous recently. As both siblings and comrades, Fei-wen and her third brother are now closer than ever. They don't really talk about it, probably because it is easier being siblings than being tongzhi.

Her father never knew about her third brother's sexuality. Fei-wen, in contrast, was officially kicked out of the house many years ago. "Lowlife scum!" Her father cursed her, "Bastard!"—as if Fei-wen's genes had nothing to do with him and as if he played no part in Fei-wen becoming a tomboy. Intense hatred flashed in his eyes; he was a man who would turn on his own kin before abandoning "righteousness."

It's all in the past now. A few days before he breathed his last, Fei-wen went to see him one last time. He didn't have the strength to curse her out or drive her away. The old man's dying eyes were so sunken into his face that he could barely see; sometimes streaks of weak red light flickered ever so slightly. It was a very different kind of hatred; its object was no longer human. When Fei-wen bathed him and changed his diapers, he just stared up at the ceiling and let her take control—he was just a wrinkly bag of bones with a wrinkly, wilted penis; it couldn't have been much bigger than her little nephew Yiji's, and he'd just turned one. "Dad," Fei-wen could not help but tell him in Taiwanese, "Such is life!" even though she knew he didn't even speak a lick of Hokkien. After he passed, Fei-wen went back to the old family home to sort through his things and found several faded old photos she believed were her mother's. When she showed them to her eldest brother, he said if both she and her third brother didn't want them they should just throw them out. Fei-wen tossed them all away without even asking her third brother.

"Does he know about any of this?" She fished a pack of cigarettes from the pocket of her jacket and handed one to third brother.

Third Brother just shook his head. Probably better this way, Fei-wen thought to herself. When their mother left, their eldest brother was twelve. If he intended to forget, it would be that much harder for him than for them. So who were they to disturb his amnesia?

...... *A-gui, your kids have come to see you*......

Although she came mentally prepared, standing on the bleak hilltop and making offerings at her mother's grave left Fei-wen at a loss. She tried her best to piece together her mother's image, but her mind was completely blank. Her memories were as sparse as the field of withering silver grass before her eyes.

...... *A-gui, this is Hong-wen, this is Li-wen, look, he's a grown man now*...... Little Chen handed them each three incense sticks. Fei-wen felt the smoke sting her eyes, she blinked furiously—suddenly she was afraid that Little Chen would mistake this as crying. To Fei-wen's surprise, Third Brother was also choking back sobs. The siblings froze on the spot like popsicles; they turned their heads away in the other direction, trying not to look at each other—if they had, each would have found the other's expression strange and unfamiliar.

…… A-gui, may you watch over these kids, bless them with good health and success…… Little Chen prayed quietly with a rapt expression. Out of the blue, Fei-wen caught a whiff of hairspray that reminded her of her father. She couldn't help but look over at Little Chen's hair. Glossy and smooth, just as she expected. The smell of Lin-shen hair wax. In the ten years she was with Little Chen, had their mother ever thought of their father because of Lin-shen hair wax? Had she thought of her children? Was she happy? Was she satisfied? Fei-wen suddenly recalled a song Jiao-jiao wrote called "The masked," which was about all the lesbians hidden among the "good wives and mothers." Jiao-jiao originally pitched it to be recorded by the company's "Fairy Princess," but there was predictably no follow-up whatsoever. According to Jiao-jiao, the company's Fairy Princess, Cynthia, is a femme lesbian. Who in their company hasn't seen that tomboy girlfriend of hers who does underground music? When Jiao-jiao was making the final edits on the music video for the Cynthia's second single, "Childhood," she secretly inserted a three-second scene: a group of little girls wearing masks and holding hands as they jump from log to log. The scene is backlit and filmed through a filtered, wide-angle lens to produce quite the eerie effect: bubblegum-pink virginity trampling on wilted, helpless penises.

She's lying, la-la-la, she's fooling you, la-la-la, the smiling mask, the crying mask, the pretty mask, and you still don't know, whether she loves you or not……

Theoretically, Fei-wen should be touched—was this not a poignant and magnificent lesbian love story on display right before her eyes? Her mother and Little Chen—yes, Little Chen is a woman, an old tomboy—a real "old uncle." Little Chen had hooked up with her mother, and the two ran off together, leaving the city they knew. Her father was cast into an abyss of shame and hate, so fathomless that he breathed his last before he'd reached the bottom. Ah, the mother who abandoned her husband and children…… Fei-wen didn't know if she should praise or condemn her. Tongzhi comrades, Xu-gui and Chen Yue-zhu, other than being a fellow tongzhi, they had no ties with her at all, right? Fei-wen tried her best to review the facts objectively, to remind herself that if they couldn't be mother and daughter, wouldn't it be enough if they were just fellow tongzhi? Yet, the ineffable feeling in her heart remained.

They ate at Little Chen's place and had sautéed oysters with fermented soybeans, braised pig intestines, cold sweet potato leaves dressed with soy sauce, and chicken soup with shitake mushrooms. Fei-wen had seen a few of these among the dishes Little Chen brought to her mother's grave earlier. Little Chen said they were her mother's favorite dishes. Though Little Chen was the type of person who didn't really make much of an impression, her cooking was impressive. Fei-wen had a massive appetite and devoured two bowls of rice in rapid succession. During the meal, Little Chen kept shooting her questioning glances, as Fei-wen had been making quite a determined effort to act as manly as possible, wanting to broaden Little Chen's horizon. Meanwhile, her third brother kept looking at Fei-wen in exasperation, asking the unspoken question, "are you fucking done yet?"

The old tomboy Chen Yue-zhu, the Chen Yue-zhu who had taken their mother away, had a bulging belly, chunky arms and short legs, small eyes and nose, and a mouth of yellow teeth stained by nicotine and betel nut juice—Chen Yue-zhu neither came close to being "cool" nor being "a good guy" by any stretch of the imagination...... Damn! Fei-wen gritted her teeth and shoved a mouthful of sweet potato greens into her mouth, not anticipating the huge clove of garlic hidden within, causing her eyes to water from the spicy sting—so much for manliness.

There was nothing left to do after the meal, so Fei-wen fished out her cigarettes again. All three of them lit up their smokes, filling the house with a haze like a dry ice effect. Little Chen smoked and chewed on her betel nuts, eyes glued to the television, not saying a word. She then boiled some water and made herself some tea, still not saying a word. Fei-wen and her third brother tried to settle into their small rattan chairs and tried not to make any startling sounds in this shared silence. Her third brother is quite tall, almost six feet, while Fei-wen is around five feet five. The greatest tragedy of being tall? It's tough to sneak in and out of places. Fei-wen dragged on her cigarette as if she was trying to inflate herself. Sucking all that hot smoke into her lungs just to keep herself warm. It took all her energy just to keep from shivering. Fuck, why was this birdshit place so cold? It was at least five degrees Celsius lower than Taipei, damn it!

Just a bit longer and then we can get out of here, Fei-wen signaled to her third brother. Her third brother just cleared his throat, "Zheng-wen sells braised pork for a living—" All of a sudden, without rhyme or reason, he said that. Little Chen just replied with an "ah," implying that she hadn't heard clearly. Fei-wen jumped in to explain.

We siblings have been close. This was her opening.

Zheng-wen was in a gang for some time before he joined the army, but he didn't seem to be one of those big shots, because other than a flat drill bit, they had never seen him carry any other "tools of the trade." He had no prospects in the gang, which probably explains why he quit after returning from the army to become a salesman selling pressure cookers, which was the most terrifying part. Fei-wen really worried about him —he managed to avoid getting killed by machete while in the gang, so wouldn't it be embarrassing if he got blown to death by those pressure cookers? Later, he switched to selling toilet bowls, office accessories, and even furniture. A few years ago, he was working as a security guard. After he got married, his father-in-law gave him a perpetual, interest-free loan to help him to buy a shop with one condition—he had to quit gambling. Three days before the shop's grand opening, his father-in-law sent him a big gift—nine booklets of secret family recipes and a pot of nine-year-old braised sauce as a blessing for a long-lasting business. Fei Zheng-wan has since been keeping his promise and selling pork feet and braised pork on rice for five years now. His biggest motivation is his fear of his father-in-law—that old man was said to be part of a real gang and had quite a lot of influence over Yunlin County. Fei-wen had seen him chopping pig feet—an old, shriveled man in his seventies, sleeves rolled up, showing off his two roaring dragon tattoos. And man, the way he chopped those pig feet— with such speed, such efficiency, and such ferocity!

Fei-wen told the story with such spectacular detail, to avoid giving Little Chen any chance to chime in. Little Chen twirled her cigarette, sipped her tea, spat out her betel nut juice, and shook a leg—when her right leg was tired, she switched to her left—she was focused on the story.

Her second brother Ming-wen died of liver disease in his last year of middle school. Fei-wen strived to keep her voice as calm and emotionless as possible because she feared that her mother's spirit might be hiding somewhere, eavesdropping and waiting to jump out and go mental on her. "It was all thanks to the Joint College Entrance Examination. The studying broke him." She immediately named the culprit with such conviction, that no one would guess she was "fabricating a charge."

Hmmm, good improvisation, Fei-wen thought, she even surprised herself. Where had she gained the ability to lie through her teeth like that? Maybe her subconscious had already tampered with this part of history, imprinted it so well that she could recite it backwards. Heaven knows, they had to keep it a secret anyway. There was no guarantee they would tell the truth even if her mother was there—it was her third brother who first sensed something wrong with her second brother, when he saw him eating New Paradise. He was really eating them, putting the whole cigarette in his mouth, and chewing on it like he was eating Eng-lung's Heart-to-heart Chewing Gum. Later, he started drinking Parker Ink, gulping it down like soymilk. He ate soap, those bars of orange lemon soap that come in the net bags tied by a string. He devoured them like they were more delicious than Morinaga Milk Caramels. He ate rubber bands, newspapers, charcoal, match sticks, Otsuka Oronine H Ointment, and Green Oil; and he also ate thumbtacks, watercolor, razor blades, and erasers...... There was nothing he didn't eat. His gastric acid was like sulfuric acid, digesting whatever he ate. He just couldn't die. Their father decided to tie him up when he started eating feces.

They lived rather miserably during those years. Their father had rushed to seize the last chance to join the manufacturing industry and turned their living room into a garment factory. He joined the loan club and borrowed money to buy knitting machines. Before they had received any orders, a group of chattering aunties showed up to work. They'd keep seven or eight knitting machines rattling away all day, churning out sweaters while their father's money flowed away like a stream running dry. Second Brother lost his mind around the same time.

The aunties stopped coming, leaving their house filled with sweaters. Finished products and semi-finished ones—most of them missing a sleeve or a collar, and way too short to be worn—all became piles of defective sweaters that wouldn't sell. The only thing that outnumbered the sweaters was the yarn—balls of cashmere wool of all colors and thicknesses, were shoved into every nook and cranny in the house, eventually spreading to Fei-wen's bed. On hot summer days, it became so stuffy and prickly that her whole body broke out in a rash.

They couldn't even sell the machines, so their father had to keep his chin up and work with the yarn and sweaters himself, trying to patch his broken dream. Every sweater counted. He went to the market and hawked his wares as a street vendor just to bring home some grocery staples at the end of the day. One night, awakening after wetting the bed again, Fei-wen heard her father hard at work on that rattling machine. After taking care of the damage, she headed to the living room to take a peek.

The rattling had stopped. Her father was talking to someone.

"Leave, just get out of here!" Her father said.

Fei-wen stood in the pitch-black kitchen and saw her father untie the hemp rope from her second brother's body and pull him up from the chair.

"Leave, just get out!" Her father dragged her brother through the courtyard, opened the front gate, and pushed him out, and then slammed the door shut behind him without any hesitation.

Fei-wen saw red flickers of rage in her father's eyes. She knew intuitively that it was hate—the type of hate she hoped would never stain her life. She returned to her room quickly, opened the window screens, and threw out every single ball of cashmere wool on her bed. Then, she laid in her bed and slept soundly till dawn.

The next morning, she awoke to discover that there had been a downpour the night before. All the cashmere wool she had thrown out was ruined. Her father beat her with a rattan switch, made her kneel for an hour, and forbade her to eat for the whole day as punishment. She was happy to pay the price (perhaps she even smiled a bit), because she hadn't slept so soundly in ages.

On the third day, her second brother's corpse surfaced in an abandoned fishpond about five kilometers away. Her eldest brother brought her and her third brother along to identify the body. Second Brother had swollen to twice his original size. His mouth gaped open like he was greeting them. Her eldest brother cried, but she and her third brother didn't shed a tear.

The solitary journey, the quest to battle hate, it all started from here.

6

"Mirror, mirror on the wall...... Who's the deadest of them all?"

Fei-wen walks up to the mirror and pauses to ponder it. Another Fei-wen just stands to the side, observing.

The long oval mirror was a birthday gift from Xiao-qing and A-bao many years ago when they were still together. Xiao-qing said, "Fei-wen, for all our sakes, please check yourself in the mirror before heading out. Don't be so unkempt all the time." She's not unkempt, Jiao-jiao said, that's just her style...... Fei-wen didn't have an opinion on any of this; not on the mirror, nor on Xiao-qing and Jiao-jiao's comments. Jesse, in contrast, was of the opinion that a mirror this big would only put a person on edge, "You'll always feel like there is 'something' appearing from nowhere in your house, haunting your peripheral vision. It's a nervous breakdown waiting to happen!" Jesse then pieced together a few scraps of leftover fabric from her sewing projects and made a huge sheet to cover up the mirror. In all these years, its ghostly face had yet to see the light of day.

In fact, it was not until after the mirror was obscured that ghostly apparitions really began appearing, putting Fei-wen's nerves on edge. The brown linen patch in the center was a piece from Jesse's sleeves. Whenever the wind blew, Fei-wen could see the milky white jade bracelet on her wrist—rough linen and cool jade. Fei-wen's palm and the tip of her fingers still remember how they felt...... The green piece at the top was part of Jesse's tulle puff skirt, the one so voluminous that it looked more like a bed curtain. One twirl at a time, dominating the dance floor at Diana over on Linsen North Road one Christmas night...... the piece below had an even longer history. It was from an aquamarine ice-patterned open-back body suit—one of Jesse's favorites for a time...... Fei-wen spun deeper into her memories, on that summer day they'd all set off from Yuanshan Zoo, crossed the Keelung River, walked past the observatory, and finally reached the Shilin Night Market. It was a muggy afternoon, punctuated by distant thunder rolling like battle drums. The witches were in high spirits. Fei-wen brought up the rear, trailing after the aqua blue ice-pattern piece all the way, staunchly and steadfastly like she was following the banner of the Queen......

The past flashes before her: those pretty eyes, that pretty smile...... Ah, talk about seeing ghosts. A single scrap of fabric is already enough to put her courage to test. She is scared of Jesse, yes, but fighting fire with fire, one day she'll become truly indestructible. Especially these last two years, after giving birth to Ya-ya and going through a divorce, Jesse's looks have changed. These rags are now precious archaeological samples, allowing Fei-wen to recall the Jesse of another era—the Jesse draped in layers of chiffon: agate green, icy blue, cobalt violet, and fuchsia pink...... These days, Jesse cuts her hair short and plucks her brows thin. Her clothes are either black or white. Since giving birth, she's had issues with her thyroid and rather than plumping up, she's basically become a bag of bones. Her complexion is pale and sickly—some might say vampiric—and she is still as venomous as ever.

The Fei-wen standing on the sidelines sighs. The other Fei-wen reaches out to pull the piece of patched fabric down from the mirror. It's the first time Fei-wen has ever seen herself stark naked.

The female body in the mirror somehow makes her feel distant. "Hi! How are you?" She greets her. She inches closer to her and cautiously touches her face. She notices she has a mole there and a freckle here. Gently, she caresses the delicate wrinkles on her neck, traces the contours of her collarbones, their ascent and descent...... She then examines the two tiny bumps on her chest, which are called breasts. Her hands circle around the nipples and areolas. She counts three strands of hair on her right and five on her left. She travels down her ribs, one by one, all the way until she reaches her abdomen. She slides her fingers across her lean and slender waistline, then her bulging and protruding pelvis. She combs the bush of curly dark brown body hair under her navel and between her two legs. Under the bush, of course, she knows, are the labia, the clitoris, and the vagina. As a matter of common knowledge, she knows that inside her pelvic cavity are two ovaries and a uterus.

She grabs a small mirror and uses it alongside with the bigger one, looking at the left side of Fei Li-wen's face, then the right, not missing a single spot. Even the insides of her ears. She checks her back and finds three moles and two blackheads. She moves on to check her armpits, navel, and anus...... The more she sees, the scarier it becomes, this body; this body that she has been with for more than three decades is so unfamiliar and strange.

Her misery is so great that the Fei-wen who is standing on the sideline is almost in tears. Having neglected her body for thirty-three years, she'd have no one but herself to blame were she to wither away on the spot. Could she not wither away though? She was sprouting gray hairs and losing sleep. It's always the same nightmare day after day, week after week. Over and over, she dreams that she is tightly bound up in her gray hair, which flows for miles like a silver stream, wrapping her into a mummy. Everyone knows she is afraid of the dark. It's no news that she keeps a dozen 100-watt bulbs on when she sleeps. On cloudy days she wilts; on rainy days she withers. Sunlight is her elixir of life—but today she blocks the sunlight from her room. With her head hung low, she paces back and forth, like a trapped beast circling its lair...... time is running out.......

Blood flows from between her legs, and gray hairs shoot up from the top of her head.

Who are they to wish her longevity?!? On her last birthday, at the end of November, Jesse gave her a gold pendant engraved with the Chinese characters for "Longevity." Fei-wen simply had to ask herself if they all saw her as a kid, like Ya-ya still in diapers, sucking on a pacifier. What good would a longevity charm do for a little ghost doomed to wither away before ever getting a chance to grow old?

That night Jesse had especially procured a bottle of Chivas, just the kind she likes, a 21-year-old vintage Royal Salute. Fei-wen finished half the bottle by herself. Even though she drank the last two glasses on the rocks, she was still completely wasted.

In the middle of the night Jesse woke her up, "Let's take a shower!"

Fei-wen, from sheer instinct, grabbed her motorcycle key and was ready to flee, but she ended up getting dragged to the bathroom by Jesse, staggering and stumbling all the way. A thousand jets of water cascaded from the shower head, hitting the ceramic tile and causing a deafening echo. Fei-wen's clothes became drenched and clung to her body. Jesse moved to help her undo her buttons, but Fei-wen lifted her hand to block her. "What? Are my hands poisonous too?" Jesse said. Yes, they were poisonous...... Fei-wen made a concerted effort to stop her, trying to speak up, but before she knew it, Jesse had already stripped her down to her tank and boxers. Fei-wen immediately sobered up and backed away, alarmed, until her back was up against the wall. Jesse kept inching closer, and Fei-wen had no way of escaping; all she could do was push herself further into the wall. Jesse's hands gently entwined around Fei-wen's back; *phew*, it turned out she was only going in for a hug. Fei-wen let her guard down and hugged her back. The cascading water became a net, trapping them—water weaving in and out between them like little fish, little translucent fish.

In the end, Fei-wen didn't get to shower. She headed to Jesse's room to borrow a change of clothes. When she returned, she leaned against the bathroom door to talk to Jesse.

"I've got some cookies in kitchen. Baked them yesterday, want some?" Jesse turned around and asked her, running a hand through her damp tangled hair.

"Save those for Ya-ya. I'll pass." Fei-wen said.

"Ya-ya isn't coming this week. She's going to Japan with her grandmother."

"How's Wu Zhi-peng then? When is he getting married?"

"Next month."

"Will Ya-ya stay with you, or him?"

"Come on, give me a break! She'd be doomed if she stays with me.......and I would be too."

Fei-wen's gaze rested briefly on Jesse's bony back. She took a deep breath, and make up her mind, "Hey, how long's it been since the last time you had sex?"

"Huh?" Jesse looked at her.

"I asked, how long it has been since the last time you had sex."

"None of your damn business!"

The two stayed silent for a while, listening to the dripping water. Seeing that Jesse was not about to say anything, Fei-wen headed back to the living room, sat on the floor, and started playing Tetris.

She heard Jesse turning off the gas on the back balcony, then blow-drying her hair, opening and closing her closet, doing the dishes, and taking out the trash. The blocks fell from the heavens—concave, convex, horizontal, vertical—like hail slamming into the ground, their rhythm pounding in Fei-wen's head. Forward, backward, left, right, flipping, twisting, they hurtled down and formed a completed line, then BOOM! —they disappeared from the horizon. The necessity of disappearance, of negative space, of self-control...... Fei-wen smelled the aroma of coffee. Jesse had been sitting behind her since God knows when.

Fei-wen had reached the final level of Tetris, and she was still playing with complete ease but stopped because it was getting so boring.

"You died?" Jesse asked her.

"It's that I can't die. That's what's so annoying!"

"Go play something else then. You've been playing this for like a century. I can't believe you're not tired of it."

Fei-wen smelled something, it wasn't the coffee......she sniffed her clothes, "Smells like you."

"Duh! These are my clothes. Of course, they smell like me."

"No, it's body odor." Fei-wen teased, though she was actually mocking herself because she was so nervous.

"You're the one with body odor!" Jesse gave her a good kick.

Fei-wen steadied her breathing and as she leaned back, she grabbed Jesse's foot and started playing with it. Jesse isn't ticklish, but every time she would pretend that she was just to play along with Fei-wen. This time, however, she didn't even react. Fei-wen pulled at toes, and tickled the sole of her foot, but Jesse didn't move an inch and just stared ahead blankly was as if deep in thought.

"You just asked me how long it has been since the last time I had sex—" Her voice carried faintly.

"It was just a casual question," Fei-wen quickly explained, "You don't have to answer. I mean it."

"Last week......" Jesse continued regardless, "With a male colleague—" With those six words, Fei-wen's world crumbled and didn't even have time to dodge the wreckage, "A few days ago with A-bao, yesterday with Huang Yong-lin......"

Fei-wen's head imploded with this rockfall.

"And Jia-xian—" Jesse kept on going, "I've been doing it with all of them, from way back then until now."

Wow—fuck!

Fei-wen tried her best to get her head around all this as the pain consumed her. There wasn't a part of her that wasn't in agony. So, it was true after all? All this time *she* was the real outsider? The sun is setting, so let's *all* make love—that harmonious paradise, that utopia of love, was not only Jesse's—all of them had joined hands and formed, such a bizarre and magnificent chain, one in which she had no place.

"How about Hong Mei-hua? Feng Duan-ru? Xiao-qing, Emma, Jiao-jiao, Man-qing, and...... Who did I miss? Was Gai-zi, Gai Shu-ting, part of this too?" Fei-wen's voice was getting shriller.

"Come on!"

"Is Ya-ya really Wu Zhi-peng's daughter?" Fei-wen sneered. If she was taking lives today, she might as well make it a massacre. If they didn't care about her life, then why should she care about theirs?

"I don't know," Jesse retorted, "Maybe she isn't mine either. Maybe I had brought the wrong baby home."

"Wow, that would suck."

"Yeah, that would suck."

Fei-wen picked up the gaming console from the floor and adjusted the game to the highest level before burying her head in it. The necessity of speed, the necessity of space, the necessity of moderation...... the concave ones and the convex ones were not the only blocks falling on her; therewere triangles, circles, trapezoids, polygons, points, and lines dancing in the sky....... Fei-wen was dazzled, and she lost her head, she lost it. Her eyes were seeing stars, her ears were ringing—Fuck! Now how am I supposed to play?

"...... Every—single—one—of—them......." Fei-wen suddenly realized, they weren't just growing old in pairs, but as a group! The cat was out of the bag; the tongzhi had been forming their little alliance and she had never realized it. When they were all sharing their elixir of life, only she was still standing in the shadows, pitying herself. Although she was reluctant to accept her reality, there was no use throwing a fit about it —so this was it? Was this the end of the game for her?

"Come on! If you're pissed, then you shouldn't be playing this." Jesse took away the console from her hands, "Shall we go to bed then? You've got work tomorrow......." She reached out to pull Fei-wen up from the floor.

Fei-wen's legs just gave out as if they were paralyzed. Just before she was about to fall over, she threw herself on Jesse as if she were clinging on to a tree. Jesse stumbled a little, but she soon regained her balance and moved to catch Fei-wen, but she was too late. Fei-wen tumbled down, her palms dragging helplessly over Jesse's shoulder blades and back. Fei-wen's knees gave out completely, and she fell to her knees. Jesse lost her balance as well and fell on top of her. Fei-wen grabbed Jesse and kissed her. Kissed her forehead, eyes, nose, lips, and chin, then she bit onto her neck rather forcefully. She tasted something salty, wet and warm like blood. She traced it to the source.......it was her eyes—Jesse was actually crying? She lowered her head and tasted them with her tongue. Yes, those were tears.

She had never seen Jesse cry, and Fei-wen herself had never cried as far as she could remember. Ah, it had been so long, the taste of tears, it was so moving—she should be crying too, shouldn't she? Mermaids of the south sea, whose tears would turn into strings of pearls ……. Fei-wen blinked her dry eyes but couldn't squeeze out a single pearl. She'd walked the tongzhi road for almost two decades, but compared to other comrades, she, Fei Li-wen was no hero. If she were a character in a puppetry drama, she wouldn't be Shi Yen-wen, that's for sure; she'd be more like Bi-diao. Hell, she wouldn't even cut it as the Dragon Goddess of the Bitter Sea.

Fei-wen lifted Jesse's shirt up, wanting to get warm from her. She rubbed her back, her breasts, and then her arms which had become as hard and lean as bamboo sticks through those years. I still love you the same, fucking Jesse…… Then it was as if Fei-wen's frail neck went limp, her head descended lower, and lower…… And finally, it was buried into that place between Jesse's legs. For the first time in those ten or so years, she kissed her there, in that unfamiliar place. Her fingers stumbled like a baby learning how to walk. One step, two steps, searching, back and forth. This strange kingdom a deep and endless labyrinth, layer upon layer, she couldn't find a way in.

Perhaps she should ask Jesse for a DIY manual or map, no? Fei-wen fell back onto the floor; pitied by the gods, that was when she finally understood how thin Jesse had become—she was so thin that there was barely fat left on her ass or even her crotch. Her pelvic bone jutted out like ribs on a bell. This should have broken her heart; she should have been like a dried fish crying over the river it lost, but it was too late to mourn. It was not just Fei Li-wen who had been withering away.

7

"Leave, just get out of here……" Someone is whispering it in her ears. No, it's not just one person, but a group of them—her mother, her father,

her brother, Jesse, Jiao-jiao, Yong-lin, and A-bao...... every single person she knows. She sees herself eating thumbtacks, fistful after fistful, and drinking ink, bottle after bottle. Now she's stuffing herself with bars of soap, hunks of charcoal and handfuls of rubber bands. "Leave, just get out of here!"—the type of hate she hoped never to stain her life. She doesn't want to be like her father, her mother, her brothers. She doesn't want to be like anyone—not even a tomboy.

She doesn't have the balls, she's incompetent, and she's sick. They're completely right about her. Everyone is making love except Fei-wen, the person who doesn't make love, the sex-less homosexual—and this is her transgression.

What could a guilty body possible have to say for itself? Shouldn't she just be dragged out and beheaded on the spot? Fei-wen stands at the starting line at age thirty-three, facing a future of aging and death. Suppose she doesn't die, suppose she lives to thirty-nine, forty-nine, or even fifty-nine, she'll have countless strands of gray hair by then. Even if she plucks them or dyes them red and green like Jesse said, what was the point? She'd have such a stooped and bent frame, a hunchback with rounded shoulders, covered in age spots and wrinkles from head to toe ...... Maybe...... Maybe in the future she would no longer wear jeans and wear those loose blouses and cotton straight-leg pants instead. Perhaps she'd even create a brand-new Zen image for herself, wearing the same hat and same pair of sunglasses for the whole year and acting so cool that people would regard her as mysterious. As long as—as long as what? As long as she hadn't croaked? A pesky old crone who just won't die? Carrying a heart that has been sucked dry by hatred, even if she's old and still hobbling about, where could she possibly go?

Anguish, such anguish.

Anguish is calming. It was through this calmness that Fei-wen finally feels the chill in her body. Covered in goosebumps, she quickly puts on some clothes, but she's still freezing. She fishes out the Jack Wolfskin down jacket she bought last Spring for a trip to Huangshan, slips on her wool socks, and pours herself a glass of Wild Turkey.

After a while, she still doesn't feel any warmer, so she puts on a sweater under her jacket and then a scarf, a hat, and some mittens. She now has on every article of warm clothing in her wardrobe. These are all her options to keep warm because she generally handles the cold well. There is a real chill in her cave. She pours herself one more glass of Wild Turkey and drapes another blanket over her shoulders, but she can't stop shivering.

So, this is how it's going to be—freezing to death little by little. Fei-wen shudders, then breaks out in a grin, "Fine. Bring it on! Do what you want with me!"

So she grabs a pen and some paper to draft her will. Staring blankly at the page, she's completely at a loss about how to begin. First things first, she'll start with her funeral arrangements, but to whom should she entrust this task? Her eldest brother can barely take a day off from his pork feet business, and her sister-in-law keeps a wide berth. Her third brother? He can barely handle his own messy life. Jesse? She can't even be bothered to care for Ya-ya, so why would she even bother dealing with a dead person? How about Jiao-jiao? Oh, forget it, she would probably play "Return to Innocence" at her funeral. Besides, Jiao-jiao doesn't owe her anything, so who is she to ask anything from her? Racking her brain, she narrows down her choices to Yong-lin and Jia-xian—Yong-lin is good at planning and Jia-xian is good at execution. Most importantly, they are both wealthy—so if she doesn't have enough money set aside for the funeral, they could afford to dip into their own pockets. After decades of friendship, even if they are not real comrades, at least they have been classmates and best friends. If Yong-lin and Jia-xian feel burdened by these obligations from her death, they could just chalk it up to karma.

Keep everything as simple as possible. No need for any religious rituals—Fei-wen suddenly remembers Gai-zi's face in the coffin, and the news she saw recently about Kong Ling-wei—the poor old tomboys had dressed themselves in menswear all their lives, but just like that, they were changed into qipaos and had their hair done up in buns (maybe even pink pearl earrings, necklaces, and bangles), looking like virtuous old ladies—how unthinkably humiliating! No, Fei-wen thinks to herself, and rushes to find the shirt and pair of pants that she wears the most often before grabbing her pen and continuing to write, "Just keep everything as simple as possible. No need for any religious rituals. As for how to dress the body, I have already prepared a set of clothes and placed them on my pillow. Please handle this according to my typical style of dress, no embellishments, please......"

Cremation. Treat her ashes as one would regular garbage. Don't bother to make offerings on her birthday or the anniversary of her death. They need not remember her. The comrades can continue eating, drinking, making merry, and building their love utopia. She, Fei Li-wen, would be lost in the mists of time......

Singing her swan song now...... Fei-wen thinks of all the things that she has wanted to do but won't have the time now. She just cannot let this go. She has been planning for so long to go to Nepal and the Netherlands. She has even looked into which alleys in Kathmandu have antique sliver shops, which stalls sell erotic paintings; and she wants to take a look at all of Rembrandt's many self-portraits. Rembrandt, the Baroque master of tragedy. She has also always wanted to take some time to learn how to scuba dive, maybe even learn to drive. She wants to save money for a Macintosh—hand-drawn layouts and printing manuscripts don't really have a place in the market anymore. Her colleague, Old K, has promised to sell her his Nikon FM2 Camera and Pentax 85-105mm lens; she could seal the deal as soon as she gets her year-end bonus...... But none of this matters anymore. It doesn't mean a thing. Nothing matters other than to keep on breathing. At this very moment, she can feel any icy tumor growing in her body, slowly spreading its poison inside her, freezing her to death bit by bit. Her limbs have gone cold and stiff, and she doesn't have the strength to hold the pen anymore. "Shit!" Fei-wen throws her pen down. Needless to say, she doesn't finish her will.

In the still of the night, Fei-wen finally summons the guts to head to Yonglin's joint to collect her motorcycle. The streetlights and the moon are shining with frigid brilliance. She's riding her motorcycle at 90km/h and makes a circuit around Taipei, stopping at all the places where her comrades live to say her goodbyes.

Before dawn, she finds herself on the steps of Jesse's apartment building. She tries the bell over and over, finally a tired male voice comes over the intercom, "Who is it?" Speechless, she just turns around and leaves.

Three days later, Fei-wen goes to the publishing house to pick up some drafts. She has grown pale and lost weight. Sporting a narrow-brimmed black felt hat, sunglasses, and gloves, she simply refuses to take them off even indoors. In the past she would only wear light clothes to the office in winter, now she is all bundled up in her cotton pants, sweater, and down jacket. Taken aback by her appearance, her colleagues gather around to check on her. "Fei Li-wen did you catch the flu?" "Why haven't you seen a doctor yet?" "Drink more water, rest more, and take more vitamins......" Fei-wen does her best to smile, nod, shake her head, and sip on the cup of hot coffee her coworker has brought to her—it's so bitter and hard to swallow.

On the fourth day her abdominal pains become even more severe, and she has to take one Panadol every hour.

On the fifth day, she adds another layer of blankets over the window, completely blocking herself off in this cave of infinite gloom. Without a single light on, she just crouches on the floor, squinting to finish a few more illustrations to make a little more money to cover her funeral arrangements. The air in her cave is stale and filled with the rank odor of cigarettes and alcohol. When she gets tired, she just collapses on the floor to sleep, but she can never sleep for long. Invariably, she'll be startled awake in an hour or so by nightmares that she cannot recall.

On the sixth day, Fei-wen heads out again and buys so many pornographic magazines and videotapes that it fill her entire backpack. Her television becomes a glass tank, where enlarged human figures with curled arms and twisted legs float before her eyes, as if they could break out of the tank at any moment and pounce on her. Flesh tones and liquid desire permeate the room, but they are never enough to fill the void in this house.

Her eyes are sunken from the severe lack of sleep. She's barely able to keep her eyes open, and her vision keeps going out of focus. Black hair. Blonde hair. No hair. Big tits, big lips, big balls, big dicks. Girl on girl, girl on guy, girl on guy on girl, from the front, from the back, from the left, from the right, from above, from below....... The volume is turned to zero because there is no plot and only moaning in place of dialogue. The sounds are more like the whimpers of beasts when they are hurt or dying. The silence allows her to be more attentive to the color and texture of the flesh and the close-ups. From this angle, all that's left are body parts. How's that for candor and simplicity?

Fei-wen starts to practice masturbating. Pity the poor soul—Fei Li-wen is thirty-three years old, and she doesn't even know how to masturbate.

Holding a mirror between her legs with one hand so she can observe, she uses her other hand to pleasure herself. She copies every move of the woman on the screen—this one has curly hair like a poodle—clumsily engages in dialogue with her own body. After a long, long while, she is still numb, feeling nothing but a dull ache. Completely numb, not feeling a thing. She closes her eyes. People say it takes imagination. Fine then, imagination, even though she is lousy at imagining.

She imagines everything she could possibly imagine. Scenes from movies and novels; Yong-lin and Emma making love; Jia-xian and Xiao-qing making love; even her father and mother, and her eldest brother with "Boba Boobs" A-Xia. Nothing. She is still numb. Exhausted, she drifts off to sleep. In a haze, she feels herself awakening as if from a lifetime of dreams. She sees herself and Jesse laying in a tangle of thorns. One moment, she's a man, the next, a woman. Jess too is now a woman, then a man. Two androgynous animals mating in all possible combinations of the sexes—female and male, male and female, male and male, female and female—as if from the moment the world was created, until the end of time, there has only been sex, and the eternal, everlasting orgasm. Orgasm is Truth. Believers kneel and worship Her!

Oh, she sees the light! This is it! The perfection of truth, benevolence, and beauty. Yes, yes, Jesse was right. Now she can finally die without regret! Fei-wen's finger fiddles with her sexual desire that has slumbered for so long, like she is caressing a newly awakened soul.

From then on, Fei-wen feels herself spilt into different individuals: male Fei-wen, female Fei-wen, both male and female, non-male and non-female, feminine male Fei-wen, masculine female Fei-wen...... Every Fei-wen is making love to themselves, over and over again, cyclically as if they are going to burn through thirty-plus years of untapped desire all at once. She is totally frazzled, to the extent that her face appears emaciated like that of a ghost that died of nymphomania—well, she's almost there —to becoming a ghost, that is—not eating or drinking or sleeping at all. Her face is ashen, almost spectral. The veins crisscrossing her bloodshot eyes are like spider webs intertwining with one another, her pupils their prey. Perhaps this is the way she really wants to end things.

With one foot in the abyss, there is no returning, no stopping, only gravity and the speed of the fall. Unless someone throws her a rope. Alas, she doesn't even have time to pray for a rope—or learn how to make one—so she is unlikely to ever get up. Her body is burning up, and she lets out a last gasp. As Fei Li-wen tosses and turns in bed, her once-black locks finally turn all gray.

On the seventh day, Fei-wen's door is pried open—someone has brought a locksmith. "What's gotten into you?" That person just starts biting her head off, while kicking at the video tapes, wine bottles, cigarette butts, and paint brushes that are scattered all over the place. From there, they rip down the cardboard and cloth curtains from the window frames before opening four windows. Immediately sunlight floods the room, leaving Fei-wen nowhere to hide. She can only lift her arms up to cover her head as she lies face down on the floor. Blades of light cut through the room, while dust billows as if there is a dust storm from a soundless attack on an invisible house in the room. This house within the house is the cage in which she feels safe. Fei-wen, who feels like she has had the wind knocked out of her, begins to dry cough.

Her head shakes violently as she coughs, and at first glance she looks like she is wearing a white hat, which glistens and shimmers under the light, but this is actually her gray hair. A whole head of gray hair, every single strand, not one is spared. Her face is flushed from all the coughing. The gray hair sets off her red face, which looks a bit like that of someone rallying before death.

That person wastes no time pulling Fei-wen up and sending her to the hospital.

Fei-wen thinks she is not going to make it out of the hospital this time, and so on her way there she keeps her eyes wide open, hoping to linger a little longer in this world, reluctant to part even with the trees lining the boulevards.

Half an hour later a physician has diagnosed that she has a bad cold, and she is then wheeled to the Department of Gynecology and Obstetrics for a pelvic examination and an ultrasound. Fei-wen feels paralyzed and defenseless when they take off her pants and move her to the examination table, but she has no time to feel embarrassed or angry. She doesn't even feel the pain when the probe is shoved into her vagina; instead, she just feels ridiculous, too ridiculous—the object that touches the insides of her vagina the first time ever in her life turns out to be this stick, and she does not even have the chance to see what it looks like.

"Ovarian cyst," Fei-wen vaguely hears the doctor announce. If she plans on getting pregnant, they would not recommend removing it and would just observe her condition periodically. If not, they would recommend her to remove it soon to avoid any future trouble...... And there is no need for her to be admitted to the hospital......

On her way home, Fei-wen finally regains her consciousness. "Do you want to remove it?" That person asks her.

Fei-wen hesitates. She has never had the faintest desire to have a baby, and she's sure that won't change. Yet, suddenly, she feels an attachment to her ovaries. They have been so committed to their work all these years, and to her their significance isn't limited to their reproductive functions. They are like companions who depend on each other. She doesn't want to lose them—if only there was a way to save them.

"So, am I really not going to die?" Fei-wen just wants to confirm that once again.

"What were you hoping for? Cancer?" That person does not have any patience. "Considering the way you're treating yourself, you're almost there."

Fei-wen smiles bleakly, not knowing if it is out of happiness or sorrow.

On the ninth day, Fei-wen has mostly recovered, after a series of injections, medication, and resumption of eating and sleeping. When she wakes up that morning, the person who sent her to the hospital and took care of her for two days is nowhere to be seen—having left her apartment, as well as her memory. Fei-wen can't understand why she just can't recall that person's face no matter how hard she tries. She can't even remember if they had met or if she had seen this person before. She can only smell their scent in her room, mixed with that moldy mixture of cashmere wool, New Paradise cigarettes, whiskey, blood, flowers, and the type of body odor one gets after staying out in the sun—the high note is Lin-shen hair wax, and the base note is the mildly fermented rusty smell of a woman's loins. Some smells are melodious like flute, some are crisp like a zither, ding-ding dong-dong, e-ya-oo-oo-ta-la...... All the smells form a composition reverberating through her room, entering through her pores and seeping into her body.

On the tenth day, Jesse pays her a visit.

"This is for you," She hands Fei-wen a bag as she steps into the house, "Skincare products. Anti-aging, moisturizing, sun-protection, and more. I'll explain them to you in a minute." And she takes a quick glance at her hair, "Do you want to dye it? I know this one type of hair dye—"

"No, I don't."

"Hm," Jesse appraises her new look for a good while, "It actually looks quite good."

Fei-wen then lets Jesse read her drafted will and go through the pornographic magazines and films, while telling her everything that she has been through these past few days, including the masturbation and sex dreams. Jesse bursts into laughter in return, "You're done for! The cherry has been popped!"

Jesse makes fish soup in that tiny kitchen with no partition, and Fei-wen studies the view of her back, gently hugged by a sweater. Jesse has slimmed down a lot in these years, and though her sweater looks loose, somehow its looseness shows off her fierce, bony figure—it is strange that Fei-wen thinks of the word "fierce," and suddenly she realizes Jesse has always been propping her skeleton up, not letting anyone touch her lest it fall apart. Her ferocity is built not on fortitude but loneliness.

Fei-wen grabs a cigarette and lights up, but she can't taste a thing after two puffs, so she puts it out before running to Jesse and hugging her from behind around the waist. Jesse pats her hand but stays focused on the stove. In less than a minute, Fei-wen realizes that she doesn't love Jesse anymore. Or she is no longer in love with her. This feeling is more like that between two old sisters—she wishes she and Jesse were sisters rather than lovers.

The sun is setting outside the window, the fresh smell of fish assails their nostrils. Fei-wen ruffles Jesse's hair, seeing the streaks of gray are peeking through, she can't help but recall Jesse's words—some of my pubes have gone gray too, do you believe that...... "Did you dye your hair?"

Jesse is dazed for a second, "Yes. When I had Ya-ya, it turned a lot grayer than before. Got it from my family. My mother was the same. I started dyeing my hair after the postpartum confinement. I had to. It was so grizzled that it was horrible. That's why I cut it short." Fei-wen remembers Jesse's straw-blonde hair which reached her hips. Now it's way darker than before. It is strange that she never noticed that for all these years.

They were silent for a while. Fei-wen watches Jesse wash some vegetables and devein some shrimp, "I'll chop the green onions." She volunteers to help.

"Come on, these are garlic scapes. Those are green onions."

Fei-wen is completely taken by surprise; she had no idea how alike they look.

"Teach me how to cook when you have time."

"Do I have to teach you how to make love while we're it?"

"That'd be great." Fei-wen turns and plants a kiss on Jesse's cheek, "When I recover, I will do it with each and every one of you."

In a letter to Fei-wen many years ago, Miss Jesse, who was baptized as a Christian when she was a child, mentioned John 8:7 from the bible. It was the passage about the adulterous woman. Fei-wen remembers that Jesus said, "Let he who is without sin among you cast the first stone."

3

Howl

Ta-wei Chi
(translated by Yahia Zhengtang Ma)

When I was a child, I read a horror story.

Once upon a time, in a house in a southern European village, somewhere in Spain or Italy, peculiar stains appeared on the floor. They were impossible to erase, regardless of the efforts to get rid of them. The splotches spread across the room, finally congealing in the spectral likeness of a human face. The owner of the house hastily resurfaced the floor, but in a matter of days, another human face, at once fierce and sorrowful, emerged in the center of the room.

In the end, a large group of men pry open the floorboards, excavate the foundations, and uncover an old human skeleton. Ghosts that refuse to be forgotten, are bound to surface in the end. When they do so silently, without even a howl, it's even more alarming.

I've never seen a floor like that. Though I've known a wall that was similar ... I'll never forget it.

* * * * * * * *

I had rented a suite in an apartment complex. It was a tiny apartment with a single small window, but at least once I'd organized things, it would be a breathable space.

Intending to hang a movie poster, I purposely left one wall blank.

I couldn't decide what kind of poster it would be, though I'd already looked into its specific dimensions. Using a pencil, I marked four points on the bare wall. They'd soon become the bounds of a second, imaginary window. But before I could decide what the view would be, the lovely blank wall had been spray-painted over with a giant, red ☮.

The graffitied ☮ symbol resembled one of those lollipop logos on the hood of a Benz, only this one had grown a sagging tail. Apparently, it was a symbol of anti-war sentiment. Taking a closer look, I realized the ☮ sign's borders went way beyond my four-pencil-point zone. A movie poster wouldn't even cover it.

My attempt to cry bore no tears. My original plan went bust. The thought of facing my landlord made me even more anxious. I had no idea how I would explain it to that nit-picking hairsplitter, she was always slithering about in search of any excuse to increase the rent. All I could do was pray she would never notice it. With no other way out, I rolled up my sleeves to paint over the sign. Yet, just like the ghostly face in the story, this ☮ refused to be exorcised. There was nothing I could do but stick a huge corkboard on the wall. It was tacky, yes, but at least it completely covered the peace sign. I'd forget about the poster.

The corkboard was surprisingly functional.

I started pinning up all sorts of memos: post-it notes, pizza coupons, receipts, lottery tickets, the business card from a blood-testing lab ... I'd even scribble the phone numbers and addresses of friends and acquaintances in the margins. Not to mention my records of who borrowed how many books from me and from whom I had borrowed how many books. I'd jot down the titles, dates, and phone numbers of the owners on little strips of paper and tack them up on this memory wall.

This memory wall was decked-out in numbers, names, and faded deadlines. At its post-it-studded foot lay an old-fashioned black telephone. Whenever a gust of wind blew into the room, the wall was like a tree, the notes fluttering like leaves. Meanwhile, the black telephone sat pensively like a monk beneath the bodhi tree. When talking on the phone, I'd sit cross-legged, eyes scanning the memory wall in search of enlightenment. When there were no phone calls, I'd still look at the wall now and then, just to recall the stories behind the notes. *Thus I have heard...*

Newspaper articles I had no time to read in detail? I'd rip them out and add them to the wall, telling the printed characters, "Until we meet again." The yellowing collages reminded me that so many people have experienced birth, aging, illness, and death; so many people have lived and breathed.

When I heard the news of Eileen Chang's death, I came to the rather bewildering realization that a person can be both dead and undead. While she was living, I believed her to be long dead; now that she was dead, she seemed very much alive.

I had the same feeling arose on April 7, 1997, when I read of poet Allen Ginsberg's death in the news. I cut out the report, photos and all, and pinned it to the memory wall.

According to the newspaper, Ginsberg was a San Francisco legend, a guru of the counterculture movement of the 1960s. In the photo, the flower-power pacifist Ginsberg looked like a twentieth-century Karl Marx. Whatever. The point is that he was a spiritual leader, a comrade. In the photo of Ginsberg, there was a circular sign behind him in the background. It was a bit blurry, but of course I recognized it—that very same anti-war peace sign. Well, I'll be ... Ginsberg had only just left us. I thought he had passed away ages ago. Another fact I found astonishing: he died of heart failure. How could such an extraordinary human being die of such an ordinary disease? I had thought the notoriously lascivious Ginsberg would scandalize the world by making a salacious exit. Perhaps he was still alive, but just living in seclusion? No, that's absurd. But then again, don't people always say that Elvis Presley never died and that his tomb in Memphis was nothing but a ruse to cover for a life on the road?

> I saw the best minds of my generation destroyed by madness, starving hysterical naked, dragging themselves through the negro streets at dawn looking for an angry fix ...

The titular poem, "Howl" from Ginsberg's *Howl (and Other Poems)* unfolds in full swing. Cascading, line after line without a period, resisting pause. Too many words to spit out. How could he bear the interruption?

* * * * * * * *

Ever since Amoeba left the anthology at my place, I hadn't so much as touched it. If not for Ginsberg's death, I might have forgotten about *Howl* completely.

It took me a while to fish it out from the space between the bed and the wall. It was easy for a slim book like that to get stuck in the cracks and be forgotten. It was only about sixty pages and pocket-sized, no bigger than the palm of my hand. The black-and-white cover was a bit dusty, and someone had changed the "O" in "HOWL" to ☮.

It was impossible not to think of the ☮ beneath the corkboard.

All this was Amoeba's doing.

I hadn't heard news of Amoeba for a long time, though.

With *Howl* in my hands, I was tempted to return it to Amoeba. Perhaps he might want to reread it after learning of Ginsberg's death. I wouldn't read it anyway.

I couldn't find Amoeba's phone number on the memo board. I didn't even know what his real name was. Everybody calls him Amoeba, but nobody seems to know why. I looked through the rows of notes on the board and called various individuals, but no one knew his number. Actually, no one wanted to add his contact details to their memory walls.

Only a few people socialized with Amoeba, but many have heard of him. Even though Amoeba never made it into the spotlight on the art scene, many in that circle probably knew that he painted. He had pieced together a few self-curated shows, all of them in small bars with few customers. He hoped the bars' clientele would view his works while drinking. The bars' owners were hoping the exhibitions would boost business. In other words, the arrangement was to be mutually beneficial. Reality ran counter to expectations.

As for what Amoeba's paintings looked like, I haven't the faintest idea, but I'd heard people who'd seen them say Amoeba's style is *wild*.

"Wild" is a decidedly empty term, incapable of describing a single specific feature. However, it was spot on in describing Amoeba. Of course he was wild. There was a half-open secret about his body—maybe this was the unspeakable quality that made Amoeba memorable. I'd heard about this ages ago: Amoeba was infected.

The gossipier men in the circle would count on their fingers and say "Amoeba's been infected for *this* many years, he'll probably be able to live with it *this many* ..." Some of them said Amoeba was skinny as a famine victim. Others circulated the rumor that centipede-shaped lesions had grown under his armpits. *That must be Kaposi sarcoma!* Their excitement grew as they gossiped. They made it sound like Amoeba had achieved a global viral monopoly, granting the rest of us immunity. I reminded myself that I'd best see Amoeba as little as possible.

And then, unexpectedly, I ran into Amoeba, and it turned out to be more than a chance encounter.

* * * * * * * *

At the time, that red sign had not appeared on the wall. I sat in my tiny apartment with its single window, my homey sense of belonging mixed with a stifling boredom that I just couldn't shake.

Those days, whenever I needed a change of scenery, I'd hop on my 50cc scooter and cruise around the neighborhood, searching for a view that would lift my spirits. I frequented a café whose neon sign flashed "San Francisco." The place had sunshine-yellow ceilings, sea-foam walls, and a counter in the shape of a gunwale. Consuming something at this café was like purchasing an exotic sailing experience. Stuck as I was in the Taipei Basin, it would do as a temporary getaway.

That particular day, I "set sail" once again for San Francisco café, arms clutching a bundle of manuscript drafts. Upon entering, I found the place rather crowded. I surveyed the room in search of a seat. Just when I was about to "jump ship," I happened to see somebody waving at me.

"Can't find a seat? Join me."

Our eyes met. Awkwardly, I hesitated. It was Amoeba!

I didn't dare to take a step forward, but Amoeba just beckoned more earnestly, impatience unmistakably written all over his face.

Bound by decorum with a desire to save face, I forced myself into the seat beside him. We knew each other, but by no means were we close—at the most we had a nodding acquittance—as far as I could recall, we'd never spoken alone. I remained speechless, waiting for him to start talking.

"Don't be a little bitch. Just sit like I tell you to. What are you scared of? I'm not a ghost—*yet*."

Hearing those inauspicious words turned my face even more of a deathly pale. I remained silent to avoid putting my foot in my mouth.

He was wearing a tie-dyed rainbow T-shirt with a radiating flame pattern, like the old-school hippie trend. Even though the place was airconditioned, sitting right next to him made it impossible to ignore the stench of his sweat. Amoeba was looking quite skeletal.

When waiter brought him a cup of black coffee, I ordered an almond milk. He looked at me. I looked back at him, wondering what he was thinking about. After what seemed like ages, I finally managed to mumble,

"Amoeba, should you be drinking black coffee? It might not be good for your health." I guess I'd put my foot in my mouth after all—I just had to point out the elephant in the room.

Judging from his sickly pallor, I thought he shouldn't be out in public. He should be laying low at home, or maybe even hospitalized. He certainly should not be sitting in a café, trying to impress people. Not only was he risking his health, he was making others uneasy with his sickly appearance. I'd heard from my circle of friends that Amoeba wouldn't go to the hospital, nor would he visit his parents. He lived alone, and no one visited him. No one would be interested or brave enough to visit someone like Amoeba.

"Must you all insist on treating me like an invalid? I'm not dying. Every inch of my body is in terrible pain—*true*. Ooh, damn it hurts! I really need to find someone who'll give me a massage."

He began to cough violently, and his face flushed red. I prayed: *Please don't let this red swollen face before me swell up and explode. If it's got to explode, then please don't let the geyser of blood plasma splatter itself on my body. Ahhhh ...*

Don't tell me I'm overreacting—the whole scene was straight out of a B-grade horror flick. In fact, I don't believe anyone else in my shoes could have dealt with the situation so tactfully—I even suppressed my instinct to dodge his spittle. As his coughing subsided, Amoeba gestured to the dingy plastic bag wedged between us.

"I just went to the art store to pick up some pigments, this imported shit is *expensive*! Anyway, I absolutely *must* hold one last exhibition.

Otherwise, I'll die full of regret—like one of those corpses that won't close its eyes." He flashed a tube of pigment in front of my eyes—showing off as always.

"Do you even get it? ... With this pigment ... I could paint a San Francisco Bay full of roses ... but it has to be this exact shade"

He spoke between coughs.

He hadn't touched his coffee—maybe my advice was beginning to register? When my almond milk arrived, he asked,

"Hey, is almond milk really all that nutritious?"

His question snapped me back to reality, and I nodded distractedly after a while.

If I was behind the beat, Amoeba was rushing.

"Let's swap! I'll take your almond milk, and you'll take my coffee."

Before I could say anything, Amoeba had already taken a sip.

"Hurry up and have some coffee!" He stared me in the face. I wasn't moving an inch.

"What? Too chicken? I didn't even touch the coffee. Why won't you try it? Do you think one sip of coffee would make you sick?"

His spit landed on my face, I was glued to the seat, too afraid to move. Scrambling for an answer, I finally said I didn't drink coffee because it causes insomnia.

"Oh no, then you have nothing to drink. Let me make it up to you," Amoeba pulled two milk candies from his plastic bag.

"These are the last two. Here you go. Eat up! Milk candies are very nutritious. What are you afraid of?"

Nothing. I'm not afraid. Honestly, I was on the verge of tears. I'd never dreamed a night at San Francisco could be so agonizing. Still, I couldn't lose my temper and curse him out. No, I couldn't do that. I just wanted to leave. My plans to write while "cruising" San Francisco had been foiled. I made a hasty excuse and left quickly.

Pushing open the door and stepping onto the streets, I was feeling exhausted as I got onto my scooter, ready to head home. Unfortunately, my troubles were far from over.

Plastic bag in hand, Amoeba had followed me out of the café. I didn't want to seem rude. I explained again, for the sake of appearances, *I really had to go home. I didn't mean to leave him high and dry*. He wouldn't take the hint.

Pointing at a bicycle parked next to my scooter, Amoeba asked, "What do you think about this bike?"

Taking a can of spray paint from his bag and shaking it briefly, Amoeba began to spray-paint the bicycle. As a the red paint shot forth like a jet-stream, Amoeba grinned, "It's much cooler painted red, isn't it?"

The noxious chemical vapors formed nose-watering clouds, sending Amoeba into another coughing fit.

I just stood there—mouth agape, tongue tied, head bobbing—caught between shock and amusement. His next question threw me off completely.

"Hey, is your place near here?"

I said yes.

"Could I come over to use your shower? I just biked all the way to and from the art store, I'm covered in sweat, and I'm too exhausted to make it home for a shower. My legs are killing me, I'll be up all night with leg cramps if I ride any further. Take me back to your place for a shower, okay? It'd be so much easier."

"Hmm, I think it'd be easier if you just went home," I said haltingly.

He just ignored me.

Can I really leave him hanging like this? I sighed and asked him to hop on behind me. The moment I felt his crotch touch my outer thighs, I felt an instant and unspeakable aversion. All I could do was try to calm down by telling myself "It's fine … It's fine…It *should be* fine?"

On the ride over, I asked Amoeba how he was planning get home, given that he'd ditched his bicycle at the San Francisco café.

"No worries. It isn't even my bike."

Shocked, I stared at Amoeba in the sideview mirror.

"It was abandoned, alright? Don't you know that the NTU campus is an infinite source of bikes? What's with the evil eye? *Come on*—don't be a little bitch."

He really had his argument down pat!

"Besides, my day are numbered. There's no point sweating the small stuff!"

What? Just because you're infected, you get to do whatever you want? I disagreed completely, but I held my tongue.

As we approached a tunnel, I'd had enough of his twisted morality, so I changed the subject, "Amoeba, so you like San Francisco?"

"*Obviously.* I stop by San Francisco every time I buy paints."

Why San Francisco?

"First of all, I love the city. I love the sunshine and the sea. I want to strip naked and sunbathe. I want to …"

We entered the tunnel lit by a river of halogen lamps. Amoeba's list flowed on, "I want to …, I want to …" Dreams ricocheted into whirs in the thundering reverb.

He raised his voice against the din in the tunnel, but his howl of desires went unheard.

* * * * * * * *

I parked the scooter in front of the apartment complex and led Amoeba up to my flat. Amoeba, however, asked me to wait a moment, pulling me into a back-alley convenience store.

I asked Amoeba what he was buying, and he said mineral water. Without thinking, I told there was no need, I could just boil water at home—The words caught in my throat. I decided not to say anymore, after all, I wasn't sure what Amoeba was after. *So what if he drinks some of my water? Who cares if he uses my glass?....*

Was he buying himself water to relieve my anxieties?

He looked me in the face and continued toward the store.

"It's not that I don't want your water. I just like this certain brand of mineral water."

Stepping into the store, Amoeba started dancing along to the music playing in the store, flapping his arms like a pair of wings. Flap as he might, he never took off, though his body looked light as a bird's. I had followed him into the store and noticed him in the candy aisle instead of the drinks section. He handed me a pack of candy—printed all over with roses.

"This is the milk candy I just gave you. I'm a big fan of it."

"Why?"

He grinned playfully, "This brand has the prettiest packaging!"

"Did you want to buy more?"

"No."

He grabbed a bottle of lemon mineral water and went to pay at the register. Caught in the glare of the harsh fluorescent lighting, his scrawny body and his gaunt face were framed in the convex security mirror. I wonder what he thought of the man in the frame.

* * * * * * * *

Before heading to the bathroom for his shower, Amoeba pulled a pack of milk candy from the crotch of his pants and tossed it to me. It had the same pattern of intertwined roses. I shot him a questioning glance. As far as I recalled, he'd bought only water. When did he slip the pack of milk candy into the crotch of his pants?

Amoeba read my face like a book, and snickered, "My days are numbered, so who cares?"

As he spoke, he sized up the blank, poster-less wall.

"This wall is too empty. It needs a mural."

"That's not happening. This is a rental. I'm planning to put up a movie poster. Any recommendations? I wanna go with something arthouse and European like Krzysztof Kieślowski, none of that commercial Hollywood crap."

Amoeba seemed to loathe the idea, "Please, don't be so tacky, okay?" Rolling his eyes, he walked off to the bathroom, stripped, and tossed his clothes back out before slamming the door.

He'd left his plastic bag on the bed. Both livid and curious, I took a peek, expecting to find some special medication—he should be on medication to manage his symptoms—but I didn't find any. Other than the pigments, spray paint, and a pack of tissues for wiping his nose, there was just a slim book. I pulled it out and flipped through it. Printed on the black-and-white cover were four letters "HOWL." It was a book of poems. Was this the collection of poems that Amoeba was reading? Handwritten in pencil in the margins of the pages were the Chinese glosses of many English words.

After showering, Amoeba didn't change back into his tie-dyed t-shirt, he just walked right out of the bathroom with only my bath towel around him. He didn't seem displeased at me for browsing his book. "I've read that collection several times. It's a must-read. But I can't lend you mine because I'm trying to memorize the whole thing. But you've got to read this book if you want to know San Francisco."

"Have you even *been* to San Francisco?" I couldn't help sticking it to him, fed up with his pontificating.

"We're *acquainted*. In fact, I just came back from there."

He grinned, showing his teeth, which were neither white nor straight.

Of course, he wasn't bothered at all; it was *I* who was getting worked up. How dare he take liberties with my bath towel! For some reason the anger was only hitting me now. Exasperated, I sighed inwardly.

It would be inappropriate to say anything, but it suddenly occurred to me that Amoeba might have secretly used my razor and toothbrush while he was in the bathroom. I guess I'd have to make a trip to the supermarket to buy replacements.

His face was rosy from the shower. He ripped open the package of milk candy that I hadn't touched and popped one in his mouth.

"You don't like milk candy? It's very nutritious."

I put the book down and mustered up the courage to offer him a ride home, hoping he'd take the hint. I heard my voice quivering and felt my confidence weakening with each word. Much to my surprise, Amoeba *rejected* my suggestion. Shit, I cringed inwardly. Why did I always let people walk all over me?

"No way! My joints are killing me. I'll only have enough energy to make it home if you give me a massage."

"I don't know how to give massages …"

"It's not that fucking difficult. What, do you only use your hands to slap your monkey?" Rude, yes, but his lackadaisical tone made it sound completely nonsexual.

"I'll lie on the bed. Just follow my instructions, okay?"

I really wanted to run out, but he was too weak to be left alone. His facial muscles twitched now and then, probably from the pain.

Amoeba was already lying facedown on my mattress, and the thought of his saliva dripping onto my sheets scared me to death. Kneeling beside him, I followed his instructions, pinching and prodding the various parts of his body with my thumbs and fists.

At first, I massaged him tentatively, not daring to be too hard. Amoeba had no qualms about criticizing me for being too gentle. I had no choice but to acquiesce to his demands to be more forceful in digging into his pressure points. His face contorted in pain, but he was also moaning with pleasure, saying I'd hit the spot.

I say full force, but honestly I was holding back a bit. Too much pressure and his slim body might shatter to pieces. Too much pressure and his inflexible muscles might get permanently bent out of shape. I found no trace of the rumored appalling lesions on his body. What I did notice was a swollen gut hanging out over his skinny frame. Was it fat or fluid? If you sliced it open, would a toxic swarm of deadly microorganisms spring forth? Was I being too mean? I was in such a state of anxiety.

With only a towel covering him, Amoeba accidentally exposed his private parts. His eyes narrowed when he caught me looking, but it didn't seem to faze him. Apart from the unusually sparse pubic hair, all I saw was a regular penis, unremarkable in its color, shape, or size—or maybe it was a bridge, between heavenly pleasure and hellish pain? One could never tell.

As the massage continued, Amoeba kept moaning in satisfaction. My arms were getting awfully sore. Amoeba could hear I was getting out of breath.

"You must be tired. I feel a lot better now—I should be able to sleep well tonight."

"*Huh?* I mean, that's great! Let me take you home now." I seized the opportunity.

"Come one, there's no hurry. Look at you, you're exhausted, you need a shower. Plus, you've taken such good care of me—I have to repay you. How about a painting? It'll only take me five minutes."

Trying to keep my emotions from showing, I declined his offer as I stepped into the bathroom. I threw my toothbrush and razor in the sink, ready to douse them in scalding hot water and disinfect them. However, I stopped myself the second I turned on the tap. Would running them under a little hot water the way street hawkers rinse dishes be enough to put me at ease? I'd be better off purchasing a whole new set from the supermarket.

While I was showering, I heard hissing sounds coming from outside the bathroom. I suspected that was Amoeba gasping, probably from working too hard on the painting to repay me.

Moments later, I heard some violent coughing.

It sounded awful! Was he really suffering very badly?

My compassion didn't last long after I remembered that he'd commandeered my bath towel. Swearing, I made do with a hand towel and hastily put on some underwear.

* * * * * * * *

When I walked out of the bathroom, I almost collapsed when I saw what Amoeba had done. I realized why there had been a hissing sound and why Amoeba had been coughing so violently.

He had spray-painted a giant red circle on the blank wall reserved for my movie poster. It was a circular anti-war sign. If it symbolized peace, why did it look so aggressive?

That was the "painting" he gave me. The hissing was from the paint canister, the coughing was from the fumes. The wet paint threatened to drip down the wall, like the tears welling up in my eyes.

* * * * * * * *

I started screaming, trying to kick Amoeba out the door. I was stamping my feet like an angry monkey, but that hardly perturbed him. He just stared back at me like a sloth, reluctant to move.

It looked like he wasn't going to leave of his own accord, so I threatened him, "If you don't get out, then I'll leave!" I regretted it almost immediately. What kind of threat was that? Who would be scared by that?

In the end, I was the one who left. The unexpected guest drove the host out.

I grabbed the keys to my scooter and left the flat. After cruising around for a while, I ended up at a 24-hour manga cafe. I laid on the tatami for a couple hours, downed two glasses of flat knockoff cola. I flipped through several volumes of *Shiratori Reiko de Gozaimasu!* unable to follow a single storyline, or even laugh at the jokes. I could only think about how to deal with Amoeba.

Still anxious, I decided to return home to check on him.

I took a deep breath, trying to calm down.

I opened the door to the flat, Amoeba was still there; so was the red ☯. He was sleeping on my mattress, and he had taken my comforter, draping it over his body and spattering it with drool. He hadn't put his clothes back on, and his limp genitals were peeking out from beneath the sheets. I tucked him in without waking him.

At dawn, the red symbol on the wall looked like a bloodshot eye, crying in pain.

I decided to take revenge.

Pulling the poetry collection from Amoeba's plastic bag, I slid it under the mattress. I had no intention of returning it.

If I really think about it, my method of "revenge" was rather subdued. All I dared do was secretly take his stuff, rather than confront him directly. Revenge? Give me a break!

* * * * * * * *

Amoeba woke up and left still very sleepy, not realizing that I taken his book.

Needless to say, I refused to give him a ride. *He can take the bus!* Sure, he's an invalid, but he's got enough stamina to wait for the bus. I'm not coddling him anymore.

Looking out from my window, I saw Amoeba walking out of the apartment complex, with the plastic bag in hand. He glanced back, and I wondered if he was looking at the sky, at me or at the big red eyeball in the room. I drew my head back quickly and saw that he'd left a half-filled bottle of water on the table.

I haven't seen Amoeba since.

I decided to throw out the bottle of water and replace my toothbrush, razor, and bath towel. I stripped off my bedsheets to send them with my comforter to the cleaners. I'd even pay extra to have them disinfected—there was no choice. While I was stripping off the bedsheets, I fished the pocket-sized poetry collection out from under the mattress. Flicking through it, I recited a few lines at random and then tossed the book aside.

* * * * * * * *

I didn't try to find the book *Howl* until I heard about Ginsberg's death. Several months had gone by, during which many more memos filled up the wall.

I'd better return the book to Amoeba. It was pointless being vindictive toward a man at death's door. Moreover, he seemed so passionate about these poems from San Francisco. On the other hand, if he truly cared so much about them, why didn't he come looking for them when he realized they were missing? Was it because he didn't have my phone number? Because he was too sick and weak to do so? Or was he too ashamed of himself to face me?

Half asleep on my freshly—and regularly—laundered sheets, I skimmed over the verses.

> *Will we walk all night through solitary streets? ... we'll both be lonely.*
>
> *I saw you, ... childless, lonely old grubber, poking among the meats in the refrigerator and eyeing the grocery boys.*

A slip of paper fell out from the pages.

It was a candy wrapper. I remembered the pattern. Amoeba's favorite milk candy. He must have used the candy wrapper as a bookmark. I just hadn't noticed it before. The front of the wrapper was printed with flowers. On the back were a few characters written in pencil that were still clearly legible after all this time.

A man's name and a telephone number: □ □ □ ***-****

The name sounded ordinary, completely unexceptional. Yet, staring at these characters, I was unable to think of any man with a similar name. I added the wrapper to the corkboard.

Nevertheless, □ □ □ aroused my curiosity. What was his relationship with Amoeba? Given my own interaction with Amoeba, so it was hard for me to believe anybody could be in a relationship with him. With a personality like that, not to mention that body, impossible! Could anybody stand him?

I had pondered these issues: Why did my friends and I panic over Amoeba and avoid seeing him? Did we seriously fear that he would pass the virus to us? I daresay that was partially true, even though we knew full well that as long as we didn't have sex with him, (who'd wanna fuck around with Amoeba?), there was little risk of his transmitting the virus. What were we so afraid of? I wasn't sure what the others thought, but I found his arrogant speech and outrageous behavior rather unbearable. Yet, I was somehow unable to resist him, oppose him, or reproach him. Amoeba had reason to be reckless. Due to his condition, healthy people like myself felt like they owed him something—we either had to submit to his demands or at most keep our distance. It was almost as if we'd stolen his youth; like if it weren't for us, no such misfortune would have befallen him. Being patient with Amoeba was how those of us who'd managed to stay healthy so far could pretend we'd atoned for our sins. Why *pretend*? Maybe because I wasn't sure if this counted as "atonement." I wasn't even sure what counted as sin.

Amoeba's face seemed to say, "I may be sick, but *you* are sinful!" How I loathed to see his face! Oh, how I reveled in Schadenfreude! How gleeful was I at his misfortune! Honestly, I wondered who could stand the sight of him.

Amoeba left a man's name and telephone number in his beloved collection of poems—a commemorative gesture that must have some significance. I was motivated to snoop. Did □ □ □ give his number voluntarily to Amoeba? Or was Amoeba brazenly vying for □ □ □'s attention? The possibilities were fascinating.

I was tempted to dial the phone number. If someone picked up, it could be □ □ □. I had an excuse that was good enough to talk to him: I'd say I'd phoned to ask for Amoeba's number. I had a book to return to him but couldn't get in touch. Perhaps he'd help me return the book to Amoeba. Through such a conversation, I could easily suss out the nature of their relationship.

Doing so was by no means inappropriate, I reckoned. After all, I had to return the book to Amoeba and this was my only lead.

Maybe I was being presumptuous, but

I wouldn't feel guilty. Wasn't Amoeba even more presumptuous for intruding into my world?

* * * * * * * *

One evening, I dialed the number on the wrapper. I deliberately chose a time when most families would be having dinner.

"May I ask for whom you're calling?" It was a young male voice.

It must be □ □ □! I rejoiced, ready to deliver my spiel.

"Is this Mr. □ □ □ speaking?" I asked courteously.

He remained silent. I cleared my throat doubtfully and repeated the question.

"No, this isn't he. He's not here."

"When will he be back?"

"I have no idea. What is this regarding?"

"Nothing much. It's just that I borrowed a book from him. It's been ages, and I wanted to return it." I quickly fabricated this excuse in response.

"Sorry, he won't be back today…"

"Okay, shall I call back another day?"

A bit disappointed, I was about to hang up, but he asked me to hold on for a moment.

I heard a hushed female voice in the background. It seemed like the man was whispering to the woman beside him.

"Mister, are you a friend of □ □ □'s?"

"Yes." It was a white lie. How else could I explain why I knew his number.

"If you're a friend of □ □ □'s, would you mind sending that book to our house, please? It would mean a lot."

Huh, I wondered, why were they making such a fuss?

"*Please*—could you bring it here in person?" It sounded almost as if he were begging.

"Our place is right near the metro—it's easy to find. Otherwise, we'll pay for a taxi for you."

I heard the woman murmuring again.

I was unsure if I should get involved with a stranger and his family. If I played with fire, I'd risk getting burnt. On the other hand, returning the book was a convincing excuse. Anyway, I could just ask □ □ □ to pass the anthology back to Amoeba.

The man gave me his address, and we formally introduced ourselves. I wrote down his contact details and tacked them up on the wall.

The man was □ □ □'s younger brother. The woman who was whispering was his mother.

"When would be the best time for me to stop by?"

"Can you come over now?"

"Right now?"

"Yes."

* * * * * * * *

Exiting the metro station, I looked for the building. It took me less than ten minutes to find the entrance of the trading company, tucked away on a quiet side-street. The office was empty this late at night.

□ □ □'s family operated a small business on the first floor and lived upstairs. I climbed the stairs to the second floor, walking slowly and clutching the railing. The walls lining the stairway were crammed with row after row of old family photos. His folks must be the nostalgic type. Clutching *Howl* in one hand, I shuddered inexplicably.

Upon entering the living room, I saw a middle-aged woman was sitting on the sofa and behind her stood a delicately handsome young man. They must be □ □ □'s mother and brother, I reckoned. I sat in the single armchair facing the tea table, on which there was tea, a vase filled with dried flowers, and—*wow*, the milk candy in flower-print wrapper!

"Please forgive our poor hospitality. We haven't anything to offer other than candy."

They thanked me for coming. I promptly replied "Don't mention it" and explained that I just wanted to return the book.

□ □ □'s mother asked if I knew □ □ □ well. Unable to say that I didn't know him, I said that even though □ □ □ and I knew each other, we hadn't stayed in touch for a while. □ □ □'s brother was still standing in the shadows behind his mother. From where I was sitting, I couldn't see his face clearly, but I knew I wanted to evade his gaze. His eyes sharp as a cat's.

□ □ □'s mother chattered on about his life—snapshots from the life of a stranger—she even looped back to □ □ □'s childhood. Sitting across from her, I nodded and murmured a few insignificant responses now and then. When she asked me details about □ □ □'s life, I kept my answers as vague as possible.

I started to sense what was happening. As an elementary school student, I'd had this experience many times. Mothers of classmates would ask how their child was doing in school. My own mother certainly went behind my back trying to get my classmates to give her information on me. This was just another variation of the same quest for information. *How was this happening again?*

"He's eccentric. He only has a few friends. He isolated himself once he fell ill …." She complained, but with a smile.

No, no, He isn't. Not at all. I repeated robotically.

"His friends won't come over here. They assume they aren't welcome, but we'd love to have them. I know ☐ ☐ ☐ never liked girls, but I don't hold it against him..."

I was anxious to leave, and then she added:

"To be honest, when you asked to talk to ☐ ☐ ☐ on the phone, we were happy and afraid at the same time. We really want to have his friends visit us to chat about his life—we don't even know if anyone has mistreated him. Thankfully, you called, and we managed to invite you over."

I have to say it was absurd. The family was trying to understand their son through his friends? What a circuitous route!

"I take it he hasn't visited in a while?" I asked.

His mother turned away from me.

I was sure she was weeping.

That was exactly how my mother cried.

* * * * * * * *

It was the standard bedroom of an obedient son. I could tell just by glancing at the certificates and medals.

In the center of ☐ ☐ ☐'s room was a pot of budding roses. ☐ ☐ ☐ had loved flowers, his mother said, that's why she was always going to the flower market to have fresh ones. As soon as the roses were about to wither, she would dry and preserve them.

☐ ☐ ☐ insisted on living alone and wouldn't let her visit, the mother continued. It wasn't until after he passed away that she visited his residence-cum-art studio for the first time. She'd collected her son's paintings and taken them back to be framed. She showed me a few of them, all of which depicted flowers. I was stunned by the aesthetics and sense of tranquility. Just a valley full of flowers—time and youth held still. No people meant no aging. Flowers never wither in paintings.

After showing me the paintings, □ □ □'s mother began rummaging through a box of old photos of □ □ □—candid shots from everyday life—she was clearly trying to prolong the exhibition. I declined immediately. I had already seen some in the stairwell. □ □ □'s young brother didn't participate in the conversation at all; he just stood by the door, silently watching us.

□ □ □'s mother protested that the photos in the stairway were all from his early childhood. This album she held was from □ □ □'s high school and university years. In one photo, □ □ □ was receiving an award at an art competition. He was awarded first prize at the graduation exhibition too. I was steeling myself for this album of the departed. Fool that I am, I didn't see the light until I opened it.

> *I saw the best minds of my generation destroyed by madness, starving hysterical naked,*
>
> *dragging themselves through the negro streets at dawn ...*

Putting *Howl* on □ □ □'s bookshelf, I bid my farewell.

* * * * * * * *

After saying goodbye, I went to catch the last train home.

On the way, I passed by a supermarket, which was about to close for the night. Looking through the glass door, I saw people scrambling to cash in on the late-night bargains.

> *I saw you, ... childless, lonely old grubber, poking among the meats in the refrigerator and eyeing the grocery boys.*

Suddenly, I heard someone calling my name from behind, I looked back and saw □ □ □'s brother running towards me. I gave him a wan smile and asked if he came to snag the last available fish. He shook his head.

"Let me walk you to the metro station. It's only a few steps away. I'm sorry my mother scared you off."

"No, she didn't."

"My elder brother hardly kept in touch with us, and no one would call for him. No one has mentioned my brother's name since he passed away. My brother was just a death notice in the newspaper. I don't even want to talk about him, but my mother keeps dwelling on him. My brother is gone for good, disappeared off the face of the earth. His body's just a pile of ash; his name has been erased. Sometimes it seems as though he never existed. People have already forgotten about him, but my mother remembers." He glanced briefly at me and bowed his head again, "That's why she was so pleased to receive your call. She has been yearning for someone to talk to about □ □ □. It's been a long time, and she's never had the opportunity."

He glanced at me again, "I was very surprised when you called us."

"Your brother left his name and number on a piece of paper that I found in the book. The moment I found the note, I wondered why he left it. Assuming it was another person's number, I didn't realize it was his own."

"In the last few days of his life, I visited him secretly without my mother's knowledge. He was busy preparing for an exhibition, but he was clearly very ill." He shook his head, then continued, "When I was poking around his place, I discovered that he left his real name and phone number in all his books, cassettes, and paintings."

"Why'd he do that?"

"Because he was scared. He knew that he was dying, and his memory was declining. He left his contact details to provide others with information about who he was and whom to call in case of an emergency, like if he were to slip into a coma."

"So, I guess the hospital contacted you immediately when the accident happened."

"Yes … sometimes I wonder if he was afraid he'd forget his own name. Maybe he left notes here and there to remind himself of his identity. Otherwise, he wouldn't know who he was." Suddenly, the brother slapped himself on the forehead and cried, "Oh, I almost forgot about something!"

He handed me a pack of milk candies, "My mom and I don't have a sweet tooth, but my brother liked these. May I give them to you as a memento?"

I shook my head. "Since it's just a memento, one piece enough. Take the rest back, so your mom can keep it as a reminder."

"No, I'd rather not. My mom has kept too many mementos," he gritted his teeth, and continued, "After my dad passed away, my mum shut down the family business, but the office still sits empty. That staircase is so packed with family photos that every time I go through it, I feel like I'm getting strangled in a time warp, slow death by asphyxiation. You know what I mean?"

"There are more photo albums than books on the bookshelf in her bedroom. My brother's room is the scariest place in the house; it's like the tomb of a mummified corpse. My mother can't bear to part with the wilting flowers, so she dries them instead. Do you want her to start hoarding candy?"

"Do you want to know how we found these? After my brother died, mom and I went to clear out his place. She brought home all his paintings and even his candy, displaying it on the table like an inedible ornament…"

As we walked into the metro station, he rushed to insert a coin for me. A plastic ticket popped out, and I tapped it to pass through the turnstile.

Across the barriers, he continued, "His blood sugar was quite low. During my secret visit, he was chewing candy nonstop. I asked if he wasn't afraid of tooth decay, but he just said that was nothing compared to his illness. He told me if he didn't binge on candy to keep his blood sugar up, he'd probably pass out. He was afraid if he fainted, he'd never wake up again. No matter how hard he fought it, one day he'd be gone completely." □ □ □'s brother was struggling to sound nonchalant, "One day he eventually collapsed and surrendered."

"Oh ..." I had nothing else to say.

As he turned to face the scattered passengers in the empty station, still trying to sound casual, he asked, "So, you and my brother were together?"

I was left speechless and tried to explain, "What? No, not at all!."

His face flushed red, "Don't take it the wrong way!"

"It's okay."

"May I have your number?" He lowered his head, and explained, "My mother might like to call for a chat—if you don't mind that is ..."

Lacking pen and paper to jot it down, he said not to worry, he'd just memorize it.

"Are you still in school?"

"I'm about to go into the army."

"Your mother will be lonely while you're in the army. You'll have make up for it by spending more time with her after you're discharged."

"No way! I can't wait to escape and never come back." He became very somber.

At that moment, the last train roared into the station.

I hesitated briefly and stepped on the train, not knowing why I'd paused.

Through the window of the car, I stared into the myriad of lights outside and fiddled with the milky candy. I decided to unwrap the candy to eat it, but it was stuck to the wrapper.

*　*　*　*　*　*　*　*

On July 1, 1997, the People's Republic of China regained control of Hong Kong. That day, my landlord told me she needed to get the flat back. I wasn't sure if I should mourn or rejoice.

It costs so much to move. I would rather do it myself to save money. Using my scooter, I transported several boxes of books to my new place. After a few trips back and forth, however, I was exhausted, so I decided to take the metro. Sitting in the car with an armful of manuscripts, I stared out the window as the train passed a familiar apartment complex. Looking down from the elevated rail, I saw that we were nearing □ □ □'s family home.

I decided to make the comforter that Amoeba used into an AIDs quilt. My idea was to embroider it with flowers, a peace sign and all the names I could remember before hanging it on the wall. In this way, another window could emerge on the wall, one in the direction of San Francisco.

Some might ridicule my seeming affectation. What difference could a quilt make? Especially if it was just hanging on a wall without anyone seeing it.

Believe it or not, some things had changed. I needed a calm narrative voice. In a mournful litany, I'd narrate the journey: I'd speak it, I'd sing it, I'd howl it from the rooftops. As for the quilt, it would compel me never to forget that I am a witness to these memories. Go ahead, call it "affectation."

Yet, wasn't it marked by a touch of affection?

AND. THEN.

Howl

I'd removed all my belongings—there was nothing left but the corkboard.

I removed the sticky notes one by one, took down lottery receipts I'd never tried to cash, the expired coupons, and the rose-colored candy wrappers. The paper had yellowed, but the characters were clear. That's when I took the mat down.

The giant ☮, red as the rising sun. Vibrant and brilliant, the rejection of war and the embrace of peace. Even after several months, the color never faded. Like blood in the veins, like wild grasses sprouting, the desire to live grows savagely, it still seems to breathe and howl.

People are born; people die. Symbols are indelible.

I howl mournfully, but it's only a whisper—unsure whom it could reach.

4

Muakai

Dadelavan Ibau
(translated by Kyle Shernuk)

I.

Dawn broke over the peak of Mount Kavulungan.[1] The morning fog dispersed, and a faint light shone down upon the just-reddening leaves of the sweet gum trees.

A young girl named Sweet Potato Leaf stood in front of Muakai's bed. She kissed Muakai and whispered quietly in her ear, "My revered chief, the one who loves you rode the spring light and has arrived."

"Who is it?"

"There." Sweet Potato Leaf gestured toward the betel nut placed at the head of the bed as she proceeded behind Muakai to comb her hair. "The one sprouting in the earth, growing in the direction of the sun, is my

Muakai," she recited quietly to herself. "The young woman is so upright that even the betel-nut trees are crooked by comparison!"

The betel nut—the sublime object that communicates the romantic passions between men and women and a proclamation of an undying love. Muakai fell into a vast grief.

"Sweet Potato Leaf, stop singing." Muakai stood up, grabbed the betel nut, and tossed it outside.

Muakai's older brother, Kuljelje, was deeply in love with her. To make Muakai realize the depth of his love, he would go to her room in the dead of night and place a betel net at the head of her bed. It's not that he didn't understand that brothers and sisters couldn't marry, but he still loved her that much. It's quite likely that the smell of the flowers, trees, mud, and even the wild game hunted down by the men were nothing more than the fragrance of Muakai to his nose. The sparrows came home to roost, and he needed to represent the people in resolving a dispute. A young man had eaten too many pigeon peas out in the fields and had fallen fast asleep atop a large rock, whereupon he let out a series of sonorous farts. It just so happened that someone from a neighboring tribe was passing by and, thinking that he was being insulted, killed the man in his sleep. Although Kuljelje was young, his ears at this time were already so old that they were of no use.

One day followed another, and Muakai's beautiful looks withered like a lily devoid of nutrients. The light was no longer beautiful nor bright to her eyes, and the twittering of the birds no longer brought pleasure to her ears. She stared into the distance at the mountain range, where the ridges appeared to enfold one another, and a boundless grief swelled in her heart.

To alleviate her dejection, she ordered the people to catch her a kind of bird called the *talavalavak*. It is a beautiful and rare species that people refer to as the Chief among Birds.

The people struggled to catch them, and Muakai was always exceedingly particular. "What? A feather is broken!" She cast the bird to the ground. "I want a prettier *talavalavak*," she said, turning to walk away. The people were left completely stupefied.

Day after day, night after night, the people surrounded Muakai, embroidering her clothes and sewing her skirts. Children sang to their hearts' contents while playing on the swings. And the men? They spent their days and nights shuttling through the mountain forests. They slept among the vales, high mountain ridges, and dangerous wild waters, never abandoning the tracks of the *talavalavak*. As they wriggled like insects atop precipitous cliffs; swung like apes among the forest trees; and ran like wild steeds over the fields, they sometimes even forgot that they were different from other animals, all *Homo erectus*. The days passed, one after another. The men used grass and leaves to insulate themselves from the cold and ate wild foods to fill their stomachs. At night, they curled up their knees and slept. When they reached the point of extreme exhaustion, they would occasionally recall that they were beings called people.

As sunset approached, a group of men who had been pursuing the birds appeared at the entrance to the tribal village. They raised their powerful baritone voices into a high-pitched yell. The women were ecstatic with joy; their men had come home. "The sun's first light shines upon the bronze knife of the creator; Muakai, our revered chief, the *talavalavak* is a beautiful bird, one that measures up to its name," the elder called Relentless Plucking loudly sang their praises. The women carried leis of flowers and sang as they encircled Muakai, as if she were a bride, and handed out betel nuts to the people who gathered around the banyan tree outside the chief's home. The men set down the nets from upon their backs and ever so carefully lifted out the *talavalavak* they had risked their lives to procure. Carrying them like infants hugged to their chests, they presented the birds to the chief. Muakai sat at the center of the circle of people, bedecked in her most splendid attire: an awe-inspiring eagle's feather had been inserted into her headdress, colored-glass beads upon her chest, a necklace, and earrings. Owing to humanity's reverence for their origins, the people closed their eyes. Everyone could smell the solemnity permeating the air and it caused them to tremble. Let's call it arrogance! She had long since ignored all of this, just as she had ignored Kuljelje. In front of the hopeful crowd, she glanced over the birds arrayed at her feet, beautiful as rainbows. Then, she declared: "There is not a single one that I want." Her face was expressionless and her voice like a bolt of lightning splitting apart the people's hopes. "I want a more beautiful *talavalavak*," she turned to leave as she spoke. The bronze knife in her hand was dazzling in the sunlight.

"Kuljelje, why don't you say something," someone from among the crowd cried out in indignation, "where has our good Muakai gone?" Kuljelje stood up to his full height and faced the people's questions. His eyes were bright and piercing, but he didn't utter a word. The people could do nothing but return home disappointed.

"What's going on with our chief?" The people were sitting on a flagstone that still retained some heat after being warmed all day by the sun. The dusk winds brushed against their hips, faces, and chests, entering their bodies. Men and women, young and old, all smoked cigarettes as they watched the red sun sink behind the mountains, falling deep into thought.

"We can't keep up these days of chasing after birds." The young man who said this was surnamed "Rainbow" and called "Relentless Plucking."[2] "To exterminate an animal completely, this is not your teachings."

"He's right," everyone expressed their deep-felt agreement.

"We are people, do I need to remind everyone of that? Where in these vast lands are we not to go?" These were the words of an older man surnamed "Directly Shining Sunlight" and called "Raise," who had wrestled a bear when he was young.

Everyone began to share whatever they knew about people, nature, their ancestors, and even the tribe's entire origin story.

"Alright! Let's do it this way. Tomorrow morning when the cock crows, we will leave this place, since everyone thinks we should not have this kind of chief." The old man surnamed "Wind Home" and called "Fast Wind" made the final decision.

In fact, people preferred to call "Fast Wind" "Forever in Front" because of his speedy ability to complete any task.

When hunting, he would often say to the young people: this tree, this flower, the path trod beneath your two feet, all of the living things in this jungle, I've farted on all of them. Even the air is mixed with the smell of my farts! He would go so far as to state proudly, "From the moment my mother pulled me from between her legs, I've never seen another person aim their butt in my direction." According to the women who worked in the fields with Fast Wind's mother at the time, the sun was just about at its zenith and everyone was talking and laughing in the fields when Fast Wind's mother sat down on the soft ground and lifted an infant from between her wide-spread legs. There had been no wind or clouds that day, then suddenly a gust of wind blew by. That little life, like a clay figurine, only then realized that his first important task was to bawl his eyes out and announce to all the spirits: I've arrived.

Fast Wind's buttocks left the flagstone and he stood up; a gust of wind suddenly raced by and dogs howled in all directions.

Night was quickly approaching.

The morning mist cleared, and sunlight poured down onto the carved wooden lintel above the door to the chief's home, just as it always did, piercing through the skylight and slowly brightening the room below. A flock of birds was singing out clearly from the trees. Muakai stretched out and cast a scornful look toward the head of her bed. Even if her mind was still like placid waters, every time this moment arrived, she still found it difficult to swallow down her saliva just after waking.

"Where has the early-morning smoke from the kitchens hidden itself away?"

She gently fiddled with her flowing, waist-long hair and used that sweet but arrogant tone, which only young girls possess, as she directed her words toward the inner room. "Can someone fill their stomachs simply by swallowing air? Where have you all gone to? Cumai (a person's name, meaning "bear"), why have you run off with the smoked-meat aroma of the millet? Uzu (a person's name, meaning "Yam Bean Leaf"), what were you dreaming about last night that made the sun unable to wake that pair of hands that combs your chief's hair? Alesau? ... Lavu? ...

The sound of Kuljelje's dry coughs carried across the house. The house was deadly silent.

Sluggishly, Muakai laid beneath the window. The sun was brilliant; the birds were twittering. She closed her eyes and stretched her back. From this noble posture she listened to the gurgling of the river and breathed in the fragrance of the early-morning air. After some time, her mind invariably began to feel shrouded in darkness, at times feeling like the rotting flesh of a corpse laid out in a cave and at others like a fledgling lost among the crisp light of the cold moon.

This isn't me! Muakai raised her head and looked at the sky, piously swallowing down her sobering saliva as she looked in the direction of the myriad spirits.

Emerging from the earth and growing in the direction of the sun, this is me, the cold bamboo atop the towering mountains. The birds soaring in the sky above never go far. If someone starts asking about it: "It's me, the cold bamboo atop the towering mountains. The sun follows you, and Muakai is under the sun."

She cheerfully recited: "Who is it? Wearing the beautiful patterns of the world and dancing upon the river valley. Ah! It's the Wu-a-kai-kai (the swallowtail butterfly)."

All around were the aromas of the Taiwanese rungia, running-steed leaves, Chinese chaste trees, wet mud, rotting fruit, and fresh sweet fruit-juice. From near and far, they all floated toward the supple skin of the young woman and entered her veins. If there was a thing called happiness, she was submerged in it. Her dark red, plump lips twitched. She turned her back to the sun and spread her arms wide. It was like she was welcoming a long-awaited sweetheart, her passionate legs bent and spread wide. The wind wriggled with abandon beneath her skirt. Muakai spread her wings, and the wind danced gracefully upon the hollow of her bare shoulders. It flitted upon her toes, her knees, her thighs, and fluttered into the young woman's dark, fervent, lonely... that deep place. She smiled.

* * * * * * *

"Muakai," I called quietly in her ear. She lightly shifted her body, then felt a jolt of intense pain from the wounds on her wrist.

"Anana (It hurts!)," she exclaimed quietly. Her head tilted to one side, and once again she was fast asleep.

"Atu-atu ti Muakai (You're really stupid, Muakai)." I sat by the side of her bed and brushed the hair from her forehead.

The contours of a life seem like they are defined by waiting for someone. One's lived experience comprises so many people, so many things. When all of life's splendor has been exhausted, someone from among the crowd smiles at you; as soon as the wind blows, you smell a certain scent. Something in your body stirs, and you know this is someone you know well.

I remember that June during the summer holiday, waking up to the birds' singing. I skipped breakfast and got cleaned up, then carried a cup of coffee outside to sit beneath the longan tree and read. It had rained heavily the night before, and so I figured that all of those people who liked me or had nothing to do—the aunties and uncles and cousins—wouldn't come gather here this early! It was rare for it to be so peaceful under the longan tree. I closed my eyes and took deep breathes of the delicate fragrance in the air. I sipped my coffee as I opened my book.

My blissful morning hadn't lasted even a minute, when a hunting dog suddenly emerged from among the flowering shrubs in the backyard and began licking my toes. "Ah! College Student, you're here!" Ah-Chung appeared in front of me looking quite strapping in his baseball cap and riding his bike, a Wild Wolf 125cc. "Summer vacation started!" I replied with a smile.

I uncrossed my legs while the dog sprawled prone at his master's feet. "Is Older Brother home?" "He's still sleeping." He parked his bike and, without asking further permission, made his way into the house. Not long after, Older Brother appeared in a drunken stupor. "I'm off to work! I had a dream that there was some leftover booze here." I tossed my backpack over my shoulder and said to the wandering Ah-Chung as he lit a cigarette, "Hey! Let me ride your bike!"

"Ah-Chung's come to chat with you." Older Brother said through a mouthful of smoke.

"I'm going to have a look at a tree!"

Our father worked in the police force when he was still alive and enjoyed flowers and nature. When he had time, he would take me up to the mountains to learn about the flora there, and I would bring home all sorts of plants and herbs for my collection. By the time I started middle school, my specimen book was already higher than my knees. For many years, when dealing with my family, whenever I wanted to leave the house, I'd just start putting on my backpack and look for a tree that could serve as my excuse.

I hopped on the Wild Wolf, started up the engine and, after a quick goodbye, was on my way.

I followed the uneven and pothole-filled asphalt road and headed north, enjoying the scenery of the open country. Randomly stopping at an intersection with a road sign, I started thinking about how someone must live there. I decided to enter the village but was chased out by a group of stubborn wild dogs. After attempting this a few times, I suddenly found it immensely entertaining.

After passing through a tunnel, a lively village appeared before me. I had a fried-egg cake and a glass of soybean milk at a breakfast shop. "It's poured for several days on end. Are the mountain roads still passable?" "I saw someone come down that way!" the proprietor said. I slowly advanced along the mountain path and passed a police box, where a big-eyed and bushy-browed officer glanced my way before burying his head in a newspaper.

The mountain road was becoming increasingly steep. The muddy road was covered with the fallen, dark-green fruit from the tung-oil trees, and the bike slipped out from under me twice. Ah-Chung's bike became a mud-mobile, and I looked like a clay figurine. The sound of a surging river surrounded me. The sunlight was blocked by the lofty acacia trees, and there was not a soul to be seen among the smells of wet earth. Winding along the precipitous mountain roads alone, I was lonesome but happy. After taking a big turn, I suddenly found myself bathed in sunlight among a field of flowering wild peonies. In response to this unexpected good fortune, I kicked my legs out as high as I could and hollered with joy. I passed through a field planted with taros and, about half an hour later, found myself slowly working my way up a slope. On a peak surrounded by mountains, I saw a lonely, large-leaved nanmu tree amidst the rising, swirling mist, towering up between heaven and earth.

"Ah! Here you are, old girl." I killed the engine and stood before the tree, opening my arms and wrapping them around her. "I'm so happy to see you!"

Just behind me, I discovered a tribal village concealed in the ravine below.

* * * * * * * *

A group of people, with flowers in their hair and in ceremonial attire, sat in a circle around a live pig, some taros, betel nuts, rice wine, and carbonated beverages.

They had stern expressions on their faces as they spoke. Men and women were busy carrying bamboo baskets containing long, narrow strips of mochi, millet cakes, and piping hot pieces of pork freshly scooped out of the pot. People were using knives to cut pieces to give to everyone, and I received a juicy piece from a woman with a warm smile.

"This is a token of affection from the prospective groom's side, which they are sharing with the gathered relatives and friends. After eating it, perhaps his intended bride will have a change of heart and agree to the marriage."

I wove my way through the watchful group of people, climbed onto a platform of layered flagstones, and sat down.

I saw the wrinkled face of an old woman sat in the host position. Her eyes drooped, and her lips were slightly parted. An ancient tune slowly rose up.

For a short while, I listened attentively. A humming sound echoed in my ears, and I looked around a few times. Except for the chanting of the wizened old woman, everything before me was just as lively as when I first arrived. On several occasions, I stood up and walked to the other side of the platform. There, I quietly sat on a vacant stone.

I knew that in the past, before any rulers appeared on this land, this platform was used to display the skulls from enemy tribes. It was the place where village elders came to negotiate and in ordinary times where children came to play and swing.

I took a look at the old woman and then closed my eyes. When the humming noise rose up again, my mind was put completely at ease. This time, I could clearly tell that this wasn't the sound of some animal or insect. I listened closer, and its gravelly quality became increasingly refined and clear.

Dawn broke over the peak of Mount Kavulungan ... I heard the voice of what seemed like a goddess singing.

"We've come to propose marriage. Why are you treating us like this, Muni?" someone said loudly as they stood up. "How long are we going to have to discuss this marriage? Until Muakai and Sapili are both old? Will you not be happy until you've buried us in the ground?"

I was lucid for a moment and then fell asleep deeply again to the sound of the ancient melodies. A light breeze blew past; among the valley of lilies dancing in the wind, a woman sat upon a stone step covered in dried leaves and rotting wood.

I thought of my deceased parents and was suddenly overwhelmed with grief.

I didn't know how much time had passed when someone lightly touched my shoulder. I opened my eyes to find the old woman who had been chanting. Her entire face was covered with wrinkles, and she looked so, so old.

"Come, drink a cup of kavava." She handed me a cup filled to the brim with pale orange liquid.[3]

"Thank you!" After taking a sip, I told her it was my first time having this.

"This isn't something we have every day," she said, "millet is precious. And if you want to drink really good kavava, you have to get lucky. And it's your luck to have come when the person who made this wine is yet to be interred in the earth: I made this wine. Do you like it?"

"As delicious as a sweet spring!" I said, and she gave a big laugh. She looked like a completely different person compared to the serious women I saw before.

She summoned the middle-aged man beside her who was carrying an earthen jar filled with kavava. He poured the old woman a full cup and said something into her ear. "Let them do as they please!" I heard her say.

"Child, what are you searching for that brings you to our fog-buried village?" she asked as she looked at me kindly.

"A tree," I replied. "I happened to be looking at a book that introduced that flora of Taiwan, and it said this tree was more than 100 years old. In the past, they used to hang the heads of the Japanese from it!"

"Then we should thank that tree," she said. "This mountain range buried in the fog is certainly a mysterious place. As for its flora, a deity lives on Mount Kavulungan, and she is the source of all life. In front of her abode is a tree, under which she stands and looks upon the people. If she sees a person she likes, she will pluck a piece of fruit from the tree and throw it to that person." The woman stood up and walked inside. Not long after, she emerged carrying shiny, round, black pit, which clearly had a mark from where it had been plucked. The old woman said it had fallen to her when she was sweeping fallen leaves as a young girl. "In the past when we wanted to build a house, you would invite the clan priest to come perform an invocation and then go up the mountain to that tree and say: 'I'm sorry. My new home requires you to serve as beams and rafters so that my family has a place to shelter from the wind and rain. Please let me take you home with me now.' Of course, everything I've said has nothing to do with the tree that you saw." Ah! She remembered something and her aging eyes focused on me. "You understood all of the song I sang! Child, I can feel the sadness in your heart."

I was completely unaware that I'd even been humming.

I told the old woman about an experience I'd had when I was younger.

When I was still an infant in swaddling clothes, my parents took me up the mountain to the fields, about a half-day's distance from the village, because they had to pick and gather mangoes. People told them it would be best not to bring a young child up to the mountains, but my parents were educated people and, once I was sound asleep, they would leave me alone in the work hut. I would cry and scream all night, and my father would carry me into the darkness to some higher ground. My mother waved her hands, "Come back! Child who runs to play in the night's cave, don't lose your way. This is your path. You are here. My child, come back." From then on, my childhood years were spent drifting along on my parents' backs. I've had a weak constitution ever since I was a child, and whenever I smelled the approach of dusk I would begin to cry.

"Which tribe are you?"

I pointed to the south, "Granny, I'm Tjalja'avus."

"Let's go! We're going to my field. Let them keep on whiling away the hours." She went inside and emerged shortly after in more casual attire.

She carried a bag of betel nuts on her back and shared a whispered exchange with an older woman sat in the corridor making leis. Then, she headed my way.

"Where are you going? The guests are still here?" someone said.

"We don't want to stick around here any longer." She took a seat on my bike and wrapped her arms around my waist; I already had the engine running.

Her friend appeared from the door behind the kitchen and took a seat on the bike, moving slowly as she went.

"Alright," the old woman said.

The two women were like brides who fled and vanished without a trace before people had the chance to stop them.

I followed the old woman's directions and kept to the river after the fork in the road at the entrance to the village, riding slowly as we went downhill. We turned a corner, and a hanging bridge appeared before us. I slowed down, but the two women made no indication they intended to get off the bike. Alright! I shifted the bike down to second gear, gritted my teeth, and advanced. The bridge swayed endlessly back and forth, but the old women were not the slightest bit concerned and continued discussing amongst themselves: "There's some leftover pigeon-pea soup on the stove. I remembered to throw some pork in my bag on the way out the door just now, too, so we can add some of that to the soup as well. Then add some wild herbs!" The other said, "The roast fish from last night is still on the rack, and we still have some kavava! The girl likes it!"

My entire body was drenched in cold sweat, and I thought I might throw up everything in my stomach.

I stopped the bike. "What's wrong? Our place is just up ahead. One more turn and we're there," the woman said with concern.

"Granny, your hands." I let out a big breath.

It was only then that the woman realized that her hands, which had begun around my waist, had risen up to around my breasts due to the bumpy journey.

"Ah! Your boobs are going to suffocate!" The two women threw their heads back and laughed. A hand reached around from the back seat and patted my breasts: "It's no big deal, it doesn't mean anything."

By evening, we had arrived at their home on the river, which was built from stone slabs. Recently gathered peanuts and taros were piled high in the shed built just outside, where there was also a basket of pigeon peas waiting to be shelled. The two women proceeded just as they had discussed on the bridge: one went inside to light the stove fire, and the other went out to collect wild herbs. "Should we light the fire inside or outside, friend?" The other said, "We've not been back in two days, let's let the house recover some of its spirit!"

I stood on the stone steps and watched the roosting birds return home in the dusk's fading light.

The moonlight that shone down was clear as we carried the soup pot outside. "Ah, the sun will come out tomorrow! We can finally get some good work done." The two women looked at the sky as they set about peeling the sweet potatoes in their hands. "You've got that right, friend!" the other said. "What happened to the Muakai and Kuljelje of old, granny," I asked.

"Ah! What happened next!" She took a sip of her soup and began to recite the tale in a voice that sounded almost like chanting.

"Brother and sister sat atop a large flagstone and looked into the distance at the endless plains while the dawn light trickled down and dispersed into the fragrant air. The people's footsteps were swift, and rising dust filled the sky; brother and sister watched in silence as the people fled. They had lost their parents when they were young and had been waited upon completely by the people. And now there's nothing left, everything scattered like dust. 'What are we going to do?' They sat on the rocks and punched them like children, looking like two abandoned orphans.

"And then?

"And then a hunter from another tribe called Sapili passed by. He killed Kuljelje and spared Muakai, who was holding the bronze knife in her hand. And just like that, Sapili remained in Muakai's village and the two of them were together. Their descendants flourished like betel palms, steadily increasing.

"Those were our ancestors, and we are the fruit from the betel palm trees, which fall to the ground and after they ripen, take root, and grow. And this process has continued all the way to my own child, also called Muakai, who is currently working in Taipei!"

"Granny, your name is Muni?"

"Yes!" she said, with an air of reverence.

"Then you are one of Muakai's descendants and also the chief of this tribe."

"Yes! The man's family who came to propose marriage today are the descendants of Sapili, whose name has also been passed down to today. The male lead is called Sapili, just as the female protagonist is our Muakai," her friend said. "Singing that kind of song, they all felt ashamed!"

"Child, your name was also given to you by your ancestors."

"The people in my tribe just call me College Student!"

Ah! "College Student." They were stumped for a second as they awkwardly pronounced the Beijing-ese and then broke out in peals of laughter.

II.

I called Muakai the day I returned to Taipei. After agreeing to meet her at her place Sunday afternoon, I scrawled down her address and then hung up the phone.

I was a little early when I got off the bus at Roosevelt Road, so I crossed the Chiang Kai-shek Memorial Hall on foot and proceeded to Ren'ai Road. I saw the bustling beverage shop on the corner of the side street and walked that way. Her building wasn't hard to find and soon appeared before my eyes, tall and sturdy. I hit the buzzer, rode the elevator to the fourth floor, and then rang the doorbell. I heard the sound of feet walking across the floor, and a woman in her thirties opened the door. Her eyes were mesmerizing.

"You're Muakai."

"People call me Hsiu-hsiu here." Her long, wet hair fell freely on her bare shoulders, and she exuded big-city sophistication.

"You bumpkin, what kind of rocks are you carrying in that big bag of yours?" She took a can of juice from the fridge and gave it to me. "Have a seat!" she said, then turned and hurried back to the bathroom.

I sat on the sofa, quietly drinking my juice while I took the items from my bag and placed them on the table.

"Granny wanted me to bring millet, taros, dried taro strips, fresh ginger, peanuts, and four bottles of kavava to give you. You can share the kavava with your friends. Granny said you were definitely missing these things from the mountainside." I said this facing the bathroom door.

I heard the shower nozzle turn on in the bathroom and the water come gurgling out. Then, I heard the sound of two people messing around. I tore a page from my notebook, wrote a short note including my dorm name and telephone number, and then left.

A week later, I received a phone call from Hsiu-hsiu at my dorm. She apologized for what happened earlier and said she wanted to get together. "8 p.m. at the pub on Zhongxiao East Road. Does that work?" she asked, "go ahead and write down the address." I told her that I wasn't someone who liked those kinds of places and that the music would give me headache. "If we go to the university campus, we can have a casual stroll or sit by the lake and drink beer and chat."

"No way! You bumpkin, haven't I walked enough mountain paths already? Please let me treat you! With me by your side, what's there to worry about? And once I get drunk, you can throw me over your shoulders and carry me home!"

I spent most of my time trying to decide if, in the end, I was actually going to go, and so I arrived forty minutes late. Her delicate face was already slightly red, and her thick, black, curled hair was exceedingly glossy under the soft light. I discovered that Hsiu-hsiu was truly beautiful. It was a beauty unique to women from the mountains, wild with a touch of rebellion but also mature and cheerful.

When I arrived, Hsiu-hsiu was sitting around a table with two other women who were around her age. The two women had identical hair styles and looked like twins; when they laughed, they both had the sweetest matching dimples. I said hello, took a seat next to Hsiu-hsiu, and ordered a Heineken.

"This is my little sister. She carried the kavava you're drinking on her back all the way from the mountains," Hsiu-hsiu said, "and in just a bit, she's going to carry me all the way home!" I wasn't sure if she'd had a bit too much to drink, but her face was bright red underneath her lightly applied makeup; she was beautiful. She was wearing a low-cut top with a Western-style jacket. And if you looked at those mesmerizing eyes of hers for a just a few seconds too long, they would lay claim to your heart.

This is Chieh-chieh, and this is Mei-mei.

"They are girl-girl friends."

"What are girl-girl friends?" I asked.

"You use that college brain of yours and think about. Tell me, in our native language isn't this what *malerava* translates to?"

"Ah! Yeah!" I took a sip of beer.

Hsiu-hsiu stood up and headed for the restroom.

"Your big sister's been feeling pretty down recently, so be sure to spend some time with her," the slender-faced Mei-mei said.

When Hsiu-hsiu got back to her seat, the music became very gentle. "I said something to the owner. I asked him to put on something that wouldn't give everyone a headache." The topic of conversation changed to our bodies. Hsiu-hsiu grabbed my breasts and said, "Us aboriginals all have big boobs. How is it that yours are so small, College Student?"

I cupped my breasts in my hands and told them, "After the sixth grade, they just never grew again!" Everyone laughed.

That evening, Hsiu-hsiu and I took a cab back to her place. We sat for a bit, then I explained that I had class early the next morning and needed to head home.

She stood up, went to the liquor cabinet, and opened a bottle of *daqu* rice wine. After pouring herself a glass, she sipped it silently. She turned and looked at me like she had something on her mind, and finally said, "What does the bible say about homosexuality? I've been dealing with a bladder infection recently. Is this retribution?

"Please forgive me," I began laugh, "but I'm not a believer."

"You won't think I'm strange, will you?" Her hazy eyes were trained on me.

"How could I? The only thing that's strange is you thinking there'll be retribution," I replied.

Hsiu-hsiu called that Wednesday afternoon and asked to see me. "Let's go back to that place that won't give you a headache," she suggested.

She was exceptionally quiet that night. There were only two other tables with customers, and the bar was playing Winnie Hsin's album *Awakening*. It was one of those plaintive songs that I'd heard before. Muakai told me it was here that she had met her lover Hak.

Later, she stepped out to take a phone call. When she came back in, she just sat brooding in silence, drinking one glass after another.

"What's wrong," I asked. She looked at me, her eyes brimming over with tears. After draining her glass, she looked like a dancer preparing to take her final bow. With a graceful posture, she raised up her glass as high as she could and brought it crashing violently down upon her head. The glass shattered, and she began to pick up a shard to cut herself. I grabbed her hands and wrested it from her grip.

The proprietor helped me to call a cab. I half-carried half-dragged her out of the bar. She struggled out of my hands and rushed into the high-speed lane of oncoming traffic; it was like she had lost her mind. I wrapped my arms around her from behind and, using sheer brute strength, dragged her into the cab.

"I'm a woman with a bitter fate, so many men and women falling to their knees begging me to love them." She kept crying like this the entire way home. "She's fallen in love with another woman."

Just as we got back, the phone rang and Hsiu-hsiu answered. Nodding her head in acknowledgement, she said, "She's with me now." She handed the phone to me, "It's like this," Granny said from the other end of the line, "the groom and his family are persistent, so we must at least discuss the matter. Come back with Muakai."

III.

We got on the pre-dawn Kuo-Kuang bus and headed south. At 10 o'clock we arrived in a bustling town at the foot of the mountains, where I booked a car and we began our ascent.

Early the next morning, Muakai and I were still fast asleep as a stream of people busily came and went: "Where's Muakai? I haven't seen her for so long! It's my good fortune to still be drawing breath long enough to see her again."

"I've painstakingly sewn every stitch in this skirt over several years. I'm giving it to her, so she has something to remember me by after I die."

At 8 o'clock, the groom's party arrived carrying a pig and some rice cakes.

They sat in a semicircle in front of the house. Muakai wore a traditional outfit that was embroidered from head to foot with designs of the hundred-pace pit viper. Granny also wore traditional garb, and around her forehead she had bound some herbs to help relieve the summer heat. She stood and recited the following story:

"Everyone knows of the bronze knife in Muakai's hand, so today I will directly speak to the experiences of our generation.

This event concerns Bali's going up the mountain to work. As he was hoeing the earth, the bronze knife fell before him. 'Cling, clang—a huge noise—right in front me,' Bali said. He returned home and told my husband, Laucu, 'The bronze knife has appeared. What do we do?' Laucu asked him to bring the knife back to the village. My husband wrapped it in a red scarf and placed it our shelf.

In the past, it was forbidden to move the stand upon which the bronze knife was placed, and it was the tribal priests' responsibility to go there to perform ceremonies. Then, Bali was working in the mountains when he suddenly rushed back and said, 'This is your Makelali's bronze knife. I'm returning it to its home now,' and then headed back to work.

Speaking about this, I can't help but ask everyone, the Japanese knew our custom of not messing around with seating positions, right? Who sits in the chief's chair? The chief has their designated place. Some among you made the mistake of offering the chief's seat to them and then making a position for yourselves, one that you've kept until today. My apologies for such harsh words, but you are a family that received the favor of those rulers.

The Japanese forced our people to move here, and no one was able to move the bronze knife from its place; so when we left our original tribe, we also left the resting place of the knife.

After who knows how many years, no one had any contact with the knife back in its original location, and no one went again to pray there. Its location was lost to us among the thick-growing grasses, up until we accidentally discovered the desolate ruins of our original tribal village and the knife was found."

A member of the groom's party stood up to refute Granny's words.

"That bronze knife was a commemorative item brought to Taiwan by the Dutch. There are foreign words written on it, the kind that a Catholic priest can understand.

The Dutch asked, 'Who is the leader among you?' Someone took them to Makelali's home, where they bestowed the bronze knife upon the family as a gift. It's not a deity, and I don't believe that that thing can run about as it pleases."

Granny was about to speak when a woman sitting next to her pulled on her hand. "I know, let me speak." The woman stood up and said, "What more is there to say? I saw the whole thing. All of you from the younger generation didn't live through that period, so please don't start talking nonsense.

That bronze knife is shiny and smooth. I saw it myself when I was young. It resembled a person, with eyes, a head, nose, ears, and feet.

While we were picking mulberry leaves when I was little, Kui took off his clothes and wrapped the knife up in several layers, then set a stone on top to keep it in place. He went to wash in the river and when he finished and went to retrieve it, the knife had already disappeared. Later on, he discovered that the knife had already run back to the clay pot on which it sits."

Someone from among the groom's party said through his laughter: "How can a thing run?"

"You all listen to what I have to say," the women carried on, "there were a lot of us there at the time and, when he went to retrieve it, it'd vanished. 'Where did it go? Where was the bronze knife?' He asked each and every one of us. Who would try to steal it?

When he went back to the Makelali residence in the old village, the bronze knife was resting on its clay pot. When Kui saw this, he never again thought to try and take it with him. It was for that reason, too, that he returned home so late that evening.

The Makelali family tore down half of their traditional stone-slab home and built a concrete room in order to receive the knife into the new space. Laucu became gravely ill not long after, and Sapili's grandfather wanted Muni to sell the knife to the [Han] plains trader who specialized in aboriginal artifacts—Muni went mad with rage.

How can you, our distinguished guests, not know about these events? All we're asking now is that you find that plains trader and return the bronze knife to Makelali's family."

"After Muni sold the knife to the lowlander, why didn't it come back of its own accord? If it's as you say it is, it should be able to bring itself home again."

"Because it can't buy itself a plane ticket." Granny said with exasperation as she chewed on a betel nut.

This village was truly foggy, and one cloud after another obscured the sun above our heads. The fog rolled in from all directions and billowed upward. In no time at all, everything was engulfed in the vast whiteness of the fog.

IV.

At 7 o'clock in the morning, Big Eyes drove a white jeep up the mountain. He said that if he got us to the city for the 11 o'clock bus, then I could reach Taipei before dark.

Granny gave me another bag full of "mountain goods" to lug back with me. As we were getting ready to leave, she hugged me and kissed my cheek, and then told me to come back from school on my next break. Big Eyes drove the car, and Muakai sat in the front passenger seat. It was the first time I'd seen either of them alone together. About three hours into the drive, we passed a shop. Muakai asked Big Eyes what he wanted to drink. "Coffee," he said. "Aren't you already dark enough!" Muakai exclaimed as she turned toward him. He smiled and showed off his yellowed teeth, discolored by his betel-nut-chewing habit, which he hoped to whiten one day. "I'd like milk," I added. We spent most of the trip listening to music, and Muakai was responsible for changing the cassette tapes. She would turn around on occasion and chat with me.

We arrived in the city at 10:40 a.m., and Muakai bought my tickets and snacks for the journey while I attended to my bags.

I waved goodbye to them. Each was standing in their own corner waving, like two completely unrelated people.

At one point, I had gone a long time without contacting Granny because my class workload became overwhelming. It was then that Muakai seemed to disappear from the face of the earth, without so much as a phone call.

V.

I placed my completed phonology exam booklet on the table and cheerfully walked back to my dorm. That was my last exam, and the semester was over.

Laying on my desk was a letter bearing my address, which was written in characters that appeared scrawled by an elementary school student; the envelope was sealed with cooked rice. I was shocked upon opening it. It was a letter composed of bent and crooked Romanized letters approximating my mother tongue, which took extreme effort to understand. The letter recounted how, in the few short months since I'd left the village, two of her friends had already been buried. It said: "What can someone like me do—someone whose body withers daily under the sun? The sparrows visiting my millet are more diligent than I!"

I threw my bag over my shoulder and hurried south.

Granny handed me a letter that she had stored under her bed, and I sat on a stone chair under the eaves outside to read it.

The rain is endless. On such solitary and lonely days, what can I do to stop thinking about you? I've searched for you in my dreams for several days now. Why am I still calling like crazy? I'm scared of myself. My darling Hsiu-hsiu, have you also been suffering such torments over the past few months? It wasn't easy working up the courage to call, but then all I heard were my own ice-cold words... I keep on hurting you, but I am also suffering.

Several hundred days have passed, and I'm still deluding myself, saying that it doesn't matter. Things will get better with time, I'll forget... but I haven't. When I close my eyes, you're still there. You look just like the first time I saw you, a matchless beauty dressed in black with tussled hair.

Even I don't know the place where my love for you is buried, its depths unfathomable.

The colored-glass bead that sits upon your chest, your despondent eyes, clear and bright like a mirror. I never knew that there were such beautiful people on this earth.

Your tribe is my tribe. My bride, you fulfilled me. You occupy the depths of my soul.

Among your people you are revered, a chief, but I tear myself apart here, one piece at a time, because of love.

And now an insuppressible gloom grows in me by the day.

Are you still there, waiting for me?

Right! You'll always love me, right! Even if you have good men and women in your life, you'll still keep me in your heart, right? Come back! Hsiu-hsiu, otherwise what strength will I have to keep on living? Love me. Even if you will still love other people, don't cut me out of your heart.

You are the only place toward which I will fly.

Hsiu, come back! I'll never leave you again.

Truly. I'll never leave you again.

Granny walked over carrying a bamboo basket. She sat down next to me and related all the things that had occurred since I left.

"That marriage proposal, the one after you and Muakai came back together. The parents and relatives of the groom secretly came to the house and said there was nothing they could do regarding the bronze knife. I figured this wasn't their main concern. This old woman knows that love must survive many trials. Sapili was in love with another woman, and that woman was now pregnant. Things being what they were, there was not much to be said.

When Muakai found out, she didn't seem the slightest bit saddened by the news.

Early the next morning a letter came in the mail; by midday she had disappeared without a trace, and I noticed she'd taken her purse with her. Did she go back to Taipei? How could she leave without saying a word? It was later that I discovered this letter on her bed, on top of which was a lock of her hair. I knew that the girl must certainly be suffering some hardship.

It was only then that I frantically searched for you! Your travels must have been difficult.

What does the letter say, child? Can you please tell me what it says?" Her expression was resolute but kind.

I didn't know what to say. Should I tell Granny that there is a person called Hak, and that this Hak person is in love with Hsiu, and that Hsiu also loves her? Or should I be more direct and say that Hak and Hsiu-hsiu are both women and love one another but can't be together, which is why they are suffering? And that after several rounds of separating and getting back together, now, they have finally decided to be together.

Or should I say that there can be love between women. Just like between a man and a woman.

I hurried here from Taipei, it appears, to tell her that Muakai ran off with another woman.

A winter wind kicked up, and the leaves on the acacia trees rustled, then fell, and floated to the ground. At nightfall, it was as if an elderly woman was walking alone in solitude into the boundless mist.

After an exhausting day-long journey, the liveliness of Taipei had faded away into nothingness. I smelled the crisp air and looked at the millet growing up from the earth. For all these years, my mind seemed weak and frail, as if it had endured the trials of some illness. The cold fog fell like a screen, descending on the light that had shone upon the eaves. A gust of wind blew, and a cloud floated past. They were germs wafting through the air, eating away at every fiber of my being.

"Muakai will come back, Granny," I said. "Her boss had some important business come up all of sudden and needed her help. That's why she left in such a hurry. She told you not to worry about her."

"Ah! So that's what it was." She looked at me and then at the letter in my hands, her wizened face breaking into a broad smile.

VI.

"Muakai," I called again quietly into her ear.

"Ah! College Student." She opened her eyes, then stretched out her right hand and took mine. "I'm sorry," she said, "I always thought that her love was true. But, after so many years, I had let myself get wrapped up in all her exquisitely wrought words and couldn't see who she was clearly anymore. Women should treasure each other, shouldn't they? I believe that, so I never interfered with her family life. I told myself I'd wait for her. That letter she sent me was like a sugar-coated candy … she teaches Chinese … does everyone who studies Chinese suffer from this problem? Don't be sad for me. Those who return from the gates of hell will always cherish oneself. You asked if I'll continue to lay low in Taipei. I think it's about time I saw the light; once I'm better, it will be time for me to go back.

Use that college-educated brain of yours and consider this: did my ancestor Muakai also love women?

There's no need for you to wrack your college brain, I can just tell you: I think so."

Long, long ago… Muakai loved women.

I held her right hand and led her down the hallway. Standing or sitting, a vast and empty gaze; the gaze of a stranger, meeting.

The blowing wind, what music does it make? The strumming of her heartstrings, what song hums forth?

Notes

1. While the original version of this story refers to a Damu'an Mountain (*Damuan shan* 大姆鞍山), personal correspondence with the author corrects this to Dawu Mountain (*Dawu shan* 大武山), which in the Paiwan language is more standardly rendered as Mount Kavulungan. Moreover, all Paiwan names in the text have been rendered in English according to the author's own transliterations.
2. The Paiwan language follows the same naming order as English; it is only in the Chinese that it is reversed.
3. Kavava is a type of millet wine common to East and Southeast Asia. Among many of Taiwan's aboriginal tribes, it is also a cultural symbol and frequently used in ceremonies.

5

Violet

Hsu Yu-chen
(translated by Howard Chiang and Shengchi Hsu)

It's a chaotic mural without a clear subject depicting scenes from a bygone era.

The entrance is hidden under the overgrown canopy of a mysterious forest like those seen the Discovery channel. Embedded in a steep rock wall is a cave several stories tall. Its contours evoke a shrieking maw; it's magnificent. A flock of bats enters the cave at dawn and emerges at dusk, forming a black cloud. Just as night surrenders the heavens, the swirling flocks synchronize. Dawn breaks in layers, and the bats flit through her music staff like the notes of a symphony. Spinning, they cast an inky net over the sea of trees.

The golden age has passed; the scenery is a wasteland. The cavern is dark and humid. From its vaulted ceiling hang the flying beasts, releasing sparse droplets of excrement, nourishing layer upon layer of shiny black cockroaches that swarm across the ground. A noxious odor saturates the air.

Eventually a visitor arrives. Crushing an orgy of roaches underfoot (*ksss ksss*), the Visitor reaches the end of the darkness. Facing the infinite expanse of wall, the Visitor reaches out and feels its dense and intricate inscriptions. Totems, characters, and glyphs stretch across its surface. The odds of making such a discovery are probably one in a million. Tiny purple beads of light shine beneath the Visitor's fingertips. As the Visitor bends over for a closer look, the beads of light seem to curve, spread, and bloom like flowers.

Have we met before?

Is this déjà vu, or the dreamscape of a former traveler? Neither, or maybe both—it's a vision of perfect truth.

* * * * * * * *

That was the second time I tried Black Cat—Ol' Kela was ditching his stash before going abroad—and it hit me like violets blooming after winter thaws.

I followed the same method as before: first take ecstasy, then, when it starts to kick in, pop a Black Cat. The table was bare except for a clear plastic bag, now empty. The two pills it had held—red and white gel caps—entered my stomach three hours ago. Glaring up at me from the sticker label was a pair of cat eyes, under them a line of Japanese kana that spelled out the English word "sexual." Black Cat was a strong aphrodisiac, but dwelling as I do in the isolation of my room, I didn't use it as such.

My body waited—waited for the space-time vortex to begin its rapid revolutions—waited with my lips cracked and dry. Although my room was air conditioned, my forehead and neck streamed rivers of sweat. Limbs paralyzed, I lay on the sofa. It was a quiet afternoon in the last days of summer. The mosaic glass windows were shimmering crystalline screens locking the warming climate safely outside. A ray of light passed through the door and reflected off the tiles; a dazzling current of liquid mercury slowly flooded the room. The world hadn't changed. I hadn't experienced a long journey full of chance encounters as I had the first time I did Black Cat...I merely surrendered, again and again, to a dizziness that kept me spinning in place.

No sensation. Should I feel fortunate? Or disappointed? My foolish plans for an indoor odyssey were a failure. A vacation day extravagantly wasted, leaving nothing but a huge blank.

Because it hasn't been considered a serious subject of inquiry, no one knows the answer: why does the same drug elicit different experiences? The notepad beside me was brimming with rich material, preserving the evidence of non-linear leaps through time. Perhaps its contents portended my unsatisfying experience? For the moment, I no longer wished to pursue the matter.

If nothing lay ahead, I'd just wait a while until I sobered up and reached the end of my indoor travels. At that point, I'd switch my phone back on, open my inbox, and reply to all my messages. Is this the likely outcome of my trip? Or is it a premature end, my attempt to sail against the winds of destiny? It's hard to say. Navigating through unknown and potentially treacherous waters, my exhausted body yearned for a harbor.

Figuring it was about over, I struggled to my feet. Seeing a little ketamine powder left on the table, I hesitated briefly. If I'd come into port eventually, what was the point of prolonging the voyage? But on the other hand, perhaps it was precisely *because* I would inevitably come to shore that my travels should be extended...

Ketamine makes you hesitate, like a philosopher deep in thought. K's original use: elephant tranquilizer. If taken on its own, K causes dizziness and blackouts. If used with ecstasy, it enhances the high. Your brain's serotonin maxes out. It's the ultimate sensation of euphoria and ease, like a volcanic eruption, magma coursing through your body. It takes months or even years of repeated use—depending on the person—to build up a tolerance. At that point, K has nothing to do with pleasure. It's a key, but nobody knows what it unlocks. When you snort K, it traverses your nasal passages and leaves a bitter residue in your windpipe, like a patch of moss sticking to the back of your throat.

K has a high-tech vibe. It's futuristic shit. It'll make you stare for ages at the objects around you: Thirty-two inch flat-screen television, empty cans of Coke Zero, platinum roam-phone, remote controls for the AC, the stereo, and the TV...*they're like rectangles covered in buttons....*

Vision takes on an entirely new meaning, as if the images cast upon my retinas are thousand-year-old artifacts excavated from an imperial mausoleum transcending appearances and pragmatics, and assembling to form a magnificent picture—a testament to the times.

History is a riddle; the future is a riddle. Both are like dreamlands. Whenever I emerge from the dreamscape, I put pen to paper, drift in a stream of confused times, aiming to plot my current coordinates, to document my mind's residual illusions. *Most dreamlands are not reality, but reality often appears in dreams.*

A common experience: you witness in the present a scene from a dream. The framing, dialogue, plot, and even your own reactions are identical to what happened in the dream. Each segment cuts out after two to three seconds; you lose connection to the network. Scientists call such experiences déjà vu. It's the outcome of a millisecond delay in the neural pathways linking the two sides of the brain. You'd have to obtain evidence demonstrating that you saw what happened before in a dream for the clairvoyant hypothesis to be tenable. To this day such proof is unheard of.

Dream transcription: is it a book of memory or a book of prophecy?

Losing the structure of the workweek with a two-day weekend, time slides back and forth without restrictions and without a way to measure it. Without fully emerging from the K-induced coma, the routine of clocking in every day and working like a dog remains a distant memory —separated from the present by several glacial epochs. Peering through a narrow keyhole, into a windowless air-conditioned room, like a blur of tangled dark brown fur, a hulking mammoth stumbles through the frame.

Can the future as prophesied represent the ultimate course of destiny? Can it represent all of our past choices, including whether to go all out or quit halfway; whether to staunchly keep our faith or wallow in lingering doubts? Eventually all paths will converge on the same outcome: cosmic synchronicity, lasting but a few seconds, crisscrossing space-time, like two civilizational systems staring at each other across a vast universe. On this side of the mirror, was there room to diverge from the path in the dream? Was there space between the tracks to make an escape?

* * * * * * *

Not unless there is evidence.

Normal workdays were a thing of the past. The first time I took Black Cat was on a weekend of one of those long-gone regular work weeks. Afterward, I vividly described it to Kela: *those crystalline violets, the future form of the human species...*

That was another small gathering. The air was dank with weed smoke, filling the twilight interior with a thick, white fog. You could say the most out-of-line shit, and it'd be safely received beneath the cloud-cover. A handful of colleagues finally got together after an overtime shift and passed around an antique jade pipe purchased from a curio shop. Bringing it up to our lips one by one, squinting to take a big hit. At the pipe's tip was a glowing red circle made of silken strands of light.

The Sorcerer, cracking the spatio-temporal code, traced humanity's rise and fall using a few limited characters. Ol' Kela listened in silence, brow furrowed, absentmindedly wringing his hands, as if he were trying to interpret an omen and getting trapped in its riddles. Eyes flashing through the smoke and shadows, vision crystal clear. Like a supersensitive nocturnal animal, he could stalk through fields of elephant grass and pause to let the quiet light of a meteor shower be reflected in his pupils.

I was fairly certain that a scene like this had appeared to me in a dream.

The Interpreter stopped speaking; marijuana's numbing effects spread from the tip of the tongue to the extremities of the body. Time froze, then expanded. The moment of sensory perception extended via an endless series of fragments, all of the shortest possible duration, repeatedly verifying the dream image: swirling columns of smoke, techno versions of folk tunes. Kela's expression was complicated: suspicion, terror, both, or neither? It was hard to say.

Is déjà vu simply a misunderstanding, a minor flaw in the Creator's grand design, or a prophetic gateway? Perhaps it's fatalism, but regardless of what I wished to cling to or forsake, chilling in a dimly lit room smoking weed was my ultimate destiny.

Being able to predict fate generates the desire to resist. The words formed in my throat: *"I've seen this before in a dream!"* I paused to reflect on whether those words were also spoken in the dream. With no time to evaluate my memory's prophetic vision, still uncertain of whether I'd already chosen to operate in reverse, the déjà vu dissipated in a matter of seconds. Ultimately, it seemed identical to what happened in the dream: it went by without substance. *Is fate really unshakable?*

I decided not to mention it. Looking around, I broke the silence: "At least this is more exciting than the last time I did 5-meo."

Everyone laughed. We were all submerged head to toe in marijuana smoke and completely relaxed. The most trivial thing could become a punchline. Kela grinned mockingly, "You must have been doing it wrong…"

* * * * * * * *

5-meo was also a gift from Ol' Kela. It's another type of aphrodisiac. In a pointed plastic test-tube mix a little white powder with coca cola, take orally.

Another scene: a Saturday afternoon in winter. Bone chilling wind. Not a good day to go out. In withdrawal after another night of too much ecstasy. My body like an empty cave. I sat alone and in silence, legs dangling over the side of the bed, as if expecting someone. On a whim, I got up, grabbed my leftover stash of 5-meo and took it straight no chaser. I sat back down on the bed and continued my solitary vigil. Straight lines began to curve; shadows emitted a shiny black light. Sweat flowing, mouth dry. Apart from these effects, nothing else. I was extremely bored and a bit nauseated. Sheets of light pierced my eyes. When the effects had worn off, my body collapsed, like I'd just run a 5K. *What kind of placebo shit was this?*

What about LSD? A thin triangular sliver no bigger than a fingernail. Colorless and tasteless when placed under the tongue. As the EDM beat on the dancefloor reverberated in my ears, the chaotic thoughts in my brain gradually began to settle. The deafening music shed its chrysalis, its crystalline melodic structure emerged in distinct registers. Visual distance collapsed; the foreground and the background blurred—it was just people chasing one another, shadows chasing light—a kaleidoscopic vision of extreme splendor. *This was everything.* Tired from all the dancing, I passed through a wave of bodies with their eyes wide shut. Arriving in a darkened corner, I selected a seat at random. *Fucking placebo...*

As Kela put it: I must have been doing it wrong. It seems to have nothing to do with the drug itself; what matters are your presumptions. Drugs that lack precision can only serve as a simple entertainment; they yield too easily to the user's expectations.

* * * * * * * *

The drug that gave me the most pointed experience: Believe.

One night during business trip to Japan, I left the group and took the Yamanote Line from Ikebukuro to Shinjuku. I wandered alone in the packed streets. A vendor had set up a small suitcase on a metal stand. At first glance, he looked like just another small-time hustler selling knockoff jewelry. Then, I saw that inside the case there was a sign written in dayglow English letters: Legal drug. Who knows whether the drugs were indeed legal. Curiosity piqued, I passed by, then circled back and passed by again, eyeing the display case. In it were several orderly rows of tiny Ziplock baggies, each containing a notecard that spelled out the name of the drug. Looping around for the third time, I finally came to a stop in front of the vendor and depended on my intuition to choose a plastic bag. Looking left and right to check for cops, I took out money to complete the transaction. I was worried that a deal so publicly visible might be a trap. If I were picked up by the cops mid-business trip, how would I explain it to my company? Clutching the plastic bag in my palm—*so thin*—I hid myself in a corner after entering the subway station. I couldn't help myself; I had to check: peeling back a corner of the tin foil package, in the dim light, I could barely make out a few sparse grains of white powder.

Fatalism: To buy or not to buy? A destiny determined prior to personality.

The pinch of white powder looked capable of washing away all my sins —that shit was *pure*. Returning from the business trip on the following weekend, I swallowed the flavorless powder. The amount was so small that I even doubted whether I'd swallowed it. I sipped some water to rinse the cracks between my teeth just in case. As I waited for the drug to kick in, I turned on my computer to organize the photos that I'd taken during the trip, sorting them into files to use in an upcoming work presentation. This photo was taken at the traffic juncture project-site; that one was from the conference meeting with the entertainment marketing department.

The drug hit me in a rush, as if it had been stirring in my body for ages, ready to erupt as soon as my defenses collapsed. My eye sockets were on fire. The pictures on the screen came to life. The meeting participants in the conference room, their backs to the camera as they faced the presenter's screen, were resuscitated, breathing again in the midst of a time pause. Shoulders in suits rose and fell gently. A few of them looked as if they were about to turn around, but continued to delay doing so.

Next, the spatial dimension collapsed. I found myself in their midst. My heartbeat accelerated as if I was on the final lap of extreme motor race. My eyelids hit the brakes, suddenly shutting everything down. The force of the kickback almost threw my soul out of my body. *Deep breaths....deep breaths...*Focusing on my breathing, I was able to recoup temporarily.

After adequate psychological preparation, I was ready for round two. Inhaling and exhaling, to center my energy, I raised my eyelids like shutters opening onto a violent storm. In what seemed like a Herculean feat, I reached out for the remote control and turned on the TV. The experience was extraordinary: all images became remarkable. It was as though I was right there, up close and personal, to each of the scenes: surrounded by the thick smoke and infernal flames at the scene of a fire disaster, taking in the spicy, steamy aromas at a competition of master ramen chefs, staring into the eyes of a beautiful female celebrity and watching her teardrops turn to broken diamonds that flowed across her pale and smooth face—you get the idea. Intense sensations buried my consciousness. I bowed down to all things displayed by the Creator.

I flipped to the Discovery Channel to explore Earth's ecological rhythms. Beneath the dense rainforest canopy, the mouth of a cave—gaping, several stories tall—is embedded into the face of a steep cliff. It used to be the dwelling of proto-human ancestors. Now it's forsaken, a mysterious corner of the world. A few shots panned up toward the vast wall at the end of the cave—how spectacular. It felt so vivid, as if I was there in person; it made my head spin.

Praise all things. Believe.

All cells in my body were willing to accept what they saw and heard. The question of belief no longer had anything to do with reality. It could be decided instantaneously in a particular region of the brain—that magnificent circuit board—its external surface crisscrossed by fine strands of neural networks. Under the effect of the drug, cranial nerves heat up like a hard drive, sorting and storing hundreds of millions of data points... *When the individual psyche achieves such an omniscient perception of reality, does "hallucination" remain an accurate descriptor?* Regardless, this step had transcended karmic causality, shattering the chronology in the database of experience: a consequence without a cause was possible. *From a sober, rational viewpoint, it sounds nihilistic and depraved; from a transcendent viewpoint, it's avant-garde and radical.*

On the streets of Shinjuku, how many additional sensations were catalogued and exhibited in that slim briefcase? Did it include the accomplishment one feels after getting rich? The feeling of witnessing great beauty? The satisfaction derived from obliterating one's enemies and satisfying one's thirst for power? Perhaps it included the solitude experienced by a set of DNA, *materializing briefly as a heartbeat before fortuitously escaping the vicissitudes of a species' history…*

It's hard to imagine the limits of humanity's capacity for invention. Is it possible that one day, thousands of years in the future—if human civilization has survived of course—someone will unlock the brains' secret mechanisms of emotional control? Humans will no longer have to experience pain, grief, disappointment, except by consent. No more wars; everyone is joyous.

How beautiful this is—a bedtime story for the human species.

Kela said: it's a pity that he didn't tag along for the Japan trip. The members of the trip were all in the Planning Department, and none of the guys from Merchandising were included. *Syncing schedules is never easy…*

I asked someone who'd travelled to Japan and spent time wandering around Shibuya and Shinjuku about the vendor, but my description didn't fit his memory. Was the vendor magically hidden, visible only to people on the same wavelength? Neither reality nor memory can be trusted. The ingredient in that innocent and pure white powder will always remain a mystery. Despite journeying for eons across the wilderness, there are just too many herbs that Shennong (the "Divine Farmer") has yet to try.

Question: is it something like cocaine or heroin?

Answer: Ol' Kela tried it once before, after which we determined it's cocaine.

Sensory Profile: Confidence—the pure joy of affirming every single part of your body. It's a first-class drug, situated at the top of the tower.

Middle-class people always get stuck halfway up the ladder; it's the case in this arena too. What to do? Call up the friend of a friend of a friend—the line's busy, can't get through. Repeat for several rounds of inquiry. No dice. Supply lines? Broken. If I could give it one more try—or a few more tries—maybe a more precise description of its effects would crystalize. For now, I'm keeping a safe distance. No matter how much I express my love, in the end, it's not meant to be.

* * * * * * * *

Actually, it's a blessing—not having any channels for buying cocaine, heroin, or any drug that induces physical addiction after prolonged use. Otherwise, the Liar would definitely proclaim complete mastery of use, while knowing full well that using them is like wading into a swamp—sinking deeper and deeper as the swamp expands—it ultimately leads to full-blown addiction and the jettisoning of life itself.

The structure of the real world, the magnificent, solid, and imposing architecture, blocks the suns' brilliant rays. The worker ants creep past in formation, their route determined long ago by tens of thousands ant ancestors. An unshakable faith, carved in the blank spaces on their genes, where a passcode has yet to appear. How could this complete cartography of life be easily overturned?

Therefore, opposing thoughts coexist in a body: *even the damage inflicted via casual indulgence must be repaired afterwards.*

Second- and third-class drugs such as E and K aren't powerful enough to turn their users' lives upside down. Still, side effects include headache, nausea, absentmindedness, and depression. The scariest part about these drugs is the toll they take on the brain. Intelligence is an external trait, akin to physical appearance. Having a high IQ is like having a pair of mesmerizing eyes or a statuesque nose. Regardless of their actual function, each beautifies the sensory world. A drop in comprehension and deterioration of memory are equivalent to slicing line after line of wrinkles across an otherwise smooth face—it's a nightmare for anyone who enjoys their intelligence. In the work environment of a major firm, if you're perceived as dumb, chances are you'll be stuck with the blue-collar label for life. Knowingly subjecting your brain to damage is like announcing to the world that you've given up.

Unwilling to break ranks. Any damage, however minor, must be repaired.

Lunch hour in a downtown restaurant in an office district. The buffet joint was packed with customers; news blared from a TV set mounted in a corner. Sharing a meal with Kela, I rolled up my sleeves to avoid sullying them on the grease stained table. I wasn't eating much: my plate held only three bland vegetable dishes, tiny portions. Mood swings could lead to the breaking of any rule, but that day was calm and uneventful, not a wave or a ripple in sight. The way Kela held his bowl and chopsticks made him look like a reclusive monk in a bamboo grove. We had way too many snacks stocked up: high fiber cookies in my office drawer and organic fruit in the breakroom refrigerator. It was like a LOHAS slogan: *hunger is a moral good not predicated on the lack of food.*

Recovering from damage: locate and repair the brain's fractured neural networks and expunge the toxic residue hidden deep in the cracks of the body. Besides having hookups for various illegal drugs, Ol' Kela also has quite a wealth of knowledge about health and nutrition.

Metabolism: If the toxins that enter the body can be successfully eliminated, the burden on the body will be relatively light. The key is knowing how to expel the excess toxins promptly. Rather than trying to repair a body that's been corroded by toxicity, it's a lot easier to cleanse as you go.

The Defenders battling to maintain their original lifestyles.

Therefore, a recipe for maintaining one's health circulates among the addicts:

Foods that contain lots of moisture and fiber boost drug metabolism. Brown rice—the key is its highly nutritious casing: high in fiber and all kind of vitamins and minerals, it's the best for adjusting intestinal metabolism. Oats are similarly well known for their high fiber content. They ease digestion and help to reduce the level of cholesterol and blood lipids. Sweet potatoes are an alkalizing food and are especially good at neutralizing any acidic toxins. Black fungus is full of collagen; as it moves through the digestive tract, it absorbs any remaining metabolites, gathering them together for collective disposal.

Detoxification: Both polyphenols in tea and lycopene in tomatoes are a source of antioxidants. Cucumbers help to maintain hydration, clear heat, and are rich in pantothenic acid, which again helps to flush out toxins. With a sweet flavor and a cooling effect, mung beans are frequently found in detoxifying patches proscribed in TCM. Also known as little ginseng, carrots lower the mercury level in the bloodstream and are a powerful detoxicant. Such a colorful variety of detoxifying sacred entities circulate from the digestive tract into the bloodstream, chasing down the residual toxins in the body—engulfing and annihilating them one by one.

Apart from dietary habits, there are also nutritional supplements. Take Gingko for example: its medicinal uses date back thousands of years. Its essential extracts are like tiny grains of gold filtered from the rapid torrent of time; they improve blood circulation and cognitive functions. Like deep sea fish oil, gingko can enhance memory and prevent cognitive decline or dementia. The classic lament of the young addict: they can't recall the first digits of a telephone number after repeating it silently once—their short-term memory is toast. That's exactly why these two supplements are vital.

Multivitamins are essential, especially the oval brown Vitamin B capsules. According to Kela, if you're still experiencing discomfort days after a bad come-down, you can pay for a vitamin injection at a spa clinic, using work-related stress as an excuse. The recovery effect is excellent. Your body is completely purified to the point where on your next trip, the high will be just as awesome as it was on your maiden voyage.

This wide catalogue of nutritional terms is no less significant than the typology of drugs. As for the question of whether the toxins have really been neutralized, there's no clear answer.

Chatting with Kela while sober was usually this extreme—our conversations inevitably centered on either drugs or health foods that would allow us to take more drugs. Besides this there was only silence. One time, when it was just the two of us, I was getting bored with the silences, so I asked in a half-joking tone where he got the nickname "Ol' Kela?" Was he still clinging a romanticized vision of 1940s Shanghai gangbanging? Ol' Kela didn't understand my question. He just knew that the name came from a novel, but he recalled neither the title nor the character to which it refers. *The present-day "Ol' Kelas" had no stories worthy of the stage.*

At the tail end of one of our gatherings, while tripping on K, Kela suddenly asked a question: *do I actually exist?* The rest of us were totally stoned, incapable of responding. The room was suffused with emotions, but no one was willing to acknowledge them. It was the boiling point between crying and hugging. But all that Kela did was silently open a tube of K, tap a small pile onto the table, and cut a line with a metro card before snorting it through a straw.

Everyone was tripping. The stage was dimly illuminated in the weak glow of a single lamp, revealing the stooped silhouette of the Addict leaning into the hit. Kela was inhaling with such force, that we could almost hear the sound of each K particle entering his windpipe.

* * * * * * * *

That's all folks.

One Saturday morning, I made a conscious decision not to do any more damage to my body. Without setting the alarm, I woke up as I would on a typical workday. Still feeling drowsy from Stilnox, I lazed in bed, trying to make up for all my lost sleep. Being able to wake up naturally is absolutely the best: I flip on my computer, put on some music, walk over to the galley kitchen and make a fluffy golden-brown omelet with two eggs and a pinch of goat cheese, serving it up on a white china plate: *voilà, breakfast.* After all that, it was time to sort out my laundry on the balcony. A week's worth of laundry from a single man fit just about right in my tiny washing machine. Around 10 a.m. I set off on foot to the MRT station, dressed in sportswear, basking in the sun on my way to the gym.

Twenty minutes on the treadmill. The rhythm of my steps was perfectly in sync with the whir of the belt. On either side, my fellow gym-goers were lined up on their machines, gazing straight ahead at their monitors as they ran on endlessly, absorbed in their personal TV worlds.

If they happened to look beyond their monitors, they'd see a wall of floor-to-ceiling windows framing a four-lane boulevard, the traffic flowing like tides lapping at the edges of the islet bus stops. A squeaky-clean world in the midday sun. Under the bus shelters, crowds gathered like delicate china dolls, still and quiet, waiting to board the vehicles that would carry them far into the distance. From whom did they take their cues? What was it that motivated these china dolls—once still and silent—to set forth on the path of survival? What was it that made these bodies on the treadmills defy exhaustion, spending so much energy to race ahead, only to find themselves running in place?

On the narrow screens of the monitors, the Discovery Channel was airing a program about a universe a gazillion miles away—two hundred forty million lightyears to be exact: a star was dying, exploding in flash of celestial brilliance, then swirling in on itself...a black hole vortex like the whirlpool of a bathtub drain. This historic scene, like some monumental landmark printed on a postcard from afar, arrived from a distance measured in light years. The green LED display on my treadmill announced that one hundred and twenty calories had been burnt. My steps continued to fall rhythmically on every downbeat. Time was converted into measurable space, stretching forward into the indeterminate distance.

Did all the people running for their lives feel positive about them? Exercise does have its benefits: promoting lymphatic circulation, expelling toxins through sweat, and fostering a sense of psychological and physical grounded-ness. Alternatively, you could join a "tribe" and gather in rectangular mirrored rooms to perform its esoteric rituals: the action-packed kickboxing of "Body Combat" or the relaxing stretches of "Body Balance," to name a few. The "work" in "workout" is ironically pleasurable for the typical office crowd: rather than staying in front of their computers, they chose to hide in this "meeting room," secretively discussing marketing strategies that likely had nothing to do with the stars imploding somewhere in a galaxy far, far away.

Complaining, just complaining—like the running they did at the gym every day, the office workers ran in circles, never mounting a true revolution. Work was Life and the root of everything. They opened their exhausted eyes every morning, only to wish they didn't have to rise so early just for a paycheck. A serious question always lurked behind this wish: what would they do with their lives if they didn't have to work every day? What would they have to complain about? Is remaining yoked to the plow the only way to dodge the question? It's always the same story: on workdays it's nothing but endless complaints, but as soon as a long weekend rolls around, they find themselves *"feeling so fortunate to have a secure job that enables them to survive in such an expensive city..."*

Riding a wave of post-workout endorphins, I left the gym practically bouncing. But is physical wellbeing an indicator of happiness? Gyms are usually near shopping centers. Is this just a plot to mine the wallets of the well-to-do, capitalizing on the post-exercise euphoria to sell more products? Or perhaps it's to satisfy the lost souls of this world who can't be consoled by the post-exercise high, desiring more and more trivial items to horde in their misty hermitages.

Violet

After wandering through the bookstore, the music shop, and some designer boutiques, I ended up sitting in an atmospheric little café people watching—staring out the window at the flow of pedestrians, the shifting lights and shadows in some obscure corner of this city, while flipping through the latest fashion magazines. There were many meandering routes to choose from, countless ways to delay my arrival at the MRT station and the return to my solitary residence at the edge of the world.

* * * * * * * *

That was the first time I used Black Cat. Lightning flashed, thunder roared, and in their wake came the drumbeat of Sunday afternoon rains, the humid spring monsoon season. A world blanketed by shadowy skies and twilight mists, plunged prematurely into night.

Any E-addict would tell you that it's pointless to take a double dose. After entering a trance, however, I give in to habit, pop a second tablet and wait for my body to start trembling again, for my heartrate to accelerate into overdrive. It's impossible to have an appetite, so I twist open a jar of vitamins and swallow a dark-brown capsule of Vitamin B to meet my basic nutritional needs. A dismal atmosphere gradually descends on the room like thick patches of fog; I lay slouched on the floor with the lights off. The dynamic sway of the folk electronica intertwines with the dense fog. Time flows slowly as I wait for the sensations to come and go.

It always happens this way: first you recklessly set out on the path to depravity, leap off the precipice of darkness, then sink into regret and self-loathing. It's only a psychological spasm, and painful convulsions will subside shortly if you simply endure them. The Depraved, emerging from self-loathing, immediately start seeking the miracle cure: an anesthetic capable of effectively obliterating the entirety of their consciousness. The cat eyes on the packaging shimmered through the shadows and smoke. After ripping open the translucent wrapper, there was no wild sex; I just swallowed two capsules with mineral water.

I waited like a corpse waiting for eons of eternal decay. I languished in front of the computer screen, listening to the same few tracks of mellow electronica on replay, browsing the same old websites, and sending a few brief greetings to distant strangers. Someone in a chat room asked a nonsensical question: "Gimme your stats: Height and weight?" Combinations of random numbers emerged in my head, and I was suddenly struck by how familiar everything looked—*I knew I'd seen this in a long-ago dream.* Now *this* is déjà vu—Space and Time extracting meaning from the chaotic skipping of a scratched DVD. I wonder if these photographic memories appear in my jottings on dreams? *Could their records be recovered?* It's difficult to determine how far away these memories were: a few months, a few years? Or are these visions of my past lives, when I roamed the earth as an ant, or as a strange fish in the depths of the sea, the premonitions being an echo of their dreams? (Or was it only a few seconds ago, simply a lag in the information transfer between my left and right brain?)

Tens of millions of years ago, did early humans also experience this phenomenon? Thinking that everything before them looked so familiar that they must have seen it before in a dream?

In a secret cave deep in the jungle, a group of ancient apes, still unable to walk upright, take refuge from the predators' chase, drifting sweetly off to sleep.

How far into the future were our cave-dwelling ancestors' prophetic visions? Were they perplexed by their dreams after waking up: an ape-like figure sits facing a glowing square plane; ten fingers tapping on a board of checkered blocks beneath the shining surface, their irregular pace like intermittent rain? How to explain that a conversation is taking place on the square surface with someone on the other end, and that day or night, almost all productive and recreational activities can be performed just by sitting there tapping before the square? Regardless of authenticity or fraudulence, the question is: how do you deal with those experiences categorized by others as fantasies or hallucinations?

Fortunately, after waking from dreams, humans never seem to have a problem forgetting them completely.

In the age of science, no explanations are valid without evidence.

Before my wandering mind could return from ancient times, my stomach suddenly began churning like a surging sea, and I instinctively sprung to my feet, staggering as I sprinted my way into the bathroom. I knelt before the toilet and began to vomit. I hadn't eaten all day, so all that came up was thick gastric juice and the dissolved Vitamin-B capsule, now a food-supplement mudslide. Both gradually spread over the beige porcelain slope, slowly sinking into still water.

Once the nausea subsided, my vision began to change. The vitamin slime swirled on the surface of the toilet bowl, and drawn down by gravity, it began to sink in into the water in dark brown strands emitting a neon glow, dancing specks of light in brilliant violet. I observe the puke strands in microscopic detail, discern the shape of each and every molecule. Each one is decorated with glistening diamond chips and take their time to bend, stretch, and burst into an alluring and futuristic violet blossom.

Circumstances beyond my knowledge and experience became incomprehensible. I struggled to my feet, the dimly lit bathroom flashing transparent before my eyes then disappearing completely. When I looked down, the floor had vanished, and my body was floating in a brilliant void—*was this Heaven?* All around me, near and far, numerous violet points of light appeared and merged into lines and planes, creating a magnificently complex prism. Had I entered an infinite galaxy? Or had I transformed into an electric current (an email?) shuttling across the labyrinthine internet, climbing every firewall in an unstoppable race to the motherboard?

I set sail into the unknown, temporarily abandoning my material possessions and physical form.

With only my partially retained senses and a few flimsy thoughts, I travelled swiftly through the violet structure. It was no longer a matter of visual perception, but rather like a near-death experience as written in myth: every scene of my life stored in Memory's database was compressed into a reel of film and played before my eyes at 24 frames per second. *Is this what an out-of-body experience feels like? So serene.* A fearsome wind erupted out of the blue, fast-forwarded the film at an increasing speed. Had my life ended just like that?

No, the sensations didn't stop there. Scenes from my life continued to play one after another, although the reels spun faster and faster, the frames stayed crystal clear. I felt I'd attained nirvana after many reincarnations.

At the moment of enlightenment, abstract concepts took on concrete forms. At the beginning, it's like thousands of long slender fish swimming along with the warm ocean currents: occasionally their bodies collide, touch and merge like two droplets. It gradually becomes apparent that they are no longer following a straight course, but are orbiting around a void. This shoal of fish continues to attract more fish like an enormous energy field. Truth and Wisdom continue to revolve, until two tear-drop shaped airstreams are left chasing each other in circles, like a rotating Tai-chi symbol. Did that ascetic pummeled by winds and pelted by rain, enduring all forms of physical torment, finally realize this in his state of enlightenment under the Bodhi tree ? (Or is this a concrete manifestation of Hegelian Dialectics?)

Could this be consciousness after death? Returning to the melting pot of souls, I become a witness to the evolution of time, space, and life. Pushing forward, seeing nothing, but sensing it's so: I embody the accumulation of scientific knowledge. My learning curve is exponential, not linear. *How astonishing!* In the future humans will no longer have physical form, existing only as consciousness.

(Thus, will there no longer be physical suffering? Will humans safely escape the climate crisis? Will the wandering souls of space and time enter us? Will we completely understand?)

Science is no longer just about time and space; like science, all souls were originally one entity composed of two elements. At first glance it seems so vast and expansive, but it only takes a little shift in thinking to move the world away from the black-or-white dichotomy. *How can two sides of the same coin chase each other? How could they possibly construct this world?* All of a sudden, everything starts to make sense: the dark side of human nature, the perverse desires, are analogous to the ecological changes of two geological epochs, emblems of a particular historical period. Neither are they good nor evil. *This Truth is so tolerant and merciful.*

A larger-scale embodiment of this phenomenon would be like attending a secret summit of humanity's the highest echelon. Instead of discussing how to increase sales, the meeting focuses on the ways to allow creatures to coexist in the coming age of prosperity. *So, what exactly is this experience? Is it a God's eye view? Did the Creator (or some kind of artificial intelligence) also experience this?*

Without warning, the violet light structure resurfaced, and the vomiting returned in full force. I opened my eyes (*were they shut this whole time?*) to find myself still on my knees and leaning against the toilet in the real world. I felt nauseated; but all that vomiting earlier had already emptied my stomach, all I could do was dry heave. Feeling dizzy and achy, I managed to stand up and walk out of the bathroom. Outside, the blustery rain had stopped. The heavens shifted, and night fell, lacquer-black.

It was such a long journey; was it really but one afternoon in human time?

My body movements became so slow and clumsy that when reaching my hand out to fetch my glasses, I couldn't grip them because of stiff knuckles. Twice, like a loose claw in the claw machine, the prize just fell out of my hand, making me feel like a rehab patient with a damaged nervous system. Suddenly I remembered work, the foundation of life. Fortunately, there were still a few hours left in the day, so I started to organize my briefcase. I came across a sealed document that I'd brought home on Friday, still untouched, but because my head was a mess, the best I could do was flip through my diary to check my itinerary for the following day. Prepare to drag this wasted body into battle.

Countless eons ago, having travelled tens of millions of light years, exhausted ape-men opened their eyes to gaze at the inky scenery of their caves.

Inside the cave, coarse rock walls stretched endlessly into the shadows; their ebony surfaces were painted with intricate totemic diagrams that would later be perceived as culture. Puzzled by the fragmented memories of their dreams, these apes became completely absorbed in contemplating their significance over and again. Then, a small figure stood upright on its feet, emerging from amongst the group of ape-men passed out like logs in the pitch-black cave, and walked slowly towards the wall, reaching out to find some blank space. Uncertain of its motivation and with limited words and symbols, it inscribed everything it had witnessed on the rock wall...

I carried on living and working. City office workers are like little spots of mold stuck on the Wheel of Time. The Violet Experience broadened my horizons, yes; but returning to the present and showing up to work in business attire, that's a true survival instinct.

That was an unspeakably foolish fantasy. After the smoke session when I'd broken character and related it at length, I knew that I would never mention it again. I'm keeping my distance from Black Cat. Haven't even asked Ol' Kela if he's still dealing. *Do I fear the voyage of no return?*

Pedestrians, heads down, like an army of ants hiding in the shadows of shining skyscrapers, quicken their steps and cross the road...

Once, in a casual conversation with Kela, I started berating myself: An addict like me who squanders time and destroys his body shouldn't be able to compete in the workplace, and one day I would certainly find myself out of a job. Yet the opposite seems to be true.

Maybe it's because I've finally started to repent? Or maybe I just don't have the courage to give up the predictable rhythms of office life? After a temporary escape from reality, I would always put in extra effort at work.

It's probably because after every drug trip, the unpleasant side effects —the headaches and depression—lingered. Like the anti-drug bill-board outside my office window, these symptoms served as constant reminders of my addiction, compelling addicts like me to redeem themselves by burying themselves in work. We addicts can't change our lives. Our excessive energy can only be spent on the treadmill, running in place.

What kind of daydreams can one possibly have when life is so stagnant? You wouldn't be too far off if you guess: *suddenly coming into some money so as not to be tied down by a job.* Retirement, which requires long-term savings, is too distant to imagine, much less qualify as a viable daydream. Unexpectedly hitting the jackpot, although unrealistic, seems more probable by comparison; it's the most seductive option, worth calling to mind over and again. After all, it's only a daydream. Similarly, if a mid-sized company is acquired by a massive conglomerate, it's difficult to say whether such an acquisition would lead to a happy ending for folks like me.

We can chalk it all up to the inevitable workings of the capitalist system: vertical and horizontal integration, competition in commerce. It was the perfect farewell: a severance package equivalent to 13 months' salary, plus a glowing letter of recommendation. My old dream of waking up in the morning for something other than a paycheck had finally come true, though not quite the way I imagined it would. This twist of fate rushed at me like the tides of time; blink, and the waters were up to my chest.

Kela and I were both cut in the first round of layoffs. Only the Admin Team would survive the merger intact, and Planning and Merchandizing were both on the chopping block. A few days after we heard the news, the acquiring firm held a special meeting regarding the merger. In a rented conference room, red velvet banners festooned the stage, at the center of which hung an enormous projector screen on which well-crafted slideshows played on a loop: Staff Benefits, Employee Advancement, Corporate Giving. It was like a promotional campaign for Heaven and Sukhāvatī.

That was a long afternoon. Our new overlords preached from the mountain top with a missionary zeal, trying to revive the sea of blank stares below. Kela and I sat together among the soon-to-be unemployed, chatting about how we planned to spend our severance money: New wheels, new digs, play the stock market, or start our own companies? To us, these words sounded like Pig Latin, like we couldn't understand their meanings. What we were preoccupied with at this moment was how we'd spend our time after we wrapped up our jobs. Neither of us had any intention of jumping straight into the job search. Kela was planning a long trip; he mumbled a few faraway destinations. I listened without saying a word. When working life comes to a halt, and you've got a little money to spare, is it *necessary* to ascribe some new meaning to life? If so, what kind?

How far can the journey take you? As Ol' Kela began to repeat himself like headlines on a news ticker, I was reminded of those violet light dots and the bright space between them...

If the managers on stage had eagle eyes, they would certainly have noticed some of the audience had spaced out and begun silently guessing their perverse desires. Due to some catastrophic extenuating circumstances, these passive souls, all of whom were destined to be eliminated from the rat race, enjoyed a unexpected break in their endless working lives.

Was this Fortune or Misfortune? That is the question.

The slideshow came to an end. Kela quietly stared at the zealous preacher on stage. When the tracks of life shift under you, Silence appears to be the only fitting response. A silent stare-down with the unknown future.

Violet

* * * * * * * *

It was the day before Kela left the country.

There were no drugs left for this lonely addict in his one-man hermitage. Despite making numerous phone calls, I was unable to find any supplies at short notice. I had no other choice but to call Kela for the first time since we got laid off. It just so happened to be his last day in the country.

Without speaking too explicitly, we both knew that this was not a bon-voyage call. Kela needed to find a buyer for his leftover stash (no doubt looking forward to something more exciting abroad). The addict on this end of the phone, however, was reluctant to ask for it. Seeing that the conversation was going nowhere, Kela suggested,

"Why not give an old colleague a ride to the airport, and collect a small pack of dope as a token of appreciation from a soon-to-be traveler?"

Afterwards all I had to do was park Kela's beater at his parents' place and drop his keys off in the mailbox.

"How about it?"

Before the conversation ended, he added,

"Think of this as a favor. I don't like friends or family to see me off at the airport. All the tears and emotional baggage freak me out."

Added explanations only made the phone call more awkward.

That was the first time I'd met up with Kela after we left our jobs.

Seeing his chauffeur looking so gaunt and haggard, Kela understood how the Addict had spent his nearly two weeks of freedom: in utter absurdity. That's why he deliberately avoided eye contact. Kela led the way, striding forward with his luggage, as if he was afraid of catching himself hesitating. Maybe my body had been empty for too long; seeing Kela clad in his travelling clothes suddenly stirred up some unbearable emotions. It felt like something was stuck in my body. I could neither spit it out nor swallow it down.

Kela took the initiative and the drivers' seat. He drove smoothly and steadily on the motorway bound for the airport. In the car, he passed me some drugs in a zip-lock bag, containing all possible varieties of ecstasy in a colorful ensemble of little pills, as well as a small quantity of powdered ketamine. On closer inspection (my heart leapt!) there was a smaller plastic pouch inside. On the exterior of the pouch were a pair of sultry cat eyes and lines of tiny Japanese kana, and inside the pouch were two red and white capsules. *This must be fate.*

Kela noticed the Addict make eye contact with the cat eyes on the packaging, noticed his conflicted facial expressions. Kela asked casually like he was breaking the ice, "Remember that time when I smoked you up, and you told me about your first trip? You talked all about that epic fantasy experience, seeing the furnace of souls and witnessing the rise and fall of humanity and all sentient beings and shit?"

How could I forget? Those glistening violet blossoms, their arches and their curves….In the end that vision had to be filed away as nothing more than a fantasy? I regret confessing everything about my experience so easily: "I was high out of my mind. Must have sounded really silly, huh?" I turned around and caught Kela nodding, a wry smile on his face.

I'd hoped that embarrassing episode would have remained in the past… now it was being used as comic relief! I rubbed my face to keep my composure. Kela sounded like he was trying to console me. "I know it sounds crazy," he said, "but if we set aside the question of truth, you say you experienced it, so maybe that means it exists?"

Visions don't come out of nowhere. They're ultimately based on reality and on the limits of the user's imagination of the universe. In Kela's words, the psychedelic fantasy worlds described by these Trespassers are paradises secretively tucked away in their heads. Perhaps these witnesses should feel proud—celebrate their return with complex and detailed descriptions of those distant unknown realms?

After all, if you want to forge a beautiful life, what you need is a beautiful mold.

After indulging in so much depravity, my body knows nothing but discomfort: thirst and cold sweats. In this state, it would be so comforting to listen to humanity's bedtime story before drifting off to sleep. As I leaned my head against the car window, the scenery along the motorway flashed past, framed in the sideview mirror. I didn't have anything particular in mind, only the comforting words any kind person would say at parting.

In a world that prioritizes scientific evidence, what significance can fantasy hold?

Kela continued, "Some things may be inexplicable by nature. Remember that time in the twilight room behind the curtains of weed smoke? When the Sorcerer was describing these unbelievably fantastic hallucinations. I was so sure I was experiencing déjà vu..."

That moment? When the dreamscape reappeared and he attempted to defy fate? Had Kela also witnessed this before in a distant dream?

Kela explained that his dream was vividly playing out in reality: he saw the Addict's red and bloodshot eyes, and listened to some incomprehensible, intense descriptions from a soul's long journey. Suddenly, the space-time Codebreaker fell silent. Time froze, then expanded. The moment of sensory perception extended via an endless series of fragments, all of the shortest possible duration, repeatedly verifying the dream image: swirling columns of smoke, samples of techno folk music, and the look of sudden realization on the Interpreter's face (Was this why Kela's had shifted between skeptical and frightened?). In the dream, the Interpreter, after a period of silence, was supposed to say, "I've seen this before in a dream!" Instead, the Interpreter, after spacing out for a while, looked around and said, "At least this is more exciting than the last time I did 5-meo." *That* was entirely different from the way it was in the dream. Under the effects of marijuana, everyone burst into laughter. In a situation like this, Kela couldn't help saying, "You must have been doing it wrong…"

Kela chuckled. Perhaps it really is true that by nature, some things may always be inexplicable.

Sitting next to the driver, the Addict's worn-out face was etched with layer upon layer of doubt. He appeared to be lost in thought, but his reluctance to speak was a sign of other issues. Kela, noticing this unusual behavior, asked jokingly, "What? Did that also sound silly to you?" I shook my head, wanting to say no, but I was unsure how best to say it. I went quiet again. Thinking nothing of it, Kela clearly viewed our conversation as nothing more than an opportunity to reminisce about dumb shit from the past. A smile continued to play across his face long after he'd finished his story. His hands rested lazily on the steering wheel, and he looked ahead at the cars on the motorway.

If I already have evidence, is it sufficient to verify inferences? To negate fate?

Time and space extend boundlessly in their own ways. Their brief convergence on these two odysseys is like this: in a mirrored maze, two beams of light travel on their own refractive courses, until at some point, they explosively collide, like sparks in a powder keg. They become deeply and intimately absorbed in each other's lives; like a gentle sigh, they leave subtle traces of change that don't obstruct their forward movement. Then, they continue in their own directions, refracting along without a clear destination…

* * * * * * * *

It is a cave with an exceptionally secretive entrance.

A short silhouetted figure treads across swarms of cockroaches to reach the cave's end. Raising its face, it peers through the gloom, gazing up at the cave wall inscribed all over with various totemic pictographs and characters, which spread in all directions like an unstoppable flood. The

Silhouette then slowly reaches out its hand to trace the flood's directions on the cave wall. The odds are only one in a billion, but the Silhouette manages to find some uncannily familiar signs and symbols on a tiny patch of wall just above the ground. *Have we met before?*

An alien language, nebulously distorted. Compared to the unstoppable flood nearby, this is more like a drainage ditch in a small alley, reeking of foul smells.

The Silhouette thinks those nebulous signs and symbols must have been inscribed at a time when fantasy could not coexist with logic and reason; science must have been the only way to comprehend the world then. Anything beyond reason would have been conceived of as a fever dream, and any writing about such illusions would have been nonsense; therefore, authors chose not to sign their names. These experiences, inscribed at the margins of the of the great murals of history, can only be considered a secret interlude not to be divulged.

The Silhouette has a strange and unspeakable feeling. After loitering in the cave for some time, it decides to leave, like millions and billions of others who have once passed through.

It is a dream in which the past or future cannot be clearly defined.

Witnesses, no longer able to conceal their sense of bewilderment, return to the wall. Bending down to pick up sharp-edged stones from the ground, they begin to inscribe everything they have witnessed, stroke by stroke, in a tiny space within a stretch of mural paintings. Sweat dripping off their brows, it's finally time to lay down the stone and call it a day. They step back to admire their work through the gloom, in the haze, words and symbols begin to wriggle, preparing to break camp, to flow in every possible direction, stretching toward infinity ...

6

A Daughter

Lin Yu-hsuan
(translated by Shengchi Hsu)

When I turn around, Dad is standing in front of the dressing room mirrors. He has stolen along the corridor decorated with prints of well-known paintings and slipped past the massive flower arrangements guarding the door. From behind, his uneasy posture reminds me of how he looked that one time he crashed at my flat.

* * * * * * * *

That Hukou[1] fortune-teller was a real straight talker. He claimed to be an expert in palm reading, not just the lines, but also the bone structure. Dad made a trip to Hukou just for a consultation. Afterwards Dad complained that the fortune-teller went on and on as he read his right hand, giving right-handed Dad no opportunity to take notes. Dad wished he'd taken a pocket recorder along, but he couldn't have operated one anyway, so he rang up and invited me to go along next time.

"Sure. But I don't want to have my fortune told."

"Come on, I'm getting mine told. Aren't you curious?" He chuckled.

"Dad, I've told you so many times not to believe those fortune-tellers, but you never listen. You've got to understand that predicting the future is disrespecting it. It's like when you want to watch a film, but heard a spoiler in advance. The more you try to forget, the more it sticks in your mind. If you can't enjoy the story, what's the point of watching it at all? Remember how that kid spoiled the *Titanic* for me? I heard him whispering 'Jack is going to freeze to death' and I was so annoyed that I poured my Coke all over him! He totally ruined it for me!

"So, no, Dad. I'm definitely not getting my fortune told," I was shouting at this point.

"Fine. Let's just forget about it," he said, and hung up the phone.

I bet you're sulking now, aren't you? I wondered as I hurriedly slipped into a maxi skirt.

Why are you being such a drama queen? Do you think I'm going to ring you right back to say,

"Dad, I'm so sorry. I didn't mean to yell at you. Please, forgive me?" Fat chance!

I didn't raise my voice because I was in a rush, but even if I didn't have time, I would have still wanted to shout some sense into you.

What do you Buddhists say about the lion's roar? You should be so lucky to hear it?

Being a Buddhist, you shouldn't buy into all that fortune telling! What's wrong with you?

A Daughter

As I apply my makeup in front of the mirror—I'm using a pressed powder foundation today—I think back on what dad told me about his first reading. I imagine it went something like this:

"You will live to the ripe old age of 92. But you will suffer a devastating misfortune at 80."

"Okay," Dad nodded.

"In the next five years, you will make enough money to build a 7-story mansion. But don't mingle with people from northern Taiwan, stick to southerners," the fortune-teller continued.

"Yeah?" Dad responded.

It must have gone like this. I need some darker eyeshadow.

"Two kids?"

"Yes! Two," Dad confirmed, sounding amazed.

In our phone conversation, Dad also claimed that apparently the fortune-teller said I will get married and then have a child in 2011. *What nonsense!* Does the fortune-teller think he is God almighty? Is he going to make me a boyfriend out of my rib?

"That's got nothing to do with me! He must be talking about Lin Jianhong," I yelled over the phone.

"How can it be about your younger brother? He only just started university, still way too young to talk about getting married and having kids. It must be about you. On another note, didn't you see how elated your uncles were when your cousins got married, one after the other…"

"Dad, my phone's about to die," I interrupted.

"Well," Dad said reluctantly, "there is something else…"

"What?"

"What do you think about me taking a goddaughter? The fortune-teller said I am destined to have a daughter in this life."

Destined to have a daughter? That darker eyeshadow has smudged my eyeliner.

"Dad, let's talk about this another time. I've gotta go."

"Sure," he said.

I sat on the bus looking out of the window. "Destined to have a daughter?" *Interesting.*

* * * * * * * *

Mom walked out on us when I was still in high school, after a nearly six-month standoff with Dad. He's aged since then.

My mom is gorgeous and has always loved dressing up. *I'm jealous.* One Lunar New Year, I can't remember the year, our family gathered at Mom's younger brother's house. We were close with her side of the family. They're in the restaurant business, and everyone on that side of the family was good with a wok, so they all pitched in to prepare the New Year's Eve meal. Fruit was served after the pig trotters, and everyone knew that was the cue for mahjong—everyone but Dad. He just sat there in silence the whole evening, keeping his distance, the same way his family distanced us from any of their Lunar New Year gatherings.

"Hey, where are those old photo albums?" my uncle's wife demanded, "get your uncle to stop his game and fetch them." She opened one of the albums with a flourish, flipped to a particular page, and then pointed her finger at the largest photo,

"Your dad was such a ladies' man!"

Really, a ladies' man?

"Look at that smile on his face!"

A Daughter

Dad's fair skin and smiling eyes showed he was the baby of the family. But all I could think about as I looked at the picture was how strict Granddad was said to be.

Dad had a petite face and dark circles under his eyes, just like me. Perhaps it's more appropriate to say that I inherited his features. In the living room, from his perch on the sofa, Dad was entranced at the portrait of a Pipa-player in a cheongsam. His expression was similar to that in the picture: peeking at the wedding gown beside him through the corner of his eyes.

Uncle's wife suddenly mimed a full-figured silhouette and said, "Your mom is drop-dead gorgeous!" Then she whispered to me, "Your dad picked the right woman for himself. She's stylish and has a huge wardrobe."

"What do you mean by that, Auntie?"

"He's jealous of her."

"Jealous? Auntie, you must be tipsy!"

"Tipsy? I can down more drinks than my husband does!" After this remark, she left to swap in for uncle at mahjong.

Ah Auntie, you're not as pretty as Mom, you must be the one that's jealous. Watching her walk away, I started to ponder what she'd said. *How can Dad be jealous of Mom? I don't get it.*

Mom left the flat before dawn when everyone should have been asleep. To this day, I still wonder if that fierce argument was only a dream. At first, I heard her screaming and shouting. *It's okay, the sun's about to rise,* I tried to calm myself down. Then there was a loud bang. She smashed the family clock, and we haven't had a sense of time since. *Everything's going to be fine,* I tried to convince myself as I tossed and turned in bed. Then I heard her cry out, "If you won't leave, I'll leave! You can keep all my clothes!" I glimpsed a white dress flash past my door. *Just stop, please!* I should have said something, but I didn't. Peering from my room,

I watched Mom storm out in tears. She ended up moving back in with her parents for sixth months or so.

There's a lot one can do in half a year, and Dad used his time well after Mom's departure. He repaired the door Mom had wrenched from the wardrobe where she kept her cherished garments. One day after school, I found Dad standing in front of the wardrobe holding one of Mom's dresses in his hands.

"Just airing them out so they don't get moldy," he explained.

"Oh," I nodded.

Several months later Mom returned to our little flat and our family bond was once again as strong as an un-rippable nylon dress. She came home with a new wardrobe and never opened the old one ever again. I can still remember every detail of the garments she'd abandoned in that old wardrobe, from tailored suits to party dresses.

It is I who discovered the secret. Aren't I a clever little thing!

Dad asked to stay at my place when he came up north for his class reunion party. You can't believe everything those fortune-tellers say. That semester, I had to perform *Romeo and Juliet* for a compulsory module. I couldn't afford any of the proper costume rentals in Ximending,[2] so I asked Dad to bring along one of Mom's dresses as a "secret weapon" for my role as Juliet. When you look like a goddess, someone's bound to get jealous. They could hate all they wanted. I didn't give a damn.

"Dad, can you bring a dress with you when you come up north? A classmate needs it for our play," I asked.

"From your Mom's wardrobe?"

"Yeah."

"The beige or the white one?"

"White."

Wow Dad, you're really clear on the details.

"No problem."

Dad arrived in Taipei with an empty stomach on a chilly evening. I offered to pick up some ginger duck soup from a takeaway not far from my tutoring gig.

"Is it going to take long?"

"Not really, about 20 minutes there and back."

"Sounds fine to me."

I set out but had to run back to the flat because I'd forgotten my wallet. I walked in just as Dad was getting out of the white dress. My return startled him so much that he ripped the rose-pattern lace on the dress's left sleeve.

"Dad?"

"Well… Yi…cheng," he stuttered, "I… I thought I'd try on the dress for you, see if it fits."

* * * * * * * *

Dad, the white dress was for me, but why would I reveal that to you? You think it's unfair that I kept things from you, but what on earth is fair in this world? It may be an eye for an eye, but never a secret for a secret.

Dad, whenever I hit the mall with my girlfriends, that's when I feel most at ease. Thank you for giving me life, and your looks: my petite face, fair skin, and dark circles like yours. You're right - we do have a lot in common.

By the way, I like the way you do smoky eyes. Keeping secrets must run in the family. I'll pinky promise to keep your secret. How does that sound?

* * * * * * * *

The drizzly rain out there reminds me of the day when CC and I visited the Albion counter. We went to check out their Body-Sculpting Sugar Scrub, all because a high school English teacher was trying to get a group together to buy some on wholesale. *Wah, so tempting, we've got to get in on this!*

That day after the play, CC paid me a compliment,

"Wow! That was brilliant. You're such a good girl"

"What's that supposed to mean?"

"I don't know, you were so...girly!"

A good girl? So girly?

I didn't get it. "So" is an adverb to modify the adjective "girly" that derives from "girl." The first part sounds like the kind of thing I'd say to get the neighbor girl to tell me all her dirty secrets. *But I thought you were a "good girl," aren't you?* It is also something my high school crush, Zhu Jiekai might say, "Lin Yicheng, you are SO girly! Stay well away from me, or I'll beat you up." Clearly, a compliment can turn into an insult, in the right circumstances. (I better not say anything about the all-boys' high school I attended. It was dirty, chaotic, and noisy. Plus it was hypermasculine and phallocentric—a dog-eat-dog environment where freaks got picked on. The only silver lining was despite our hideous uniforms, the boys still looked great!) *Girly*, how I wish I could transform into just that: a good *girl*, how I envy your ability to evoke new meanings through these beautiful metamorphoses! When I turned around, Wang Zeyuan and Kang Wanting, the most envied couple on campus, had taken off their costumes and were just heading out. "Catch you later!" Seeing Wang putting his arm around her slender waist as they left, I was suddenly filled with frustration. *Damned boys! Don't be so set in your own way of thinking. Let me tell you something: Girly* is far more transformational in its shape and meaning than you can ever imagine!

A Daughter

Girly isn't just an adjective determined by fate. *Good girls* aren't simply modified nouns.

I'm a warrior. I'm so pleased with my argument to speak up for all *femmes*! But when I looked to CC for more compliments, she just sat there quietly at her dressing table. Still in her Romeo makeup, CC's neck, fingers, and her brows caught my attention. *How strange! If I am "so girly" as she said, how come I don't have her exquisite fingers? Why do I have prominent brow bones and an Adam's Apple?* I decided to ask, "CC, we girls…"

"Ju-li-et! Are you stuck in your character? We girls?"

"That's what I said. WE girls."

"Li Yicheng, you did look great in that white dress, but you're not a girl." I knew she was annoyed because of the way her chest rose and fell… CC's breasts and wide hips always reminded me of a textbook illustration of Inanna, the Mesopotamian goddess of fertility, a ceramic sculpture with three sets of tits.

"If I'm not a girl. Tell me then, what qualifies you as one? Did you have to pass an exam? Please tell me, CC. I want to take the exam, too!"

"Don't be ridiculous! Lin Yicheng, you're a boy!"

"But I've been a girl since I was little."

"Then you're probably what they call transgender," she shrugged.

"Trans-gen-der?"

"Exactly."

"So I'm transgender?"

"I guess so."

She walked away with a medieval-style paper dagger swaying back and forth on her curvy waist.

Thank you, CC. I can finally see why I often get stuck in-between.

On that strange afternoon the sun and the moon were both high in the sky. Zhu Jiekai, a born leader, commanded the class to force me to straddle the bottom rail of a sliding window. I loved him, so I didn't try to run. Two big guys who played center on the school's basketball team held me down. I clung to the stainless-steel window frame trying to keep my balance. *If I fall, I'll die, and I'll never get to be with Zhu Jiekai.* CC, I had no choice but to stay alive and accept what he was about to give me.

He moved back ten meters or so, stretched his legs, and sprinted towards me like it was the last ten meters of the 100-metre dash. He always looked so adorable when he broke a sweat. "Go to Hell!" He shoved the sliding window shut, crashing it right into my crotch. "Fuck off, you queer!" The blood vessels throbbed on the muscular calves that made him the school's sprinting champion. "Die, you sick pervert!" *Zhu Jiekai, I can't let go, otherwise I'll die. You are so strong, yet so gentle. You don't need to apologize for giving me so much pain, because this is my first time.* "Fuck off and die, you ladyboy!" *I cannot thank you more for what you are doing. You must know I love you, because now you are working like a sculptor to cut those unwanted parts of me. Look, Jiekai, there's blood streaming down my legs. Farewell to those two dirty balls.* "Fuck off to Thailand, Lin Yicheng!" *Harder, Jiekai, harder. Nothing will be in the way once those extra bits are removed! Oh yes, now you are in. It hurts, but I always hoped you would be the one.*

The bell rang, Zhu Jiekai paused his assault. He stood there panting and glaring at me.

CC, he looked at me, and his eyes welled up. *Jiekai, my dear, why are you crying? Real men don't cry. I know, they must be tears of joy!* I am so happy that we feel the same way about our first intimate experience.

Everyone but me then left the classroom for the 6K time trial on the sports field. I couldn't move, so I stayed on the windowsill as if I were waiting for Jiekai's return. But he just kept on walking and disappeared into the stairwell.

A Daughter

There were many things I never had the time to tell CC.

That day at the Albion counter, the saleswoman put some of that sugar scrub on the back of CC's hand. "Hey girl," CC sounded surprised, "this is real sugar and it's violet scented!" I pinched a dab from her hand and tasted it. *It's so sweet.* I stealthily adjusted the fit of my heels—It wasn't easy to find heels in my size. *Thanks CC for tracking those down for me.* Although it left her hands a little dry, she was very satisfied with the sugar scrub, telling me, "Hey, your turn." *My turn? Yay! I love sweet things!*

When I hopped onto the stool, a nearby salesman whispered to his colleagues, "Well, well—looks like we have a *new-half* here... another chick with a dick on the scene." *He called me a "new-half"—that's the same Japanese word used for the pretty Korean pop singer Harisu and the stunning Japanese model Ayana Tsubaki!*

"How dare you call him a *new-half*, you fag!" CC blasted out.

"Give me a break, missy. A man in a dress shopping at a skincare counter? How is that not a *new-half*?"

"Shut up, you dirty homo! Why don't you go back up the Hershey Highway. How gross!" CC swept the sugar scrub testers off the counter.

"That's gay bashing! I'm going to sue you!"

"Go ahead. Who started all this anyway? I'll put in a formal complaint to the store about *you*!" *But CC, was he really insulting me? I want to be a "new-half"; both Harisu and Ayana Tsubaki look fabulous.* She continued, "Well, being a homo isn't any better!"

Are you implying that being a new-half is bad, CC? This reminded me of that night after the show, CC shrieked when I followed her into the restroom. "Lin Yicheng, this room is for girls only, get out! If you want to change, you can do it in the boys room!" *I guess I'm not a girl like you, CC. After that day at the mall, I decided to cut ties with CC.*

Dad, it's a pity that CC had to reveal her hidden thoughts that way. She didn't have any chance to hear mine. I asked for a girls' high school uniform without name embroidery at the recycling center down the alley.

"For your younger sister?"

"Yes, she'll be thrilled."

I bought some honey tea and headed home. It was probably best to keep things private, so I shut myself in my bedroom and closed the windows. Using Mom's sewing kit, I started to embroider my name, character by character on the shirt: stitch by stitch, *up and down, in and out. Just like that, easy-peasy.* When I marry Jiekai, we'll do it just like this on our wedding night. First character, my surname, Lin—This is how it should look, 林, two trees standing right next to each other like a couple. *Jiekai, I love you, of course I'll take your surname if you'll marry me!* Second character, Yi— I have a big heart like the bodhisattva Guanyin who apparently has two manifestations: one as a man, and the other a woman. *Guanyin, hear my prayers. Please help me cross over—* I'm holding this needle like an incense stick. Third character, Cheng — *With all my heart, I promise I'll be a good girl* ...voilà, *finished!* The three characters did not quite align, but that didn't matter. I would still look great in the uniform. I closed the curtains, took off my hideous boys' uniform and put on my new one. I'd transferred myself to the "National Bedroom School for Girls"! I twirled around, checked myself out in the mirror, sipped my tea, snapped some selfies, and took a nap. When I woke up, it struck me that Mr. Sun should also take a look at this pretty girl. I opened the curtains, just as a butterfly flew past. *How ugly! It's just a worm with glued-on wings. You're certainly not as pretty as I, butterfly.* But my excitement was short-lived: there is no name embroidery on girls' uniforms. I began to remove my name from the shirt, character by character. First, Cheng. *What a silly mistake that was...*Then, Yi... *Just get rid of it...* Lin—There was a knock on my door. I tucked the uniform away before I could finish, leaving a solitary 木 standing above the shirt's pocket. Its better half has been uprooted and died.

A Daughter

"The neighbor across the alley said there's a girl in your room?" Mom asked.

"No there's not!"

"Be honest with me."

I didn't respond.

"Girlfriend?" She wasn't going to give up.

"Yeah..."

"And, where is she?"

"She had to go."

"Had to go? Right." Mom sounded relieved, perhaps because there was no fire to fight. She continued, "Remember to treat her with respect. Don't be like your dad."

"Dad, did you hear what Mom just said?"

"Why don't you invite her for tea sometime, or perhaps a meal?" Mom raised her voice on purpose and shot me a mischievous grin. *Shit. She could see the flap the green and black uniform hanging out of my wardrobe.*

"Is she as pretty as me?"

"No, Mom. You're the most beautiful woman I've ever seen."

Mom, I was being genuine when I said that. You are the most beautiful woman, and that's the main source of my stress. I envy of the curves that run from your neck to your breasts, and from your waist down to your hips. I wish I could see you in my girls' high school uniform. You want me to work hard and have a bright future, I just want to know from looking at you how stunning I can become. Come to think of it, Dad, I can see why uncle's wife said you are jealous of Mom; I'm jealous of her too. But things never go as one hopes. "Your momma's sleepy, I'm going to take a snooze." She covered her mouth and gave a sonorous yawn towards my wardrobe.

I bet you did that on purpose, Mom. Please, save the acting to me! I wish I could cast a spell to steal her voice! That beautiful soprano. If I had that voice, there would be no need to waste any more money on voice training. I could fly flawlessly up to a feminine key, like on a karaoke machine. After that, if I ever got kidnapped when she receives the ransom call, she would hear me crying for help in my gorgeous soprano: *Please, Mom, they've taken me...Mom, come and save me, mom, mom, mom....*

* * * * * * * *

"Dad, hurry up. Mom is waiting with everyone in the banquet hall."

It is rude to keep all the guests waiting. After all, they have come to congratulate me on my wedding day. I want to give them my thanks and best wishes like a fairy descending from heaven in a rain of petals.

"Okay." Dad was taking off his blazer.

What on earth? Why is he taking so long? Suddenly, I realize Dad is slowing down with age, and I am suddenly hit by waves of guilt for being so abrupt and disrespectful. *How embarrassing! Have I completely forgotten about filial piety?*

"Dad, there are two more shirts for you." I remind him in a much gentler tone.

"Thanks."

Nothing, not the arrangement of the artwork or those magnificent bouquets, deserves my attention more than what I see now. All over the pale skin on Dad's back are clusters of age spots blossoming like coppery flowers.

"Dad, I'll touch up first if that's okay?"

"That's fine."

Touching up can be a pain. Being pretty takes work. Despite some voice training, my voice still cracks from time to time, but I don't care.

A Daughter

Life's too short to waste on perfectionism. People often mistake the scar from my Adam's Apple surgery for a love bite. Whenever that happens, it stings a little; so to lighten things up, I would immediately cuddle up to my fiancé and respond, "I wish!" People suggested I get cosmetic procedures, like a nose job, lip lift, and cheek augmentation. But, thanks to you, Dad, my petite face means there is no need to mess about with my jaw line and cheek bones. And you, Zhu Jiekai, I don't have any feelings for you, not anymore! You failed to seize my family jewels, so I gave them away myself. Wait to hear what I will whisper into your ear when I see you at your table for the toast: "Guess whose name is etched on my dilator? My husband's, not yours. You had your chance, but you didn't take it, did you, sweetie?"

Pinky promise, this is our secret.

* * * * * * *

Naughty secrets, you must be a hunk; hunks are usually naughty. I discovered Dad's instant messenger when I was on his computer the other day. Dad, you are quite tech savvy for your age, aren't you? I nosed around in his chat logs and decided to say hello to one of his contacts.

The contact ended up sending over dozens of photos of Dad in Mom's dresses. One by one, these photos filled up the entire screen. Must be Dad's secret admirer. *What a weirdo!* I made a face at his profile picture on the screen. *But Dad, I can see that white dress must be your favorite; it looks amazing no matter how you change your poses. I love it so much, too. I always thought that dress outclassed everything else in that old wardrobe whenever I put them on. Dad, don't you fight for the dress with me....*

But there may be no need to fight after all. *We can always take turns wearing it, can't we?* Dad has left the dressing room in his suit, and my husband and I are getting ready to go back out for the toasts at every table. Mom is seated at the top table with uncle's wife nearby; CC and Zhu Jiekai are at two different tables at the far end of the banquet hall. *How much money did you two put in your red envelopes?*

"Getting married is a once-in-a-lifetime thing."

"I am so lucky to have him as my loving husband."

"My dad? My younger brother will look after him."

But does Dad really need any looking after? Maybe not. Look how happy he is! As I touch up, Dad is there in front of the mirror trying on my wedding dresses—one isn't enough at a wedding in Taiwan. The fortune-teller's prediction was right on: Dad *is* destined to have a daughter in his life. But that's not all, because Dad himself, or should I say *herself,* is destined to *be* a daughter.

The gown's zip is stuck halfway on Dad's back, faintly revealing her blossoming age spots through the layers of lace. Dad, there is a lot for you to learn about being a woman. You remind me of my old self, still getting your head around laces and underwires, but you will learn sooner or later. You want to be my Mother, and I—as your daughter—will give you all my support. In the next life, if there really is one, we can swap places so I can be your Mother. We will reincarnate with a renewed mother-daughter bond.

I put down my brow pencil and run my hand down her back to force the zip closed. Those dark coppery blossoms are now buried under the white fabric.

"Take your time, Dad. I have three more dresses for the evening."

Notes

1. Hukou township Hsinchu is a city in northwestern Taiwan.
2. Ximending is a fashionable district in Taipei.

7

A Nonexistent Thing

Chen Xue
(translated by Wen-chi Li and Colin Bramwell)

"Honestly, this Cambodian clinic is bothering the hell out of me. Yesterday, I was so furious that I could barely think."

"Wait, what? Cambodia?"

"Well, recently we decided to have a baby, so we've been preparing for that. There's a problem with our sperm, though. They say the delivery from our bank in the US will get seized by Cambodian customs. The clinic isn't allowed to collect it for us, so it'll have to be returned to the US. The sperm won't survive."

"*Having* a baby? Are you going to have a baby?"

"Artificial reproduction. We've been planning it for more than half a year. I made appointments with the gynecologist, took Chinese medicine to prepare my body for the strain of pregnancy, participated in experience-sharing workshops for lesbian mothers, bought the sperm from a bank in America, and, finally, I found a clinic in Cambodia that will do artificial reproduction. I've scheduled time off work and everything. Now, after all this, our sperm gets revoked, just like that. I'm so angry."

Earlier that day, they had gone to a karaoke bar. Afterwards, in high spirits from singing for five hours straight, they went to get something to eat. Xiaomeng brought up the topic of pregnancy. They were six friends, all lesbians. Xiaomeng and Gege were a couple, as were Anton and Wanqing. Kay was single and masculine. Xiao Jin was more feminine in the stereotypical sense. Although she had a boyfriend, she wasn't completely straight: she loved Beyoncé intensely. None of the women had children. Their ages ranged from 30 to 40 years old, but they all looked much younger. They talked about pregnancy and childbirth like a teenager might talk about a sci-fi or fantasy novel.

Wanqing had found out about Xiaomeng and Gege's plan a little earlier than the others. Their news didn't come as a surprise to the group. Xiaomeng and Gege had been in a stable relationship for five years. Recently, they went to the Household Registration Office and registered for a civil partnership. Gege had just turned 40 and badly wanted children. In the past, she had dated both men and women. Just before meeting Xiaomeng, she had ended a relationship—six years of cheating and abuse. Her masculine ex-girlfriend was horrifically possessive; anticipating that her desire for children would overwhelm her, Gege was sure that she would marry man once the relationship was over. Fortunately, she met Xiaomeng relatively soon after the breakup. She found that she much preferred being in romantic relationships with women. But having a child with another woman brings up issues.

"I used to think about contraception all the time. I never thought that pregnancy would be so complicated."

"Isn't it just the merging of a sperm and an egg, ultimately? Find sperm, problem solved?"

"I don't want to search for something like that so casually. And I wouldn't want to ask anyone I know."

"I heard that 'formal marriages' are very popular in China. Marry a gay man and have a child. All-inclusive package."

"Yeah, but that may bring up the thorny issues of custody later on. It's so much easier to go to a sperm bank."

"And you have to think about the eggs too. Like, with me, a child from my egg would definitely have some problems, even though I'm still young. My genes are, well, problematic."

"Our plan is to buy sperm from an American sperm bank. We'll try my eggs first, and I'll carry the child. I'm determined to have one."

"Is there any other way?"

"Millions of ways. I could have your masculine egg in my feminine womb, or my feminine egg in your masculine womb, or both our eggs together in a different womb. Everyone has their own way of doing it. Some couples take turns to conceive; others look for surrogates. There are many ways."

"So how do you get pregnant?"

"Well, I'm at the age where conception becomes more difficult. I've heard that some people can get pregnant by using a syringe to inject semen. They go to the clinic and just ask them to inject it straight into the womb. That improves your chances of conception. But you're still looking at less than ten percent."

"You could just go to a bar and pick up a guy. Like in the movies. If you really want a child, you could have a one-night stand."

"Isn't that stealing?"

"You'd have to pierce the condom."

"Not exactly safe..."

"The safest way is to go to the hospital for artificial reproduction, like any infertile couple. The success rate for that route is up to fifty percent, these days."

"All the physical conditions for having a baby get worse at my age. I would have gotten pregnant earlier if I'd known. But I never met a partner that I could have a stable relationship with, let alone children."

"If you're young, you can freeze your eggs. You'll still have the chance to give birth later."

"Well, I didn't think of children until now, but I'm still interested. Can you tell me more?"

"Okay. So, in Taiwan, artificial reproduction is only an option for straight couples, which is super irritating. If you're like us, you have to go abroad. It's best to go to the US, of course, but you're looking at spending over a million Taiwanese dollars on the cost of travel, surgery, and so on. Many Chinese lesbians fly to the US to reproduce. Some packages even get you a green card."

"I heard that you used to be able to do it in Japan, but that's not possible anymore. The first viable place I thought of was Thailand. Then I went to an experience-sharing workshop and a mother told me that it's forbidden there. The only option in all of Southeast Asia is Cambodia."

"The only reason I'd think about going to Cambodia would be to see Angkor Wat, not to conceive a child. It's absurd."

"The main problem is the budget. Going to Angkor Wat—no, going to *Cambodia*—for conception costs up to five hundred thousand Taiwanese dollars. We had to do a preexamination in a fertility clinic in Taiwan. And now we are told that our sperm is 'unacceptable,' and we can't transport it to Cambodia. So we've just decided to do it in the US. I don't even care about the money. If we have to spend all of our savings, so be it."

"To prepare my body for being pregnant, I spent twenty, thirty thousand Taiwanese dollars on Chinese medicine. Took it for half a year. It's so expensive—conceiving a child."

"And even more expensive to raise one, remember? It's a real burden."

"That's what my parents said. I discussed it all with them. My sister was the first to object. You know, they all accept my relationship with Gege. But, when it comes to having children, they're dead against it. They told me that my current life couldn't be better, having a baby is expensive, you won't be able to have such a good life as before. Blah, blah, blah. They brought us up without *any* support, of course. Even when they made little money, they never asked anyone else for any assistance. My mom asked, don't you already have a cat? Fuck!"

"My mother's even weirder. The first time I told her, she was quite happy, saying it would be nice to have children without marriage. You can depend on the child when you are old, she said. Now when I go back to my hometown and ask her again, and she rejects the idea, saying she's too old to help me with my child, I'll struggle in the future, life is good now so why change it…"

"Finance is also an issue. For instance, you guys now live on the fifth floor without a lift. When you have a child, it'll be exhausting to run up and down the building."

"We'll have to move out, then."

"Even with all these difficulties, we still want to have a child."

"How do you select the sperm?"

"Fortunately, Xiaomeng has pretty good English. She examined the donors, one by one, at this American sperm bank online. After a long discussion, we finally decided to have an Asian child—Japanese or ethnic Chinese. You can see the childhood photos of the donors on the website. Some were really adorable. Height, weight, blood type, birthday, IQ, education, hobbies, all clearly listed. It's hard to choose."

"So you want to have a mixed-race kid?"

"Yeah, Gege looks like she's of mixed race anyway."

"We searched for the right donor for ages. Finally, we narrowed our selection down to two: one is half-Japanese, graduated from Harvard, Libra, energetic, works as some kind of musician. Reading the evaluation on the website—you have to read the whole thing pretty carefully—they said he's good-looking, and they're rarely that direct."

"There was this other one, with big eyes, he caught my attention. He looks a lot like me. A quarter ethnic Chinese. His childhood pictures are so cute, and he fits the bill in a whole bunch of other ways. Here, I'll show you his photos."

"It's hard to choose. They're both adorable, but in different ways. I don't know how you'll choose."

"Yeah, we're a bit hesitant."

"But the Japanese guy is Type A, whereas the one with the big eyes is Type B."

"Does blood type really matter?"

"I can't get along at all with Type B."

"Why?"

"Don't you think Type B people are indolent?"

"I get along well with people with Type B."

"But the Type B donor is allergic to pollen. He gets really bad hay fever. And hives."

"Then I choose A."

"I couldn't imagine blood type making much of a difference, really."

"Some people even select the sex!"

"I've heard you can choose twins."

"Don't say that. Two children would be impossible. We can't afford it."

"What about astrology?"

"They don't mention that in the profiles."

"But we'll avoid giving birth around the time of Virgo or Cancer."

"If you conceive in September, you'll have a Gemini baby, right?"

"Aries and Gemini get on pretty well. It should be fine."

"I don't want a Virgo."

"When there are so many choices in front of me, I can't help but take them all into account. I wonder if it's wrong to determine so much from a donor's profile. But I know that, when people choose a spouse, they take all sorts of things into account too. It seems as if people fall in love, but actually it's just another choice they're making."

"When you're selecting a spouse, your instinct acts like a sort of filter…"

"Some people find it too cruel to choose a baby based on the sperm donor who is a stranger. It seems unnatural, so they talk about getting sperm from an acquaintance, but artificial reproduction is essentially an unnatural process. To seek out a stranger's sperm is part of that process. I mean, it's unnatural for me too."

"But some people even screen embryos for sex and to rule out genetic defects. I couldn't do that, though. It would be torture."

"Do you know much about the whole process?"

"Sort of. But now I feel like I'd prefer not to know."

"Typical Aries. Escapist."

"When I was twenty-five, I went through this weird stage where I constantly wanted to be pregnant. It didn't have anything to do with the people I dated. It wasn't about sex, either. I couldn't put my finger on it, but I had this feeling that something in my body was telling me to get pregnant, to have a child. Back then, I had this constant urge to find a man so that I could have a child—but only for that reason."

"But you can still get pregnant now!"

"The impulse is long gone now. It only lasted a year."

"I know the feeling. When I was thirty-five, I felt totally miserable that summer. I'd just ended that horrible relationship, and I was constantly thinking about having babies. My ex-boyfriend wanted to get back together with me, so I lived with him again for a while. I had nowhere else to go. Whenever we had sex, all these memories came back. Having sex with a man was so easy. Easy. If you want pleasure, then it's easy pleasure, like turning on a tap and watching the water flow out. If you don't use a condom, you'll have a baby. Simple. But is it so simple, to be straight? Sometimes you turn on the tap and you find out there's no water left. After a while, I felt like I just couldn't love him anymore. And that was okay. We were on and off for a while. I knew that eventually I'd end up with a girl. It was really clear to me that we weren't in love anymore. Whenever I looked into his eyes, I saw his hopes for a future: a future where, after a while of continuing to get along smoothly with each other, we would get married, and so on. He thought I'd be a good partner, an ideal mother, a wife. I could tell that he thought it would be nice to live with me. I saw the same thing: my life being settled, and all other possibilities cancelled. That was our last chance to start over again. I was thirty-five. If I didn't marry him, I would soon be over the age to bear children safely. After we separated, he complained that I always saw him as a Plan B. Sometimes, when I think about all the work it takes to make a child, travelling a thousand miles around the world and such, I'm not sure why I didn't just go for it back then and have my baby with him."

"Because of true love?"

"I'm never going to really know my sperm donor, though. It's not like I can fall in love with him. But we never felt that it was weird, to be browsing the personal information of various sperm donors, night after night. We were looking for the most suitable sperm to make our baby. *Our* baby."

"Our love—love itself—isn't based on blood relations, but on something deeper. For example, even though our child will be created by an egg with a stranger's sperm, I know that I will love her. I would prefer a girl, of course. If we could choose, we would all choose a girl, right? This is our child. Even though my participation in this does not involve me being pregnant and passing on my genes this way, I am still intimately related to her. I know I can love her."

"But we still want to choose a plan where the information about the donor is open—where they are traceable. If the child grows up and wants to find their blood relatives, that way she can find out who her brothers and sisters are. We can't be sure about what the child will think about her relationship with her father."

"We'll discuss that with her when the time is right."

"I have no urge to reproduce. But, sexually, I feel strongly that I would like *my* partner to have *my* baby. Specifically, I want to seed a part of me inside her, although I'm not biologically equipped to plant that seed. It feels like my whole body is full of impulses, though, and these can be transformed into millions of sperm."

"Is that a biological instinct? Continuing the family lineage?"

"Possessiveness, in other words!"

"No, it's a much more abstract feeling. I can't put it into words. When I have sex, I feel fully devoted—I feel like we've merged. I want to merge with her completely."

"How possessive!"

"You're not getting it! Sometimes what you don't have can be more real than what you do have. To an extent, I see myself as transgender."

"What, you mean you want to have a cock? And sperm?"

"No, at least not the kind thing that flows out when you turn on the tap. I'm talking about deficient ownership. A non-existent thing. Nothing meaning something."

"Fictional masculinity?"

"Not fictional. It's real. It can't be compared to the operations of specific organs."

"I've felt something similar, I think, but I've also felt the potential for motherhood in myself. I think I could be both."

"So, you want to do both, penetration and receiving?"

"All you think about is sex."

"I can't understand it without conceptualizing it that way, making it about sex somehow."

"This whole biological dimension makes the situation much more disturbing for my mother. She doesn't know how she should approach her prospective grandchild. Finally, she accepts that I'm in a partnership with a woman, but now I ask her to imagine a grandchild who has no biological relationship with her. She told me outright. She doesn't know what to do."

"A lot of people adopt children and love them. Can't your parents understand that?"

"Yeah, I told them that. They are still in shock."

"Some people believe that, if they break up after adopting, they'll be left with nothing."

"Love is an adventure, not an investment."

"I don't know how other lesbian couples handle it after they separate."

"I saw this story about a lesbian couple on the news. They conceive a child: masculine egg, feminine womb. Then they break up. The woman who gives birth to the child—the feminine womb—becomes, under law,

A Nonexistent Thing

the child's only parent. She gets custody and finds someone new. Now things become difficult for the egg donor, because every time she wants to see her child, she has to make an appointment. There is also no chance of her being able to adopt her own, biological child formally."

"The legalization of gay marriage and adoption still remains an imperative."

"I'm just looking forward to the birth."

"You know, after all this talk, I want to have a baby too."

A baby, a baby, a baby, a baby.

With the conversation still midstream, she drifts into the past. She was twenty-five years old and never thought much about being pregnant, but she burned herself out with sex day and night, finally conceiving. She vaguely recalls the expense of having a child—now about a half million Taiwanese dollars. But in the past she couldn't give birth, couldn't bring up a child, couldn't get married. She had only to continue her impossible relationship with her boyfriend because she couldn't leave him. Maybe she loved guys just because she was influenced by (or possessed by) hormones and pheromones, and maybe she gave up and left because they didn't like condoms and children. She couldn't tell if they even used condoms. She eats quietly at the table while everyone talks about children *and how there is no male, no father,* and *how we can still give birth and bring up a child.* But that is not me, she thinks, it is impossible for me to have a child—not in the past, present, or future. That year she had an abortion, and she loved a man with whom she couldn't get along or break up. She couldn't have his child, and he would never understand why. On the day of the operation the doctor did an ultrasound scan on her abdomen to capture this little spot. *This one* and *did you see that* and *I didn't see clearly,* but when she saw it, it was just a small throbbing spot. The doctor said she was definitely pregnant, but to the untrained eye it seemed like just a tiny, almost invisible spot on the scan. This little black spot was life.

Why did every relationship have to be so tragic? Why did they all just end like a nuclear explosion when all she wanted to do was to love someone? She never expected that she could live well after she reached forty. Everything exploded so violently back then, but now her life is still as water. She recalls lying on the operating table waiting for the anesthetic and thinking that she didn't need it—she was already paralyzed. Sex had become a reflex action for her. It couldn't awaken or move her anymore, so she had sought more and more of it, to confirm the existence of love. The lights of the operating table dazzled her, but that black spot was like a new mole on her skin and became indelible in her mind. She smiles and listens to her friends talk about a baby costing all your savings *like half a million, eight hundred thousand, a million Taiwanese dollars, all that money with no guarantee of success.* But how easy it was in the past: like putting a coin in the slot of a claw machine and grabbing a doll and pulling it out. She recovered after a few days. She drank a lot of herbal soup—or was it chicken soup? Eventually, it was as though nothing at all had happened.

Many voices shout in her body. She remembers her womb was removed three years ago, so nothing they are talking about applies to her. She hears an uncanny voice roaring in her mind, and she cannot calm it, this voice that has wounded her memory continuously: *I am a woman, yes, and unable to reproduce.*

Her partner is saying *nothing means something now*. It's as though she can feel her sadness: a squeeze of the hand draws her back to reality. Those intermittent voices quieten, and she remembers that nothing means something and that she has no uterus. *But so what,* her partner seems to say. *What is important is that you survive.*

What is important is that you survive. You have transgressed death and mania and constant disease and survived. All that has occurred between you and your partner shows that the deepest and strongest loves are not built on feelings of passion that crush bodies and shatter bones, but on the holding of a partner's hand when all dreams become disillusions,

A Nonexistent Thing

and your life stands still because of sickness, pain, disaster, and all that cannot ever be resolved. Holding hands enables you both to weather the rising tide, the storms, the endless nightmares.

The problem is not whether you were with a man or woman, but that you were unable to understand yourself properly. You were so fully broken that you couldn't afford another life, and it took you a lifetime to realize that. Now you tune back into the conversation again. You realize that you care about your lost child, and you want to say goodbye to him or her in your mind. You hope your friends can have the baby they want; you hope you can bury the broken child in your heart, the nonexistent womb in your belly that bore a nonexistent daughter. And now, within this short, almost indiscernible memory, you feel the small thing gently beat under the scan of the ultrasound again, and the one eternally missing thing in your life is now existent, for a time. Lub-dub, lub-dub, lub-dub. What is important is that you can write. Write her out.

Nothing means existence.

About the Editor

Howard Chiang is an associate professor in the Department of History at the University of California, Davis. He has written two monographs on China, forming a duology of queer Asian Pacific history through the lens of knowledge production. *After Eunuchs: Science, Medicine, and the Transformation of Sex in Modern China* analyzes the history of sex change in China from the demise of castration in the late Qing era to the emergence of transsexuality in Cold War Taiwan. It received the 2019 International Convention of Asia Scholars Humanities Book Prize and the 2020 Bonnie and Vern L. Bullough Book Award from the Society for the Scientific Study of Sexuality. *Transtopia in the Sinophone Pacific* proposes a new paradigm for doing transgender history in which geopolitics assumes central importance. He is the Editor-in-Chief of the *Global Encyclopedia of Lesbian, Gay, Bisexual, Transgender, and Queer History*, which was awarded the 2020 Dartmouth Medal by the American Library Association.

About the Translators

Colin Bramwell (MSt, University of Oxford) is a PhD candidate in the School of English at the University of St Andrews.

Shengchi Hsu (MA, University of Salford) is a PhD candidate in Translation Studies at the University of Warwick. His thesis investigates the translation of gender and sexuality in Howard Goldblatt's translations of Taiwanese novels in the 1980s and 1990s. He has been a Further Education lecturer, teaching ESOL, English, and Teacher Education in both Taiwan and the United Kingdom.

Wen-chi Li (MSc, University of Edinburgh) is a PhD candidate in the Institute of Asian and Oriental Studies at the University of Zurich.

Yichun Liu (MSc, University of Edinburgh) is the founder of RoHo Language Consultant Company. As an educator, she has devoted herself to teaching English in Taiwan for more than a decade.

Yahia Zhengtang Ma (Master of Translation [Enhanced], The University of Melbourne; MA, Beijing Normal University) is a PhD student in the Asia Institute at The University of Melbourne. He is currently translating an excerpt from Xia Mucong's *Military Dog*.

Kyle Shernuk (PhD, Harvard University) is a Postdoctoral Research Associate in the Council on East Asian Studies at Yale University. His research focuses on issues of ethnicity and indigeneity in Sinophone literature and film.

Jamie Tse (MPhil, HKU) is a tutor at the Department of Comparative Literature at the University of Hong Kong. Her research interests include Hong Kong literature and cultural studies, existentialist literature, postcolonial theory, and game studies.

About the Editorial Assistant for Translations

Greta Hagedorn is a graduate student at National Taiwan Normal University in the Department of Taiwan Culture, Languages and Literature. She holds a BA in Chinese from Georgetown University. Her research interests include Taiwanese queer literature and film.

Cambria Literature in Taiwan Series

General Editor: Nikky Lin
(National Taiwan Normal University)

A Taiwanese Literature Reader edited by Nikky Lin

The Soul of Jade Mountain by Husluman Vava, translated by Terence Russell

A History of Taiwan Literature by Ye Shitao, translated by Christopher Lupke

A Son of Taiwan: Stories of Government Atrocity edited by Howard Goldblatt and Sylvia Li-chun Lin

Transitions in Taiwan: Stories of the White Terror edited by Ian Rowen

Queer Taiwanese Literature: A Reader edited by Howard Chiang

Printed in Great Britain
by Amazon